Rainstone Fall

Also by Peter Helton

Headcase
Slim Chance

RAINSTONE FALL

Peter Helton

Constable • London

Constable & Robinson Ltd
3 The Lanchesters
162 Fulham Palace Road
London W6 9ER
www.constablerobinson.com

First published in the UK by Constable,
an imprint of Constable & Robinson, 2008

First US edition published by SohoConstable,
an imprint of Soho Press, 2008

Soho Press, Inc.
853 Broadway
New York, NY 10003
www.sohopress.com

A copy of the British Library Cataloguing in Publication
Data is available from the British Library

UK ISBN: 978-1-84529-649-0

US ISBN: 978-1-56947-525-6
US Library of Congress number: 2008018088

Printed and bound in the EU

1 3 5 7 9 10 8 6 4 2

Chapter One

What we called a studio at Mill House was really a leaky old barn at the top of the meadow, with the rattly windows I'd botched into one side creating on all but the brightest days the kind of medieval gloom Caravaggio would have killed for. It was a stormy afternoon in October and I'd lit the pot-bellied stove for the first time that autumn. Despite rainwater dripping into old pots and buckets here and there it was quite cosy. My world smelled of freshly brewed coffee, of logs and wood smoke and Venice turpentine, and I should have known it was too good to last. The stove was temperamental at the best of times but in this kind of weather it tended to puff smoke at you like a startled dragon. There'd only be a few hours of thin light left today and I was impatient to get on with some work. Simon Paris Fine Art had offered me a show in February. It was the graveyard shift, of course, but since I had missed my usual autumn slot through a complete lack of new paintings I couldn't really be choosy.

The wind-up radio, never the best of receivers down here in the valley, howled and crackled. I turned it off. The forecast had been for fifty m.p.h. winds with gusts of up to seventy but in here it sounded very much like they had got it wrong. It was a lot worse than that. The whole structure creaked and boomed. Rain hammered against the streaming windows.

The door slammed open and Annis flew in. 'Blimey, it ripped the door right out of my hand.' She pushed it shut against the rain and leaf-laden wind, pulled the hood back on her cagoule and the cordless phone out of a pocket. 'Client for you,' she announced, holding it out to me.

Annis is a painter, like me. Thankfully that's where the similarities end since it is mainly the differences I appreciate: unlike me she is five foot eight, female, strawberry blonde, lithe and athletic, has a beautiful butterscotch voice and perfect poise. A few years ago when she was still an art student she simply appeared at Mill House unannounced, a bit like a cat really, and has been living and painting here ever since. What do you expect me to do about it? She works with me on the private eye side of things when she feels like it. And we do share a bed sometimes but it's by no means an exclusive arrangement since there's also Tim. Of whom more later.

'Are you going to answer the phone or just stand there staring at me?'

'I'm too busy to take on clients right now,' I protested. I folded my arms in front of my chest like a stroppy kid and refused to touch it.

'Okay.' She tossed the phone high in the air and shrugged her shoulders. 'You tell him that.'

I caught it just before it dashed itself to pieces on the floor, pressed the talk button and acknowledged my presence with what I hoped was a discouraging grunt.

'Aqua Investigations.'

'Giles Haarbottle here, I trust you remember me, Mr Honeysett?'

Haarbottle worked at Griffin's, the insurers, who often came to us to sort out the trickier cases, things they wouldn't want their own staff to do but were happy enough to let a mug like me take on. I just wasn't in the mood. And yes, I did remember him but hadn't been pining for his company.

'I'm not sure why I still call you,' he complained. 'You turned down the last two jobs we offered you recently and we had to find other agencies to fit us in. But we do appreciate the work you do for us, when you can be bothered.'

I walked over to the draughty windows and stared out at the house and the outbuildings through the rain and swirling leaves. All the trees I could see from here were waving at me like overexcited lunatics. Even though I should have known better by now a small part of me still believed that wind was caused by trees waving their branches about. The big oak at the top of the meadow had already dropped several that would eventually end up in the fireplace.

'It's a surveillance job that could run for a while, so we need to negotiate rates accordingly. We were judged to be liable for compensation in the case of . . .'

I wasn't even listening. What kind of a moron would want to take a job standing at street corners in this kind of weather? Answer: the kind of moron who watched with disbelief a patch of tiles on the roof of his house come loose, slither and tumble, then pulverize as they hit the ground. Oh, no, please don't do that, that looks expensive . . .

I must have spoken out loud because Haarbottle asked: 'Pardon?' At the same time a fist of wind picked up the barn roof, gave it a good shake, then ripped off a selection of tiles and corrugated metal.

'I'd be delighted to take the job,' I shouted over the sudden noise as debris and rain clattered over everything, including me. Annis was already rushing around, rescuing canvases and covering our easels with sheets and rags.

'Splendid.' Haarbottle did sound surprised. 'Let's meet tomorrow lunchtime like civilized people,' he suggested. 'The Bathtub at one?'

By first light the storm had blown itself out and left behind a damp, bright and messy day to survey the damage in.

7

Both the house and the studio had developed bald patches and debris lay everywhere. Broken tiles had landed on the roof of my black DS21, known alternatively as a 'fine classic Citroën' (by me) or 'that Frog rust bucket' (by the guy who does the welding on it). Of course if the whole roof had slithered on to Annis's battered and equally ancient Land Rover you would hardly have noticed the difference. The willows by the mill pond had fared worst, shedding many limbs, several into the pond; that would need clearing now. A collection of branches and a plug of leaves and other debris had accumulated in the mill race too and the stream went noisily through, over and around it. The sagging outbuildings on the other side of the yard hadn't fared too badly, I thought, or perhaps they were so dilapidated I just couldn't tell the difference. I had called a firm of roofers first thing in the morning, along with everyone else in Bath, it appeared. Around noon three guys bounced down the potholed track to the house in a shabby lorry densely loaded with planks and ladders. They largely ignored me, spent half an hour fixing cobalt blue tarpaulin on both roofs and got back into the lorry. While the driver performed a twelve-point turn in the puddled yard they said they could only do emergency repairs right now and would be back one day, perhaps, if I promised to hand over my life savings. Which sharply reminded me: I didn't have any.

I left Annis in the studio at her easel, muttering darkly about 'blue light' and 'subaquatic conditions' under the snapping tarp, then got into the car and followed the roofers up the track. Everywhere lay twigs and branches and I spotted two more blue tarpaulins on roofs in the valley before I'd even reached the London Road. While I joined the slow procession into town I lost count of the scaffolds adorning house fronts. Keeping two-hundred-year-old houses standing upright was quite a job in itself and high winds didn't help. Many a decorative urn that in the eighteenth century was firmly anchored to the parapet was now secured by little more than a smudge of rust. And once a few tourists had been flattened by bits of the famous masonry . . .

Such cheerful thoughts helped to pass the time pleasantly until I got into the centre. It was too late to be creative about parking so I drove straight into the constipated bowels of the multi-storey affair next to Waitrose. I got lucky and shoehorned the DS into a space just vacated by a car half its size and thirty years its junior and walked out the back door on to Pulteney Bridge, which might look like the Ponte Vecchio from the back but presents a very English front. Then I took a left into little Grove Street.

The Bathtub Bistro was doing good business this lunchtime but I'd booked my usual table by the upstairs window. It was one o'clock and Haarbottle hadn't arrived yet. I didn't mind. I wasn't really looking forward to the job and sitting in the Bathtub was no hardship. I liked the place. Even though geographically it was smack in the centre of Bath it had a slightly secretive atmosphere, as though you'd only just discovered it. I often met clients here, since I didn't keep an office in town. Something was different though, quite apart from the fact that Clive, the owner, appeared to be ignoring me. I didn't realize what it was until he eventually appeared at my table and stuck a fragrantly frothy cappuccino under my nose.

'Don't say I never do anything for you,' he said meaningfully.

It took me a moment. 'You bought an espresso machine! At long last!'

'Anything for the Great Detective.'

'Now my life is complete. I'm waiting for a client. In fact here he is and he wants . . .'

'A double gin and tonic, if he may,' Haarbottle intoned, stiffly as ever, setting down an imitation leather briefcase as gently and precisely as though it contained the meaning of the universe written on bone china. Every inch of his tall figure was precise; greying hair plastered down in a side parting, miraculously uncreased raincoat which he now hung up carefully, blue M&S suit, blindingly white shirt sparking with static and the palest of pink ties. He waited until his G&T arrived, then gulped half of it down in one. Then he snapped open his briefcase and extracted a fat lemon-yellow file adorned with the Griffin logo.

'It's quite straightforward, as I explained on the telephone yesterday . . .' he began.

'Yes, do you mind repeating what you told me then? I wasn't really listening,' I pleaded.

'Wasn't really . . .?'

'Well, my roof was flying away at the time.'

'That can be quite distracting, or so our clients tell us. Remind me, did you insure your residence with us?'

'No. What's more I have the sinking feeling my house insurance lapsed.'

'Lapsed?' Haarbottle shuddered theatrically at the thought and dispatched the other half of his gin and tonic. 'It's not like Catholicism, you know. There's no such thing as "lapsed". You're either insured or you're not.'

'I was afraid you might say that. So what have you got for me?'

He flipped open the file and withdrew a six by eight photograph. 'James Lane. NWNF-ed our client –'

'N-what? Do speak English.'

'No win, no fee, the latest craze imported from across the pond. Claimed he fell down the stairs due to a torn bit of carpet while visiting a friend who lived in rented accommodation. Hurt his back and head. Claims he's permanently in pain, has problems balancing and now walks with a stick. A "nerve" thing. Utterly bogus.'

'How d'you know?'

'Five years ago he made a fraudulent insurance claim. Small stuff, pretended he had his camera nicked on holiday when actually he'd sold it.'

10

'How did you get to know about that?' I asked.

'Insurance companies do talk to each other sometimes. Anyway,' he turned the picture round and slid it across, 'that's your man.'

The photo showed a round-faced bloke in his mid-thirties with straggly, untidy hair, wearing a suit. He was leaving a building which from much experience I recognized as the magistrates' court. His smile was aimed at something outside the frame but definitely not the camera. Naturally, since the photo was a grainily enlarged black and white print, he looked guilty as hell, but then so would my Auntie Edith.

Haarbottle liberated a sheet of A4 from the file. 'Thirty-four, divorced . . . lives by himself in a two-up-two-down in Larkhall.' He handed it over. 'It's all there. What we need is good, intelligent surveillance, not expensive round-the-clock surveillance, okay? I don't want to know if he snores but I do want to know if he is faking it. Correction: I know the bastard's faking it. You just get me the proof. It's costing us a fortune to finance his life of leisure.'

'Did he have a job?'

'He used to work in a garage fitting exhausts to motor cars. And can we have video footage if at all possible? Judges do like a bit of video footage. So do the defendants. Show them a video of themselves doing naughty stuff and they change their plea to guilty very quickly. Saves a lot of time and money. Nail this little toerag for us, will you?'

What ever happened to 'innocent until proven guilty', I wondered. We haggled over my rates for a bit in a long-established way in which surprise, affront, regret and final acceptance were satirized rather than faked. Once we'd agreed and Haarbottle had fastidiously signed a crumpled copy of my standard contract, amended in the relevant places in biro, he folded away his stuff, climbed back into his coat and stalked out into the rain without paying for his drink. I'd stick it on my expenses somehow.

11

I sighed. *Surveillance.* Detective work rarely got more tedious than that. And since all my gear was at home and there was little chance of me starting work this instant I turned my full attention to the lunch menu. Detective work has its perks.

Chapter Two

What did I say about morons standing at street corners in bad weather? That's exactly how I felt: stupid. What a stupid way to earn money. I was sitting in my car, in the Oriel Hall car park, from where I could just make out James Lane's tiny terraced house in Brookleaze Buildings, where it skulked behind a riot of unchecked vegetation that, along with the National Collection of Broken Kitchen Gadgets, cluttered the tiny front garden. All the houses along the narrow street that faced the infant school and New Oriel Hall had back doors but since presumably he was unaware of being watched I hoped this wouldn't be a problem. Surveillance of course was really Tim Bigwood's speciality, Tim being the third member of Aqua Investigations, my small detective agency. I could only just afford to employ him at the best of times. His day job as an IT consultant for Bath University, mixed with his expertise as a retired (or so he says) safe-breaker, made him an excellent addition to the team. Tim's winning ways with all things locked were very helpful in the detection business, especially if you didn't mind bending the rules a little, and anything to do with pinhole cameras and sound bugging was a Bigwood job. But if I employed him at the going rate for watching Lane I'd never pay for my roof repairs.

It was cold in the car. I had to open the window to stop it steaming up, which didn't improve the temperature. 'Oh, *please* come out,' I implored. 'There's nothing but crap on telly, I checked.'

First upstairs, then downstairs the lights snapped off and Lane's front door opened. 'Blimey! It worked!' Mr Lane negotiated the cluttered few yards to the pavement with the awkward side-to-side movement of someone with a dud leg, using his stick. As he crossed the street and came towards me through the car park I let myself slither down in my seat and closed my eyes, pretending to be asleep in case he saw me. Through the open window I could hear him splish past on the wet tarmac. After a minute I slithered up again, got out and followed. He was wearing a hooded waterproof, faded jeans already darkening with wet at the bottom and black trainers. He looked thinner than he had in the picture taken last month outside the courts. His pace was slow, syncopated by a thin black walking stick in his right hand. I kept well back since he didn't look like he was about to sprint off. He made his laborious way along quiet St Saviour's Road and disappeared into the Rose and Crown. Things were looking up. I hung back a while and let several people go in before following inside.

It was only eight o'clock but the place was already busy. I'd always liked the Rosie. The decor looked like it had survived from the 1930s rather than been bought wholesale last year. The heating was on. Someone had had the excellent idea of putting the radiators on the outside of the bar and turning the pipework into footrests so that wet and grumpy detectives could warm themselves. The narrow tables along the walls were fully occupied and it took me a while to locate my quarry. He'd already been furnished with a pint of beer and he had found a wooden chair in a corner near the little fire. Ignoring the music and the loudly talking groups of people around him he pulled a hardback book from under his rainproof, opened it at a marked page and started reading. It was the kind of pub where nobody would dream of disturbing you. In fact there was another lonely book reader perched on a barstool, looking absorbed and oblivious to his surroundings.

I called Tim on my mobile. Mixing business with pleasure had always been my preferred way of working. It took Tim all of ten minutes to get here in his black Audi TT from his tiny flat in Northampton Street. He never needed much encouragement. A gang of girls was noisily leaving just as he arrived and we pounced on their table full of empty Bacardi Breezer bottles.

'So, an emergency night out at the Rosie? It was short notice but naturally I dropped everything,' Tim said as he parked himself opposite me with a pint of Löwenbräu and a giant packet of parsnip crisps. I pointed out James Lane, safely engrossed in his book.

'Oh, him.' Tim nodded his woolly head. 'I've seen him in here before. Sometimes with mates but mostly by himself, reading. So you think the walking stick's just a prop?'

'A walking stick's always a prop.'

'A stage prop, you pedant.'

'That's what Griffin's are paying me to find out.'

Tim had been tugging with his broad fists at both ends of his crisp bag which now suddenly yet predictably split open, decorating our table, our beers and our neighbours' beers with deep-fried parsnip shavings. 'Help yourselves, everyone,' he offered.

This was one of several mysteries surrounding Tim. His tiny flat with its dust-free banks of computer hardware and pathologically clean, gadgety kitchen contrasted so sharply with the mess that happened when you let Tim anywhere near food that I'd long suspected he ate in the shower. With the water running.

It was quite a while ago now that Tim and I discovered we had more in common than a love of pubs, food and risky jobs, namely: Annis. Whether Annis was eventually going to own up to sleeping with both of us even if I hadn't walked in on them one night is another question I never asked her. That she managed to induce us to share her favours rather than make her choose between us is a measure of her persuasiveness. There were certain conditions

15

attached to this arrangement though. One was that 'Three is Company'. The other one was the kind of discretion that precluded the comparison of notes. We quickly learned to ignore, too, the fact that Annis seemed to make all the decisions in this affair and treated her like a force of nature. A bit like weather, really.

We talked about the weather for a bit – there'd been a lot of it recently – while I kept an eye on Lane. He was so engrossed in his book, he groped around for his pint rather than take his eyes off the print. Tim interrupted his description of how the trees in his neighbourhood had suffered in the storm and tapped my arm. 'That kid with the black curls has been staring at us, I think he wants to talk to you.'

He looked too young to get served in a pub but took a fortifying swig from a pint of lager as soon as I looked up. He wore the latest evolution of pre-ruined jeans and holey sweater and was being nudged towards us from behind by a bottle-blonde girl in a similar outfit who if anything looked even younger. Both wore expensive trainers which suggested they were in the Rosie by choice, not because they couldn't afford a night in a more fashionable city centre pub. 'Okay, okay,' he complained to the girl over his shoulder, then composed his most streetwise expression and came up to our table.

'Ehm, hi, ehm, the, ehhhh landlady said you're a, ehm, private dick ... ehm ... tective.' The girl behind him turned her eyes heavenwards and stuck her studiously bored face into a pint of bitter. I hoped for his sake that they were friends. It would last longer that way.

I nodded encouragingly at him, don't ask why. 'She's right.' I'd once helped the landlady to find out who was pinching her empty kegs, gas-axing them in half lengthways and turning them into cut-price barbecues. Drinks were still on the house. The boy was blocking my view of Lane so I told him: 'Why don't you sit down.' He did. The girl did likewise, tucked her hair behind her ears, crossed her legs and focused her eyes into the middle distance.

Nothing to do with her. The bloke looked at her for help, saw he wasn't getting any, took a deep breath and said quickly: 'There's going to be a murder. Or, or two even. I think.'

'Tell it properly, tell him what you told me,' the girl urged impatiently. She took out a blue tin of tobacco hand-painted with stars and moons and proceeded to roll a fat cigarette.

The boy pulled his dark eyebrows together in concentration and stared deep into his pint for inspiration. 'It was last Sunday, ehm, at night. I was out late and, eh, walking home up the hill and they came out from the footpath. It was dark so they didn't see me and they were talking and, ehm, one said something about someone called Albert having been "nosing about". "Just like the old witch," said the other one, "sniffing around at night." And then the other one said, "Maybe we should arrange for them to have a little accident."' He looked up at me, visibly relieved at having finished this long and involved story.

'Wha eshi-nashy?' asked Tim through a mouth full of parsnip crisps.

'What else did they say?' I translated.

'Nothing. I mean I don't know. I just stood and waited until they were gone completely. I didn't want them to know I'd heard.'

'Did you recognize them?'

'It was too dark. They were big blokes though.'

'Did they have any particular accent?'

'Didn't notice any accent,' he mused.

Probably local then. 'How old did they sound to you?'

'Older than me.'

'That narrows it down to forty million people,' I complained.

Tim came to his rescue. 'Older like him?' He pointed at me. 'Or older like me?' he asked smiling, being a comfortable ten years younger than me.

'Oh, old like him.' The boy pointed at me. How rude.

17

'That *does* narrow it down,' Tim assured him.

'Doesn't matter. And where did this happen?' I asked distractedly because Lane had got up. But he was only walking to the bar, using his faithful stick.

'Down the valley, just past the Lane End Farm turn-off.' He pointed his thumb over his shoulder in the general direction of Swainswick.

The girl set her pint hard on the table and blew cigarette smoke at me. 'You're not going to do anything about it, are you? You're not really listening. I knew the police wouldn't but aren't you supposed to help people when the police can't be bothered or is that just on TV?'

'No, no, it's a bit like that, I guess, though nothing's quite like it is on TV. Especially murder. So what would you like me to do about it?'

'If I knew what to do about it I'd do it myself,' she snapped, suddenly no longer bored. '*You're* the detective, you're supposed to know what to do in a case like this.'

A case like this? 'Two blokes talking on the way home from the pub, probably pissed ... Do you know any Alberts? Who might be nosy? Or a witch?'

'I don't know any Alberts but there can't be that many, can there? It's an old man's name, no one's called Albert any more,' she pointed out. 'But I do know an old witch. So does Cairn.' She nodded in the boy's direction. 'Lots of people know about *her*.'

'Do they now. And what's her name?'

'I don't know her name. We just call her the Old Witch. Actually she's not *that* old. More ... old like him.' She pointed her chin at Tim, who stopped smiling at her.

'And has she had an accident lately?'

'Well, I don't know, do I? I haven't seen her for ages. So she could be dead, couldn't she? No one would know.' She fixed me with steady gas-blue eyes. Her friend nodded tiny nods.

'And where exactly is her place?'

'Give him the map,' she instructed him.

He half stood up so he could pull a bent piece of paper from his back pocket.

I took it from him and stashed it in my jacket. 'Next time I have a spare moment I'll check it out.' I was planning on not having such a moment for a long time.

The boy looked relieved for a second, then worried again. 'So that's it, we hired you? How much is it going to cost?'

'What? Oh . . . ehm.' I looked at Tim for help but he just raised one eyebrow, something else I wished I could do.

'Look, I'll let you know,' I said eventually. 'Don't worry about it, okay? What are your names?'

'I'm Cairn, she's Heather.'

'There's some kind of pattern there,' I mused.

'Our mum's Scottish,' said Heather.

'Ah, brother and sister,' I concluded.

'Wow, you really are a detective then,' she said drily.

'No doubt about it. I'm Chris and the big woolly one's Tim. And now, if you don't mind . . . we were in the middle of discussing another case . . .'

'Oh, okay. We come in here quite a lot,' Cairn assured me.

'Come on.' Heather dragged him away.

'So, are you going to check it out?' asked Tim when they were out of earshot. He was hunting about for bits of crisp between the bottles on the table.

'Are you kidding? Not until I find the morning headline screams "Nosy Albert Has Little Accident".'

James Lane did nothing more interesting that night than visit the Gents at regular intervals. If anything, his reliance on the walking stick seemed to increase with each pint he drank. During one of his toilet breaks I walked over to his chair and pretended to warm myself by the little fire while checking out his reading material. I nudged the book off the chair with my knee so I could pick it up and read the title. *The Great Crown Jewels Robbery of 1303*. Whatever gets you through the day . . .

* * *

19

Bribery doesn't deserve all the bad press it's had. Hey, bribery can be fun! That morning I bribed Annis with her favourite breakfast (hot croissant, quince jam, five-minute egg and a cafetière of freshly ground Colombian coffee) to drive me back to Larkhall where I'd left the DS in the Oriel Hall car park the night before due to a certain degree of inebriation. I'd flagged down a passing minicab and offered the driver the entirety of my cash reserves for a lift home. An expensive exercise since it's quite a few miles from there to Mill House but anything was better than losing my licence. A private detective without a car was an impossible proposition.

I enjoyed feeding her anyway. She always attacked food as though she hadn't seen any for a week. Her disposition invariably sweetened while she demolished what you put in front of her and she always had that is-there-any-more look at the end of it.

Annis topped up the fuel in her ancient Landy, always a good idea with a beast that drank more than its fair share of the dwindling oil reserves, then sat fiddling and mumbling behind the wheel. Eventually she persuaded the thing to start.

'Full moon soon,' she explained. 'It's always temperamental round the full moon.'

I didn't say a word. I was long used to Annis's firm belief that the thing was alive and needed to be treated like a slightly batty elderly relative. Secretly I thought it was just a ruse to deter people from wanting to borrow it.

I had less success with trying to talk her into going halves on the surveillance of James Lane. 'I didn't tell you to take the job,' she rightly but annoyingly pointed out as we rumbled along the track.

'The roof needs repairing. Both roofs. How am I, how are *we* going to pay for it?'

Annis frowned. 'How have we always paid for stuff?' she wondered.

'Sold a few paintings, found some money in an old tin somewhere, that kind of thing.'

'Oh yeah. Well, you check the old tins while I do some work in the studio, if you don't mind. Seriously, you're not the only one who needs to crack on with some painting. I promised the Glasshouse Gallery in St Ives four canvases for a mixed show and they only want to show new work. So do I of course. I'm afraid you're stuck with this surveillance thing for now. How's it look so far?'

'Like a man walking with a stick.'

A few minutes later I waved her goodbye in St Saviour's Road, out of view from Lane's windows which overlooked the car park where I'd left the DS. I walked the last few yards, sauntered along the line of cars while scanning the house for signs of life. It was a dank, dark morning and I registered with relief that the lights were on downstairs.

I fumbled in my pockets for my car keys. Nothing. Not there. Then I registered first with disbelief and then with a feeling like a punch in the gut that the car wasn't there either. Gone, disappeared. Twenty parking spaces in the row and every one of them taken. Not a Citroën among them. I clearly remembered which space I'd left it in. That one. Or that one. Next to an old mud-coloured Volvo estate. I was beginning to feel stupid pacing up and down in front of the cars carrying the essential bit of private-eye kit, my thermos flask of black coffee. A couple of shoppers walking past gave me suspicious looks. There was only one thing to do, even for a private detective.

If you ever need a demonstration of polite boredom then report your car stolen (though wait until it *has* been stolen, obviously).

'You're not going to send someone out here?' I moaned.

'There really wouldn't be much point, Mr Honeysett. I'll take your details now but you'll still have to come into the station and fill in the form . . .'

Great, just when you're stranded without a motor. I don't know what I had expected, a SWAT team and a vanload of technicians dusting the world for fingerprints of the nefarious car thieves and a counsellor for my post-automotive stress . . . What I hadn't expected was a load of nothing. Now completely deflated I gave the guy the details. He was unlikely to be a police officer himself and there was no telling whether he took the call from Bath, Bristol or Bogotá. 'The DS21, that's the one with the swivelling headlights, isn't it? Nice . . .'

Looking up from my misery I saw that I'd nearly missed Lane leaving the house. I told the guy I'd come down to Manvers Street police station later, terminated the call and followed my target left. After only a few yards he sat down on the bench by the bus stop at the Larkhall Inn. He was dressed like the night before in grey waterproof jacket, jeans and trainers and this morning was carrying a blue shoulder bag. He stood by the kerb, blearily looking at the wet tarmac. Two women were also waiting, one with a pushchair already folded up and a listless child standing snottily by her side, and a guy in a raincoat I recognized as the other reader from the pub was sitting on the bench. I went and pretended to study the timetable. Then I actually *did* study it and realized I couldn't make sense of it at all. One of those small yellow buses drew up. In the corner of my eye I could see Lane shuffling forward. It suddenly occurred to me that I might have to pay hard cash to use this service. Lane seemed to have some kind of pass that allowed him to ride for free. I got on whilst hunting around for change in my pockets. Nothing. I didn't think they'd accept plastic so kept furtling about and eventually located something promising deep in the lining of my leather jacket. I apologized to the driver while I stood, thermos between my knees, one of my arms halfway down a torn jacket pocket, clawing for the money. At last I managed to close my hand on the coins and pulled them out: two shillings.

'Excuse me,' I said feebly to no one in particular and got off the bus which pulled eagerly away with Lane on board.

Shillings? Just how old was this leather jacket? This was getting ridiculous. I unscrewed the top of the vacuum flask and took a draught of hot black coffee. It cheered me up just long enough to find the post office and use their cash machine to furnish myself with some readies. When I got outside the heavens opened again and I got soaked before I'd even decided what to do next. I hadn't been without my own transport for more than fifteen minutes and I was already heartily sick of it. If I ever caught up with who had taken the DS I'd happily throttle them. I was sorely tempted to call for a cab but taking taxis everywhere wasn't going to help pay the roofers so I padded along in the rain to the next bus stop near the surprisingly large church and hopped on the first one that came along. It ground up and rattled down hills and seemed to be going in circles without really getting anywhere but it was dry and it beat standing in the rain, though only just.

'The DS21, that's the one with the swivelling headlights, isn't it?' asked Sergeant Hayes, looking over the completed form. I'd finally made it to Manvers Street police station.

'It is.' It was. The DS had four headlights, two of which turned left and right as you turned the wheel, lighting your way around sharp bends.

'Probably joyriders, Honeysett. If you're lucky then they didn't set fire to it at the end of the night.' He flashed me a grin that bared his white but uneven teeth.

'I didn't think joyriders would be interested in a thirty-year-old left-hand drive. And why are we calling them joyriders? They're damn car thieves and I don't feel any joy.'

'The joy's all theirs. Until we catch up with them, that is. We're allowed to ram them now to stop them, like the Americans. They call it the PIT manoeuvre,' he said cheerfully.

23

'*Ram them*? I don't want you to *ram them*, it's a classic car!' I protested.

'I've seen your car, it's a tatty old heap, Honeysett, and I'm sure the MOT on it is dodgy. If we do find it we'll make sure it's roadworthy before returning it to you.'

That's the problem if you're on grunting terms with the Old Bill, they start taking liberties. My relationship with Avon and Somerset's finest had always been a little strained. Hardly surprising since our interests often overlapped uncomfortably. But unlike many other private investigators I wasn't an ex-police officer and so hadn't got a lot of friends on the inside on whom I could rely to feed me information or avert their eyes when necessary.

Just then a door opened to the left of us and an all too familiar figure barrelled into the office: Detective Superintendent Michael Needham. I had to fight the urge to duck. The Superintendent didn't approve of Aqua Investigations since he rightly suspected that we sometimes fell off the tightrope of legality he himself seemed to walk so effortlessly. In one respect it was more than a suspicion: he had always known that I owned an unlicensed WWII revolver, a Webley .38, and had spent years patting me down trying to catch me carrying it. Then a few months ago it had been fired in a typically messy episode of Aqua business and had promptly been confiscated, together with all our personal effects.

Needham dumped a file in someone's in-tray and was safely on his way out again when kind Sergeant Hayes called: 'Morning, sir! You remember Mr Honeysett, don't you?'

Needham stopped in his tracks, turned his big, mobile face towards me and gave me an evil stare. I had the feeling he'd known I was here all along. 'He's hard to forget. What's he doing here?'

'He's become a victim of crime, sir.'

'Make a nice change for him.' He disappeared through the same door and shut it hard behind him.

'How is your corpulent Super these days?' I asked Hayes, who wasn't exactly skinny himself.

'Lousy of mood and short of temper. But I'm sure seeing you here cheered him up no end.'

'What's eating him? This year's crime figures out?'

'He's got a medical coming up in three weeks and has gone on another diet. He's like a bear with a sore head when he doesn't get his two sugars in his tea. Personally I think it's the artificial sweeteners driving him round the bend . . .' Hayes suddenly put the brakes on his indiscretion, remembering I was only a meddling civilian. 'Okay, that's fine.' He ran his eyes down the form. 'It's more than likely then that someone stole the keys to your car while you were at the Rose and Crown. Unless you left them in the ignition, of course. Ah, ah, ah.' He stopped my protests with a calming gesture. 'It's easily done and we come across it all the time. Now don't worry, I'm sure it'll turn up,' he added reassuringly. 'It's not the kind of motor that gets nicked to order after all. What state it'll be in is another question.' He gave me his sweetest smile.

Back outside I turned up my collar in a feeble attempt to keep pneumonia at bay and scooted along Manvers Street. The rain was back, driven by a wind that seemed to come from all directions at once. Everyone else was hurrying too with hunched shoulders or fighting umbrellas more a hindrance than an asset. By the time I got to York Street and pushed open the door to the steamed-up Café Retro I felt clammy and miserable and in need of comfort. I found a tiny table at the back. When the waitress appeared I ordered a large mug of hot chocolate and a bowl of chips. The Retro was, as the name implied, made to look like it had been there since time immemorial with the aid of imitation marble, fake gilded mirrors and distressed waitresses, but now it had been here for so long it had taken on a genuine patina of its own. It seemed an age until my order arrived but it was worth it just for the chips. I drowned them in ketchup and took comfort by the handful. Losing the car was bad enough but while I was filling in the form for Sergeant Hayes I'd realized how much stuff I'd left in it: video camera, binoculars, Dictaphone, CDs, sunglasses . . .

The big café window was blind with condensation and the door opened constantly with people looking in, hoping to find a table just to get out of the rain. I called Annis on my mobile; I was in no mood for getting soaked at a bus stop. She answered grumpily and my request for her taxi service didn't exactly cheer her up but the offer of hot chocolate finally swung it. After a short while I put in the order and made sure the waitress took the empty chip bowl away so it couldn't damage my culinary reputation. French fries, *moi*? When Annis splashed through the door her hot chocolate had only been standing on the table for a minute which puts the respective speeds of the disgruntled painter and harassed waitress in perspective.

'What a sight for sore eyes,' she said and sank her face into the mound of whipped cream. She had hardly got wet in the rain which could only mean one thing. 'I'm parked right outside on a triple yellow. Any parking fines payable by the passenger,' she slurped.

We ran the few yards across the street and jumped into the cab of the Land Rover. She had a fabulous moustache of whipped cream. I leant over and kissed it away. 'Thanks for coming to the rescue once more.'

'That's okay. I was getting a bit fed up anyway. Smoke from the stove, blue light from the plastic tarpaulin and the flapping noise it makes, it's enough to drive you potty.' Annis did her mysterious ministrations and mumbled her invocations and the Landy burbled into life.

Some unexplained bottleneck in Broad Street had slowed traffic to a crawl. A number 7 bus was shipping water as it took on a few bedraggled passengers at the corner with Green Street. And there he was. 'Look. See the guy about to get on the bus with the hood up and the shoulder bag? That's James Lane, the guy I'm supposed to be following.'

It looked like the same few people who had left from Larkhall in the morning were coming back on the same bus. I recognized the snotty kid and his young mother and the bloke in the raincoat.

'I'll let the bus pull out then, shall I?'

'Don't bother, I know where he's going and the bus'll only go round in circles.' I settled down to a good moan about traffic jams, the state of public transport, the price of roof repairs, the apathetic police response to my car crisis, the freak weather and that bit of hard skin on my middle finger that annoyed me. In fact the unusually violent bouncing action Annis got out of the Landy as she flung it down the track to the house made it completely impossible to chew at it. 'Whehehewow what aaaare youhoohoo dooin?' I managed.

She turned into the yard and scraped to a halt by the outbuildings. 'I was trying to shut you up, Honeysett, you've done nothing but moan from one end to the other. I come all the way to pick you up and you're trying to bore me rigid in return. What do you have to say for yourself?'

'Sorry, let me make it up to you,' I suggested suggestively.

'Mm . . . okay then. Get into the kitchen and fix me a decent lunch. I'll be in the studio.'

Chapter Three

'Yes, you look utterly ridiculous,' Annis answered lazily, the duvet drawn up under her chin against the chill of the morning. Her hair was spread invitingly across the pillow and I suddenly felt like taking all this gear off again and getting back in beside her, but duty called.

'What? Ridiculous? Not . . . cool? Stylish? Dashing?'

'Yes, dashing, that's it,' she cackled. 'You look like you're about to *dash off* somewhere. Like the Western Front, in one of those biplanes held together with string.'

'Well, that's all the biker gear there is.'

'I know. But perhaps you should dispense with the goggles. I think Lane might remember you like that: black open-face helmet, long hair, goggles, tatty black leather jacket, gauntlets, jeans and clumpy boots.'

'Well, I don't have a choice. I either use your Norton or follow him on roller blades. You can't follow a man on the same minibus more than once unless he's blind.'

'I know. Just make sure you don't drop the machine, now that it's been repaired.'

A few months back Annis had crashed her 1950s Norton after someone had sabotaged the brakes, landing her in hospital. Both Annis and Norton had been beautifully restored, the bike with the help of the Norton Owners Club, but Annis's enthusiasm for riding the thing had somewhat diminished. In fact, she hadn't ridden it since.

I wasn't exactly overexcited myself. A fine rain was falling when I wheeled the Norton into the yard, and the air had turned noticeably colder. I had to work the kick-starter only five or six times before the engine fired, which wasn't at all bad for a fifty-year-old bike that didn't get used much. The people who restored it had fitted a pair of working exhaust pipes, a not unimportant detail since before the accident it used to sound like a Sherman tank. Even so it was noisy enough.

I hadn't ridden a bike for ages but by the time I reached the other end of the valley I had got used to the gear change and the lack of a CD player and could concentrate on other things. How much time was I going to devote to the limping Lane? Several shortcuts to finding out how disabled he really was came instantly to mind but none of them were exactly ethical and at least one of them contravened the Dangerous Wild Animals Act of 1976.

I cut the engine just before I reached the Oriel Hall car park, coasted in and chained the bike up out of sight of Lane's house. All this faffing about had made me quite late this morning and no sooner had I found a relatively sheltered spot than Lane left the house, dressed entirely the same as before and carrying his blue shoulder bag. I walked to the street corner and peered round. He had hobbled to the bus stop again and the bloke with the raincoat, who seemed to be a regular himself, made room for him on the bench.

I got the bike, sat with the engine idling at the exit to the car park until the number 7 bus rattled past, waited a couple of minutes, then followed.

The bus really did go round in circles, cranking up Claremont Road and taking the less than scenic route through the estates of Fairfield before revisiting Claremont and grinding on into town. I hung well back and stopped several times to allow for the excruciatingly slow speed of the thing.

Lane got off in Walcot Street. I quickly parked the bike opposite the Pig and Fiddle and followed on foot. I didn't have to walk far. He disappeared into the Podium, an understated little shopping centre, and soon I was gliding up behind him on the escalator to the upper floor that housed, among some cafés and restaurants, the central library. Naturally I hoped that Lane had a secret job as a limbo dancer at the Indian restaurant but of course he went into the library, returned a couple of books, then disappeared between the shelves. The place was full of school kids sitting on the floor, working at some kind of project. I followed Lane into the history section, kept my eyes on the books until I picked him up in my peripheral vision, then casually looked him over. He was checking the shelves against some notes on a scrap of paper. His walking stick hung over his left forearm. He moved sideways along the shelf but there it was, that awkward jerk of the torso, as though the right leg refused to move by itself. The man had a limp. Either that or he was a very good actor indeed; it's difficult to dissemble while concentrating on something else entirely. I'd come quite close to him so I picked up a book at random: *Britain at War, Unseen Archives*. I got so engrossed in the black and white photography that when I looked up again Lane was gone. In a panic I scooted round the shelves and eventually spotted him at the issue desk. I ditched my book and walked closely past him while he was busy exchanging pleasantries with the young librarian who was issuing his books and I managed to read a couple of the titles: *Witchcraft in the Middle Ages* and *A History of Sculpture*.

Best to wait for him downstairs, I decided, and left the library. I was already on the downward escalator and just calculating whether to tell Haarbottle that Lane was most likely a genuine case when I caught sight of two ugly blokes blocking the exit at the bottom. They had just let through a woman with shopping bags and now plugged the gap again looking up at me with expressionless faces. Both were quite tall, both had short hair, wore dark rainproof jackets and gave me the creeps. The escalator carried me inexorably towards their waiting, unwelcoming arms.

One of the men I'd never seen before, the other was Detective Inspector Deeks. Sod this for a laugh. I turned around and started running up the downward escalator, not making much headway but at least I wasn't going any further towards the goons. Fortunately I was the only one on the thing at that moment. I looked over my shoulder. The other guy had started running up after me and was making headway just as slowly but being halfway to the top already gave me a sure advantage over him. Once I hit terra firma I could leg it down the back stairs and disappear into the underground car park before he had a chance to catch up. Suddenly the escalator stopped. My frantic running motion tipped me forward and I landed painfully on my front. The next second it started going down again and by the time I was once more on my feet it had deposited me and the running bloke, who had also fallen, in front of Deeks who still had his finger on the emergency button.

'Just as well one of us has brains, isn't it?' he said with a theatrical sigh and stuck his warrant card into my face. I had to lean back to read it. It didn't tell me anything new. I looked at him with little interest and much loathing. Deeks had been Superintendent Needham's preferred sidekick for years, something I'd always found hard to fathom. For a start he was not a thing you wanted to have to clap eyes on every working day of your life. Especially first thing in the morning. He was one of those blokes who probably wanted to look like his dad when he was twelve and by the time he was sixteen had succeeded. There was no way of telling how old he was. Forty? Sixty? His face was long and jowly, his eyes dark and narrow and his scar-puckered nose nearly hid his ungenerous, thin-lipped mouth. His bad breath alone was enough to make me want to go on the run. His attitude to civilians in general and PIs in particular was one of profound contempt. He brought his cadaverous face close to mine and wafted his halitosis up my nostrils. 'A word.' Several came effortlessly to mind.

He grabbed me by the arm so he could lead me aside to the window of a silversmith's shop. 'This is Detective Sergeant Sorbie,' he introduced the other officer, who was peeling chewing gum off his trouser knee. The DS looked equally unpleasant with an unhealthy pallor, an inept shave and tired, bloodshot eyes which seemed to have problems fastening on to anything in particular. 'You've been traipsing after James Lane, sitting outside his house in your car, even following him to the pub,' Deeks continued accusingly.

'Don't tell me he made a complaint,' I said, wondering how Lane could have clocked me so quickly.

'He didn't. *I'm* making the complaint.' He drew me further back and pointed out Lane who was just then stepping off the escalator. Only a few seconds later the ubiquitous bloke in the raincoat appeared from behind one of the large fake columns and followed him out of the building. 'DC Howell. A bright new detective constable, good practice for him.'

'So you're having him followed as well. Care to tell me why?'

'None of your business. Who's paying you to sniff about?' he asked.

'Sorry, client confidentiality.'

'Bollocks.'

'Tough titty.'

'Stop fucking me about, *Mr* Honeysett, or I'll be forced to arrest you,' he said in an unpleasant singsong.

'I'm not breaking any damn laws by following Lane until he takes out a restraining order against me,' I said, serious now.

'You're interfering with a police investigation.'

'You'll never make it stick. Especially since I demanded clarification on the matter and was refused. Your sergeant here's my witness.'

'You what?' grunted Sorbie.

'Look, we're bound to follow him for the same bloody

32

reasons, aren't we?' I said reasonably. 'I'll show you mine if you show me yours.'

Deeks considered for a second. 'All right, let's go and find a bike shed somewhere.'

Five minutes later in the Green Tree, just around the corner from where Lane was still waiting for the bus with his personal DC in attendance, Deeks lifted a pint of Janglepaws or some other odd-sounding stuff to his pale, floppy lips and slurped. I stuck my nose into my Guinness to help me through this. I couldn't believe I was sitting at the same table as Deeks without a tape recorder running. DS Sorbie was staring glumly into his glass of reconstituted orange juice.

'Okay, you first,' Deeks said.

'N-nn. You first,' I countered skilfully. Kid's stuff.

Sorbie groaned.

'Does he have a hangover?' I asked.

'Doctor told him not to drink with his medication. But DS Sorbie likes to try everything once.'

'Laudable.' I didn't ask what DS Sorbie needed medication for. Lots of things by the look of it. 'Okay, no big secret, Griffin's, the insurers, want to know if he's faking his disability which they are forking out for.'

'Same here. I believe Lane's always been a part-time fraudster. He's got two convictions for fraud, one insurance, one benefit, though neither are very recent. Which doesn't mean he's not been at it in the meantime.'

'So why are you interested at all, surely you must have better things to do than to keep small fry under surveillance?'

'I certainly do. Only the landlady who got sued for damages by the little toerag is the Assistant Chief Constable's ex-wife. She's only a recent ex and he wants to impress.'

'I took the job because my roof got blown away. I believe I have the purer motive: money.'

'You'll do as you're told. Don't underestimate my career plans, Honeysett.'

'What about you, DS Sorbie? Do you have career plans?' I asked pleasantly.

He gave a pained and joyless grin and nodded. 'When I'm not too busy trying not to puke in your Guinness, yeah.'

'Well, it's a job and I have to make a living, guys, just like everyone else . . .'

'Too right, you'll never survive on your art, mate, I've seen the crap you paint.'

Everyone's a critic. 'Okay, howsabout we'll take it in turns to watch Lane?' I suggested. 'Saves on the man-hours and we'll let each other know if he suddenly starts jogging round the park.'

'I'll think about it,' Deeks said and took a long slurp of his pint, then set it down precisely on its beer mat. 'I've thought about it. *You have to be shitting me.* I'm telling you to piss off out of it. But I'll make you an offer, and you'd better take it 'cause you won't get a better one: if *we* catch him line dancing we'll give you a shout. And another piece of advice: you really should take the goggles off inside.'

Next morning I was watching Lane's house as usual, only even more carefully. Two things had made me suspicious: the chummy offer to let me know if they found anything on Lane and the frankly unlikely fact that Deeks had paid for the drinks. Not at all normal behaviour for the fuzz, as I liked to think of them. Sounds cuddly, doesn't it? They were to get less cuddly before the day was out. In the meantime I was getting soaked under the inefficient shelter of a near-bald tree in the now familiar car park, waiting for Lane to make an appearance. It had started to rain again when I'd set off for Larkhall and not stopped since. It was that annoying kind of dancing rain, so fine it wafted about on the breeze and there seemed an endless supply of it upstairs where the sky was a featureless slab of wet cement.

It wasn't until after ten that Lane left the house. Again I made sure he got on the bus, then started up the Norton and followed the by now familiar bus route into town, just to make sure he didn't get off before then. He had his blue bag with him and went to the library once more. He returned some books and walked on into the history section where he browsed, picking up books, reading the blurb or the index, then returning them to the shelf. Another batch of school kids was there and *Britain at War* was still on the shelf so I opened it again. If his surveillance went on like this I might get to finish the book in tiny increments. This time I made sure I didn't miss him leaving. He exited the Podium at the back, where a couple of wooden picnic tables stood deserted, crossed the road and disappeared into the Victoria Gallery. The large sign over the entrance read *A Half-Century of Sculpture. An exhibition of American and European sculpture from 1905 to 1955*, sponsored by this, that and the other.

I waited a minute, then followed inside with a stony heart. Did it have to be sculpture? Being a painter I wasn't really wild about it. Especially this piddly stuff. If you must do sculpture (and I really don't see why) make it big, make it heavy, do it properly. And preferably outside somewhere.

Lane was taking a clockwise turn through the exhibition space. On the walls were some drawings and photographs of stuff they couldn't get in here, an awful lot of blurb about the history of sculpture and how Duchamp's urinal had changed everything. (Surely if one *pissoir* can revolutionize your entire discipline you're in trouble, *non*?) I skipped most of it, keeping one eye on Lane. There were things plonked about everywhere: some guy's reinterpretation of a *pietà*, better luck next time, mate; a couple of de Kooning things that looked like he left them on top of the stove too long, should've stuck to painting; two rather witty wire things by Picasso, should've stuck to sculpture; some motorized Alex Calder stuff that was ever so slightly

35

bent which gave it an art-schoolish feel. The unavoidable Mr Moore was represented by some reclining, sorry, recumbent lump with holes in all the right places, and the centrepiece was a small contorted bronze by Rodin on a plinth. The whole exhibition looked like the stuff had just been dragged out of storage and no one had taken the time to give it a dusting. The names were all there but the examples, apart from the Rodin, were rubbish.

Lane seemed to think the same. He didn't linger over anything in particular until he got to the centre where the little Rodin dancer stood, presumably because it was recognizably human, I thought uncharitably. He spent some time admiring it from all angles, then made for the exit. It was no hardship to tear myself away and I followed him outside into the dancing rain. Lane took a left up Bridge Street, then turned his back on the Abbey and walked to the post office where his bus stop was. I had a pretty good idea where this was going and I had no intention of tagging along again. Not once had he given the slightest indication that he didn't need the stick, not a single lapse and no exaggerations either. He just looked like a guy who had a slight problem in the walking and staying upright department.

I scanned the street for anyone following Lane. I could still hear Deeks say 'brand new detective constable, good exercise for him' but I couldn't see any evidence of a tail on Lane. Or perhaps the DC was better than I'd thought. I didn't much care because I was starving by now and had been running around long enough. A reward was in order so I steered a course towards the Abbey Church Yard. The rain and the lateness of the season had cleared it of tourists but all too soon it would be sporting a giant Christmas tree. I crossed to the Pump Room. *Water is Best* some abstemious wit had chiselled on top of the sandstone façade, in ancient Greek no less. Yes, water was all right, I'd called the business after the stuff, but right now I felt I'd seen enough of it. I was shown to a table near the low stage where the

Pump Room Trio were playing Mozart at an unobtrusive volume. Here, everything was calm, relaxing and reassuringly expensive. As always the service was swift and efficient. I ordered Eggs Benedict and a pot of Earl Grey and sat back to enjoy the salubrious surroundings. By the south window a bloke in Georgian costume still dispensed the warm mineral water that came out of the ground here but there weren't many takers today. Apparently the water that bubbles up is an amazing twelve thousand years old. It tastes like it, too.

It didn't take long for the perfectly proportioned columns, the splendid chandelier and the excellent ambience of the room to convince you that you were indulging in real luxury, even before you looked at your bill. The tea arrived first. My stomach gave a delicate rumble as the waitress poured the first cup for me. Naturally as a private eye I was supposed to drink mugs of stewed tea and eat eggs-over-easy in a 'greasy spoon' somewhere but apart from the fact that you'd be hard pressed to find such an establishment in Bath it just wasn't my style. *This*, I was telling myself, as the white-aproned waitress wended her way towards me with my Eggs Benedict, *was my style*. Just then dirty jagged shadows fell across the pristine white of the table linen. The waitress slowed, then stopped.

'Thank you, we're not hungry,' said DI Deeks. The waitress hovered uncertainly.

'And he's about to lose his appetite,' added DS Sorbie, pointing at me.

Quite the comedy duo. There was no sign of hangover in Sorbie today; he was well shaven, neatly pressed and frighteningly alert.

'What's up with you two?' I asked, annoyed because the waitress was retreating with my order towards the manager at the cash desk.

'We bring glad tidings,' Deeks said. 'We found your car.'

My heart sank. 'Did they trash it? Where'd you find it?'

'Not much damage but then I'm told it wouldn't have looked much different before you said you lost it.'

'Very funny. Where is it?'

'In the middle of a field in Lower Swainswick.'

'So it's not a total write-off? They didn't torch it?'

'No,' said Sorbie reassuringly. 'It'll be just fine. Once we've scraped the dead body off the back seat.'

Chapter Four

The car zipped fast up Lansdown hill. DS Sorbie was driving, I was in the back of the big Ford with Deeks. Neither of them answered any of my questions though where we were going was becoming obvious when Sorbie screeched right, down a minor road which soon turned into a network of muddy farm tracks. 'We really want a Land Rover for this kind of thing,' Sorbie complained as he cranked on the wheel to avoid the worst ruts and holes.

'Dream on,' Deeks encouraged him. He turned to me. 'Now, I should really have cautioned you at the Pump Room only the Super said there was no need. But you do anything stupid or even think about doing it and I'll cuff you, clear?'

So Needham had put in a word for me. Obviously not a huge one or I'd be finishing my Eggs Benedict just about now but a word nonetheless. 'Yeah, no sweat.' Then I gave an involuntary groan because as we splished past yet another cluster of dripping farm buildings I could see it there below us. Smack in the middle of a gently sloping field of pasture stood my car. Three doors were open. The tracks on two sides of the field were clogged with police vehicles: Land Rovers and saloons and a noddy car, vans, a minibus and an ambulance. There was a large white tent in the field, just below and to the left of my black DS21. Police tape fluttered everywhere.

When we got there Sorbie simply abandoned the car on the track and we all got out into the thin rain. We hopped and zigzagged and took unnaturally long strides to avoid the puddles and waterlogged ruts until we got to a uniformed constable stoically guarding the remains of a wooden five-bar gate. It looked like someone had driven the DS straight through it. It also looked like it was half rotten anyway which meant somebody had been lucky; only on TV do wooden gates simply crumble when you drive through them. The small field was bordered by hedgerows on all sides and this appeared to be the only way in. Scene of Crime Officers were busy along the hedge, around the car and the tent, all in their white space outfits. At the entrance to the tent stood the bulk of Superintendent Michael Needham, sensibly clad in a blue rainproof over his suit. He'd stuffed his trousers into a pair of black wellies but even so he'd managed to get his suit splashed with mud. His deep-set intelligent eyes under thin, dark eyebrows dispassionately followed our slithering progress up the slick slope. Needham's sparse grey hair was closely cropped, his broad face pale and tired, his mouth set in impatient contempt. By the time we got to him the bottoms of our trousers were dark and heavy with moisture and mud.

I noticed Needham had lost a bit of weight recently yet I preferred him when he wasn't on a diet. Diets really did make him grumpy. He missed his Danish pastries and absolutely loathed tea without sugar. Just now he took a sip from a plastic mug, pulled a sour face and splashed the remainder of the grey liquid on the ground, which probably meant it was missing that vital ingredient. He dropped the mug on to the trestle table behind him without looking where it fell and attracted my full attention by grabbing my arm hard. 'You're in deep shit this time, Honeysett, so no arsing about. Do exactly as you're told, touch nothing, answer all questions in full, stay behind me. Got that?'

'Got it,' I agreed soberly.

'Deeks, Sorbie, stay here.' Needham talked to them like they were a couple of hounds.

I followed him up to the Citroën which stood, mud-spattered and with a crumpled bonnet, just above us, nose pointing to the right. Forensics were still busy all around and a bloke with a large video camera took sweeping panoramic shots of the valley.

The offside rear door was closed. Inside, against the window, slumped the body of a man. A blue and white face below a mess of bloody skull pressed against the pane. Blood streaks and mud nearly obscured the glass. There was a hand print in the middle of it all. Someone was moving around inside on the back seat and two technicians in moon suits, both women, were standing by the open door on the other side.

'Let's move round,' said Needham who was quite sure-footed in his boots. I slithered on. 'Give us some room,' he said to the techies, who stepped well back to allow for Needham's circumference. 'So you left the body but took the car keys,' he said to me conversationally.

'I didn't drive the damn –'

'How're you doing in there, Prof?' Needham called.

Professor Earnshaw Meyers, the white-haired Home Office pathologist, was sitting comfortably on the rear seat next to the slumped corpse. 'Just finishing,' he said, scratching away with a fountain pen on a pad of forms on top of his fat aluminium briefcase that was lying across his knees. I stuck my head around the corner. Meyers looked absolutely ancient, with sparse white hair and parchment skin, but apparently he'd always looked like that and was nowhere near retirement age. 'Mr Honeysett,' he said by way of greeting without bothering to look up. We had met before. He finished scribbling, pocketed the pad and pen and slid his bum out of the car. The smells of blood, urine and faeces that came out with him nearly made me retch.

'What have you got for me then, Prof?' Needham said chummily. 'And don't make it too polysyllabic, I'm not in the mood.'

'One dead male, aged between sixty and sixty-five, I'd say. Not particularly tall but you'll get all that later. Trauma to the front of the skull, abrasions to the face and hands. Could have been an accident but –'

'Did you run over him, Honeysett?' Needham interrupted.

'As I told Deeks –'

'Go on, sorry,' he said to Meyers.

'His injuries appear to be consistent with having been involved in a vehicular accident, though his head injury suggests some kind of attack prior to that. Could turn out to be the Gobi. I estimate the time of –'

'Wait!' I said. 'The what?' The *Gobi*? What was he talking about? The desert? Some kind of ghost?

'Good Old Blunt Instrument,' Needham supplied. 'Did you hit him with your car jack?'

'I never saw the bl—'

'Sorry, Prof, you were saying about the time of death?'

'About six, seven hours ago. Sometime between five and six this morning.'

'You said it could have been an accident. So he wasn't killed in the car?'

'Oh no. It looks very much like he entered the car after he received his injuries. And died quite some time later. Enough time to move about and lose a considerable amount of blood. That's all I'm going to say at this stage.' He nodded to us. 'Gentlemen.' Then he took off down the hill, swinging his aluminium case like a schoolboy on a field trip.

'Right,' Needham said. 'Who is he, Chris? Don't touch the car.'

I bent down, hands on my knees for support, and took a long look at the dead guy. Even before his accident or fateful meeting with the Gobi he'd been no oil painting. He had large fleshy ears, now looking waxy, practically no lips and false teeth. I knew this because his mouth hung open and the upper plate of his dentures had fallen down, giving him a double row of shark's teeth at the bottom. His sparse, bloody hair still had some dark in it. He wore a cream weatherproof jacket and olive green, well-worn cords, now half pulled down after Meyers had taken the rectal temperature. Accident or murder, there was no dignity in the man's death.

I shook my head. 'Never . . .'

'. . . seen him before in your life,' Needham finished for me. 'All right, let's go and we'll have a nice long chat down the station.'

The Bath cop shop is a no-frills concrete lump of ugliness, sitting shamelessly between St John's and the Manvers Street Baptist Church. No amount of flowerpots on the outside or corporate colour scheming on the inside was going to dispel the air of architectural depression that the concrete walls sweated out. Even the Superintendent seemed heavier, slower, unhappier when walking its hard-wearing carpets and looked gloomier than ever once we had all settled in a cheerless interview room. Deeks was there too. After he had done the preliminaries with the tape – time, date, who was there and the fact that I'd waived my right to have a solicitor present at this stage – Needham began to patiently ask me the same damn questions over and over. How come my keys were missing? When had I first noticed I'd lost them? When could they have been stolen? Who was the dead guy, where had I met him, did we have an argument, what did I hit him with, did I run over him? Perhaps I was going to drive him to hospital and he died on the way and I panicked? Completely understandable, he assured me. Best come clean now, save us all a lot of bother. Or did I find him already hurt and then decide to give him a lift? Did I crash through the gate then bail out when I found he had croaked on the back seat? Deeks supplied the odd question but mainly it was the good old Needham–Honeysett ding-dong. Cop-shop tea arrived and was drunk – Needham produced a plastic dispenser of sweeteners from his pocket and stirred in a hailstorm of them with his biro – while my stomach rumbled indelicately in protest and then it all started again from the beginning with exactly the same questions. Their patience and capacity for going over the same ground for hours and hours always astounded me and drove me up the wall. Which is of course where they wanted me. There was no way Needham thought even for one minute that I had bashed the guy's head in, then stuffed him in the back of my car and parked it in the middle of a field for someone to find. If he did then police would be swarming all over Mill House by now and I'd be wearing paper clothes while all my gear was on its way to a forensics lab in Chepstow to be analysed for traces of blood. But of course he still had to do the due process and good copper thing and I was all he had so we spent the afternoon angry and bored at the same time, with rumbling sour stomachs from too much tepid quick-brew while futility filled the space between us like a fog.

All this was eventually followed by a written statement. I hung around for another half-hour waiting to sign the printed version. Needham grabbed it from under my biro almost before I'd finished my signature. We were all as irritated as each other. 'Right, you can go. We'll do it all over again as soon as we know who he was.'

Naturally I didn't say so but I had the unenviable certainty that the dead man's name was Albert.

The one good thing about autumn and winter as far as I could make out was the plentiful and cheap supply of pheasants. For many landowners it was the shoots that kept them from going under and new ones were springing up everywhere. Pheasant shooting had become the fashionable pastime for townies now. At some companies it had even replaced paintball games as a team building exercise. They taught their employees to shoot, then took them to the country and let them blast pheasants out of the sky to boost their morale. The staff's, not the pheasants', obviously. (It struck me that you had to be quite sure of your staff's loyalty to hand them all a shotgun, though.) It was rumoured that at some shoots the bag was so great that the majority of it was simply buried. The upshot (sorry) of all this was that the price of pheasant was tumbling and had now fallen to that of non-cardboard chicken.

It was dark and still raining by the time I left Manvers Street behind. By now I was seriously hungry. I just made it to Bartlett & Sons, the butcher's in Green Street, before they closed their doors, then rattled home on the Norton with a brace of pheasant strapped to the tank. When I splashed into the waterlogged yard I could see light up in the studio – Annis was working late. I was thoroughly wet and cheesed off with the day, and famished. I stabled the Norton and promised myself that I'd devour the first edible thing I clapped eyes on when I got inside. I walked into the kitchen. At the end of the long table stood a big stripy pumpkin, an annual gift from one of our neighbours in the valley. Not exactly convenience food. Okay, the second thing then. I found some seriously ripe cheese oozing on to a plate in the pantry and set to work on it. I instantly felt better. Not exactly at one with the world but better. I could faintly hear the phone ring in my little office in the attic but had no intention of answering it. Now or ever.

There's nothing wrong with just shoving pheasant in the oven as long as you drape some streaky bacon over it to stop it from drying out but I felt I needed a serious treat. After a shower and a change of clothes I grabbed the big oval casserole, browned one of the birds in oil and butter on top of the stove and flamed it with a good splash of

45

brandy. Then I chucked in some herbs from our straggly herb garden by the kitchen door and ladled in a couple of pints of stock. Some double cream, just a criminal amount, would finish it off nicely. I stuck the lid on and shoved it on the back of the stove to simmer. Then I poured myself a brandy, put my feet up on another chair and tried to relax while listening to the pot bubbling on the Rayburn. It didn't work.

Dead bodies, especially bloody ones, can have that effect on me. So who was the dead old boy in the back of my car? How did he get there? What had killed him? I could leave that question safely to Prof Meyers. But should I have told Needham about Albert, about Cairn and Heather's attempt to hire me? Should I have told him about 'the witch' and the conversation Cairn overheard? It would have sounded like I'd made the whole thing up and I'd probably still be at Manvers Street answering useless questions. I sat up again and gulped my brandy. It didn't have to be Albert, did it? No. It was the same area Cairn had been talking about. So what? And even if it was the aforementioned Albert what was I supposed to do about it?

I exchanged my empty brandy glass for a bottle of Pilsner Urquell and started wandering restlessly about the house. I continued the discussion with myself since I had the not unreasonable suspicion that I was going to have to give this talk for real in the near future. By the time I'd climbed all the way up to my cluttered little office in the attic my Accumulated Guilt Quotient had reached a seasonal high. It's the only explanation for what I did next. When the phone rang again I answered it.

Chapter Five

'Hello? Can I speak to Mr Honeysett? Please!' It was a female voice, tearful and fluttering with nerves.

'Speaking.'

'They've got my son, they kidnapped my son, you have to help me. They'll kill him if you don't!' the voice rushed at me.

'Is this a wind-up?' I asked, despite my instant bad feeling that it wasn't. I just wasn't ready for another dose of trauma.

'No, you must believe me, please, Mr Honeysett. You can save him, make them give Louis back. I read about you. You brought that woman back that everyone thought was long dead but you stole her back from the kidnapper. You must get Louis back for me.'

And here was the problem. A while back I had stumbled on a woman being held prisoner in a disused railway station and ever since then my phone hadn't stopped ringing; people wanting me to find all the stuff missing from their lives, anything from a brother lost in World War II to an iguana called Knut. But until now no one had asked me to bring back a kidnap victim, which was just as well because I hadn't a clue how to go about it.

'You have to go to the police, Mrs . . .'

'Farrell, Jill, my name's Jill. But I can't tell the police . . .'

'Only the police can deal with abductions safely and professionally,' I said firmly. 'They have specialists for this kind of thing. Even if the kidnappers told you not to go to the police you still have to do it. I really cannot help.'

'But they said to call you,' she said, crying now. 'They told me to call you!'

'What? Rubbish. Who did? The police?'

'No! The people who took Louis! I got a letter through the door. It says, I'll read it, it says *We have your . . .*' Her voice wavered, then recovered. '*. . . son. If you want to see him again alive do exactly as we tell you. Do not call the police. Involve them and he dies. Here is what you will do. You will arrange a meeting with Chris Honeysett, a private investigator, and tell him to expect my instructions. If he refuses to get involved the boy dies. Speak to nobody else.* And then there's your number. I called your number all day.'

'And what's the demand?' I asked.

'I don't know. There isn't any. I don't have any money, Mr Honeysett, I only just got a part-time job, starting next week. We've been living off benefits. I don't know what they want. Perhaps they took Louis by mistake, maybe they got the wrong child, perhaps when you tell them I don't have any money they'll let him go. You must tell them that. They must have made a mistake. Please say you'll help. Can I at least meet you? We only just moved here from Bristol, I don't know anyone in Bath yet.'

This couldn't be happening. My stomach turned over, my hands were sweating. And I felt like I'd had a long day already. I rummaged round my desk drawer for some cigarettes. Nothing. I'd given up and thrown them all away during an uncharacteristic fit of optimism.

'Where are you? Are you somewhere safe?' I asked.

'Where is safe? I'm at home. I rang your number all day, I left messages on your machine, I –'

'And where is home?'

'Harley Street. Please say you'll come, Mr Honeysett. I don't know what to do, I'll go mad if you don't. They'll kill him.'

'All right, I'll come and have a look at the letter. I'm not saying I'll go along with this but I'll come over. Now, I might not be alone when I arrive, I might have one of my associates with me. Don't open the door to anyone but us. I've shoulder-length hair, grey-green eyes and I'll be wearing a leather jacket, okay?'

'Okay.'

'I won't be long. Just sit tight. What number are you?'

I wrote it all down and hung up with a heavy heart. This needed the woman's touch. I hammered down the stairs and was going to run up to the studio but Annis was already in the kitchen in her paint-encrusted work gear making tea, adding a few more paint smudges to the kettle. 'Hiya,' she said tiredly, then did a double-take. 'You look . . . terrible. What kind of a day have you had?'

'Well, they found my car.'

'Oh good.'

'With a dead guy in the back.'

'Oh dear.'

'They didn't charge me with anything.'

'Oh good.'

'Just now a woman called.'

'Oh yeah?'

'Her son's been abducted.'

'Oh shit. Seriously? Abducted? And she's calling you?' I widened my eyes at her.

'Yeah, of course she's calling you, everyone remembers you found Nikki Reid. You told her to go to the police? You did tell her to go to the police!' Her fingers tightened around her mug as though she was getting ready to throw it. We'd gone through quite a few mugs recently.

'Of course I did. She's not having it. It was the kidnappers who told her to contact us.' I thought I'd slip the 'us' in there early.

'The kidnappers? Us? What, as go-betweens?' Her grip on the mug relaxed. 'That's really strange.'

'I know. You'd have thought they'd have preferred some-one helpless and panicked. I said we'd be over straight away. She's all by herself.'

'Damn, damn, damn. I'll get showered and changed. Sod tea, make me some strong coffee. Quick mug and we're on our way.'

I made a cafetière of very black mocha. Once Annis had emerged damp and shiny from the shower we gulped some of it standing up, then rushed across the muddy yard to the Land Rover and rumbled off into the rain. We peered through the two minuscule arcs cleared by the wipers on a windscreen otherwise blind with gunk and rain.

'Where to?' Annis asked, cranking the wheel this way and that, avoiding the biggest holes and ruts on the track more by memory than sight.

'Harley Street.'

'That's just one along from where Tim lives, I know it, past that little church in Julian Road. So tell me again what she told you.'

I did.

'Do we know how old the kid is?'

'I never thought to ask. Does it matter?'

'Yeah. A teenager might have more emotional resources to cope with a situation like this. A young child ... it doesn't bear thinking about. And she says she's poor? Then what the hell can they want?'

More than anything else it was that question that filled me with dread and foreboding.

Harley Street had a mix of old and new houses, where WWII bombing had left its scars. Annis pulled up in front of Jill Farrell's house. It was a small, dispirited-looking thing in a row of five similar ones on the steeply sloping street. We passed through a little gate and the tiny front garden of leaf-littered lawn and blown-in rubbish. The door opened before I'd touched the bell.

The woman in her early thirties who opened it looked us

over nervously. 'You gave a good description of yourself,' she said.

'I'm Chris. This is Annis Jordan, my associate.'

'I'm Jill.' She was a tall and angular woman. Her wide-open brown eyes were red from crying and haunted with fear. Her short hair was a bright henna red which accentuated the pallor and tiredness of her skin. She wore a shapeless grey tracksuit and tired trainers. Her hands shook and fluttered as she guided us in. 'Come in, through there.' The narrow front room smelled stale and smoky. It was sparsely furnished with a blue sofa and one blue armchair, a rickety coffee table and a big old-fashioned telly on a stand in a corner by the window. On top of the TV stood several china and glass pigs. There were more pigs and piggy banks on the chimneypiece. The walls were bare and white. Cardboard boxes crowded the corners.

'We haven't even finished moving in yet,' Jill said, bewildered. 'This is it, this is what came.' She pointed to the white business envelope and the sheet of paper on the table next to a saucer full of cigarette ends. The address read *To the mother*. I picked up the A4 sheet. Fingerprints wouldn't matter here. Nobody left fingerprints on a ransom note. Except me just now of course.

It was printed on standard paper in a large font. I read it through, twice. It contained nothing other than what she had read out to me on the phone, yet seeing my name and business number there sent a chill through me and I actually shivered.

Jill noticed. 'Sorry it's so cold here. I haven't figured out how to work the night storage heaters yet. It's a council place. They said they'd send someone to check them but I'm probably just too thick to use them. We had gas fires before.'

'When did you first realize Louis was missing?'

'Straight away this morning when he didn't come back. I sent him to the shops to get me a packet of ciggies and a pint of milk and he never came back. I went down the shops myself after a while, furious, because I'd given him my last tenner and had to get money from the cash point. I looked everywhere up and down Julian Road but it started raining. So I went home.' Her face crumpled. 'I was so angry with him,' she wailed. Annis offered her arms and they hugged awkwardly, Jill sobbing. They sank on to the sofa together, Annis keeping a supportive hand on her arm. I emptied the armchair of newspaper-wrapped crockery and put it all on the floor, then sat down myself.

'Sorry about the mess.' Jill dabbed her eyes furiously with a wad of tissues from inside her sleeve. 'I was still unpacking.'

'No problem. How old is Louis?' I asked. These sober questions made me feel like a police constable and bought some thinking time, yet at the same time I knew they were probably fruitless.

'He's just turned fifteen in August.'

'You had him very young,' Annis said.

'I was only nineteen when I had him.'

'The father's not around?' I said, still sounding like a policeman.

She shook her head. 'He's never been around. And just as well.'

'Does Louis go to school?' Annis asked.

'No, he quit school, he hates it. He's thinking of going to catering college, though. He's a bright kid. Wants to be a famous chef on TV. He cooks for me sometimes but it always costs a fortune, he can't cook anything simple.' She looked up at me. I was here, therefore I was in charge. It didn't feel like it. It felt like being sucked out to sea by a treacherous, unseen current. 'You'll get him back for me, won't you?'

'Do you have a picture of Louis?' I kept on asking the kind of questions I thought I ought to ask, though quite what I was going to do with Louis's photograph I had no idea.

52

'Just a minute.' Jill left the room and we heard her footsteps on the stairs.

Annis puffed up her cheeks and let out a lungful of air. 'What a nightmare. What a depressing place. It's freezing in here.'

'Do you know how the night storage heaters work?'

'Yes. They store electricity at night when leccy is cheap then heat the house during the day while you're away at work and stop working the moment you come home.'

'Ingenious,' I conceded.

'It's a crap invention. I'll see what I can do.' Annis fiddled with the heater under the window for a minute. 'That should do the trick.'

Jill returned with a small picture in a chunky, brushed metal frame. It showed Jill with a boy on a park bench with dense foliage behind. She had her arm around her son and was smiling. The boy looked at the camera with a stop-embarrassing-me face. He looked like a happy kid with straight dark hair cut very short, wearing jeans and a plain grey sweatshirt.

'That was a couple of months ago at Bristol Zoo, so it's quite recent.'

Inspector Honeysett would have said, 'Can we keep this, Mrs Farrell? I'll make sure it's returned to you,' but I just set it on the table and mumbled about him being a good-looking boy. Annis had a look at it too. I noticed both of us handled the picture gently, reverentially, as though the kid was dead already. If I didn't make the right decision now then he soon might be. I had to buy myself some time until I could see what this was all about.

I gently quizzed Jill about herself. She'd left another council place in Bristol's Fishponds area behind, along with an ex-boyfriend, and had struck lucky being rehoused to Harley Street.

'Did you break up with him?' I asked.

'Yes. None too soon neither. Stew's a lazy sod who does a bit of gardening work when it suits him and watches telly all day when it doesn't and Louis was beginning to pick up bad habits from him.'

'How did the two get on?'

'A bit too well, actually. Stew constantly undermined me when it came to Louis. Filled his head with his crap home-baked philosophy, turned him into a difficult boy. That's one of the reasons I dumped Mr Stewart Tanner.' She spat the name out with considerable force.

'Could he be behind this? As a kind of revenge? Could he have taken Louis to get back at you?'

'Stew? I doubt it. Not if it means getting off the sofa. And I didn't leave a forwarding address. I think he's too apathetic to get worked up about being dumped. Being dumped isn't a new experience for him. He's useless but kind of cute, that's the problem. He's probably got some other dumb girl cooking his tea already and in six months she'll dump him too if she has any sense.'

I picked up the note and wandered over to the window with it, trying to think. All kidnappers will threaten to kill their hostage if you involve the police. You ignore it and call the police and comply – or pretend to – and you pray a lot. Yet this was subtly different. There was no ransom demand as yet. The only demand was for Jill to contact me and for me to 'get involved'. I was here. I was involved.

'Why have they done this, Mr Honeysett? Why did they want me to call you? You must have some idea!'

'I'm afraid I haven't. As I told you on the phone, we'll have to call the police, it's the only way.' I pulled out my mobile.

'No! No, we can't, they'll kill him!'

'They won't kill him as long as they think they'll get what they are asking.'

'You don't know that, how can you know that! We're *not* getting the police involved.' Jill stood up, agitated.

Annis rose too and put a gentle arm around her shoulders. 'It's the only way, I'm afraid.'

Jill shrugged her arm off. 'He's *my* son. No police! It's *my* decision.'

Annis and I looked at each other but for once the silent communication seemed to fail. Jill was right, it was her decision. I couldn't make it for her. Yet I was here. I looked at the ransom note again. The demands had already been met: get Honeysett involved. I turned my back on the women and looked out on to the street. It glistened darkly in the rain that drummed a violent tattoo across the nests of black swollen bin liners on the pavement. There was a square bit of paper stuck under the windscreen wiper of the Landy. I looked at it for a bit, dismissing the possibility of a parking fine – too late in the evening. I checked my watch: ten to eight. A flyer then. None of the neighbouring cars had one.

'Do you have anyone who could stay with you? A friend or a relative?' I asked.

She hesitated. 'My sister, I suppose.'

'Where does she live?'

'Trowbridge. But I'm not sure. We don't exactly get on.'

'Think about it. Now what's your phone number here?'

'I haven't got a landline yet.' She gave me her mobile number.

'Keep that charged and topped up, please. The note says they'll contact me. I think I should wait at my place. The sooner we find out what it's all about the better. Perhaps they've already left a message. Now, would you like someone to stay here with you?' I was aware that meant volunteering Annis but she gave me a nod of approval.

Jill shrugged. 'It's okay. I might call my sister. But should I tell her?'

'That's up to you, of course.'

'I'll think about it.'

Annis and I got ready to leave.

'About the money, I will pay you, of course. It might take me a while but I'll pay.'

55

'Who said anything about money? Don't worry about that now,' Annis reassured her.

On the windscreen of the Land Rover waited a folded envelope shoved into a little sandwich bag. I snatched it from under the wiper. Looking up at the house I could see Jill silhouetted against the light. I waved and we got into the cab.

Annis just sat for a second or two, letting out a deep breath through puffed-up cheeks.

I prised open the sandwich bag.

'What have you got there?' she wanted to know.

'I think it's from him.' The envelope had *Honeysett* written across it in large computer-printed letters. I quickly ripped it open and pulled out the single sheet of paper. *Return to Mill House and wait for instructions.*

Nothing else. I looked around. People with shopping bags from the Co-op round the corner walked along Julian Road. There was no one in Harley Street just now. Blank windows and drawn curtains everywhere. Whoever we were up against was confident and on the ball and was here, had walked past this house a few minutes ago, might even be watching. I tried to look confident and unconcerned in case we really were being watched.

Annis started the engine. 'Should we get Tim in on this? We could pop in.'

'Not yet. Not until we know what it's all about. Just get us back to Mill House.'

'Okay. But this is serious shit, Chris. It really scares me.'

Chapter Six

The last bulb that ought to have been illuminating the yard had apparently burnt out. We splashed from the Land Rover to the door from memory.

'What's that awful smell?' Annis asked in the hall.

I raced ahead to the kitchen whence the smell emanated and in my eagerness to knock the casserole off the heat managed to burn my fingers twice. At last I got hold of the oven gloves and lifted the lid on the pheasant. One for the forensic students. I'd scatter its ashes later. In the meantime I opened the back door to air the place.

Listening on the stairs I could hear the faint bleep of the answering machine in the attic office. Out of breath from rushing upstairs I listened to all the messages but Louis's kidnapper had not left one. I fixed my little voice recorder on to the cordless office phone with a couple of rubber bands (I'm terminally low tech) and sat it on the kitchen table by the fruit bowl. Drinking mugs of tea and coffee we sat and stared at it, willing it to ring and dreading it at the same time. Annis distractedly chewed through a few apples and I tested my dental work on a concrete pear.

Two hours later we were still sitting there, waiting. From time to time one of us would ask a question or make a remark but it always faded into bleak silence after a minute or two. We had talked ourselves to a standstill. What was keeping him? Was it a him? Was it one person or several? I didn't suppose it was all that easy to snatch a teenage boy off the street. Could it all be a sick joke? Could the ex-boyfriend be behind it, whatever Jill had said about him? And what if he didn't get in touch by phone? We'd both drunk too much coffee by now and I had started coughing from chain smoking. Even Annis had absent-mindedly puffed through one or two. I didn't care to remind her that she'd given up years ago.

I walked to the front door and checked first inside then outside for another envelope. There was nothing but darkness and the smell and sound of soft rain falling. The electronic warble of the phone back in the house made my heart miss a beat. I slammed the door shut and ran back to the kitchen. Annis stood, holding the phone out to me. I started the voice recorder and quickly checked the clock on the wall: it was half past ten. I pressed the talk button. 'Honeysett.'

'Listen carefully, Mr Honeysett.' The voice sounded far away, like a long-distance call from the bad old days. It was too scratchy and faint to have much character beyond the tone of impatient arrogance, and sounded almost robotic. 'We have got the boy, Louis. You do exactly as we tell you and he might just survive this.'

'There's no money,' I protested. 'The mother's on the dole so you –'

'Do shut up and listen. We don't want a pissing thing from the mother. We just needed a kid. It's you, shithead. We're hiring *you*. Get it? The boy's life is the fee we're prepared to pay for your services. I'm sure you'll agree that's an offer not to be missed.'

I sat down heavily. Annis did so too, never taking her eyes off me. 'I'm listening.'

'I knew you would!' said the triumphant voice. 'You're the caring type, by all accounts. And here's the little job you'll do for us. You know Barry Telfer?'

'Know of him.' One half of the delightful Telfer brothers. Heavyweight villains both of them, only brother Keith was doing time right now. 'What about him?'

'Know his house up Lansdown?'

'The 1930s modernist pile?'

'If you say so. Clear out his safe. It's in his office upstairs.'

I jumped up with surprise and indignation. 'You're winding me up. You can't be serious. I'm not a burglar.'

'Oh yeah? That never stopped you before. You've got a reputation for getting in and out of interesting places, so just do it.'

All through this exchange Annis's eyes burnt fiercely across the table at me. 'How is the boy, Louis?' I asked. 'I want to know that he's unharmed. At least let me speak to h—'

'Shut the fuck up, Honeysett!' the voice bellowed. 'You don't make any fucking demands 'cause you got fuck-all to bargain with. The boy's just fine but if you fuck us about, if you as much as *think* of dropping this one on the pigs, we'll fucking cut him into ribbons, that clear, arsehole?'

'Crystal. Calm down. I'll do it. There's no need to harm the boy. Now, what am I likely to find in Telfer's safe?'

'You'll see. Try Thursdays, he goes and plays cards at the Blathwayt Arms. And bring the lot, every sodding little thing you find, I don't care if it's old ticket stubs and snotty tissues. When you've pulled it off, we'll know. We'll be in touch. Sooner you get to work, sooner the boy gets home to mummy.' The line went dead.

I let the receiver clatter on to the table. 'They hung up. They said the boy was fine but they wouldn't let me talk to him.' I somehow felt that this, and *every sodding little thing*, was my fault, that somehow, through what I was, through who I was, I had made this happen.

Annis clearly read my mood. 'What do they want us to do?' she asked quietly. 'Did I hear something about burglary?' I noted the 'us' with relief.

'You heard right. Nothing too strenuous though,' I lied.

I quickly dialled Jill's number before I had too much time to think about things. She answered immediately and I explained, tried to reassure her.

Her voice steadied. 'I know I have no right to ask you to do anything criminal but I'll ask you anyway. I'm his mother, I *have* to ask you. In fact I'm begging you.'

'I already agreed to do it.'

'Thank you, Mr Honeysett. You just have no idea –'

'I think I probably have, actually. And don't be so quick to thank me. If it wasn't for me you and your son might not be in this situation. We'll keep in close contact. But prepare yourself for a wait. It will be days, perhaps longer.'

'I think I might call my sister now,' she decided.

I terminated the call and repeated to Annis all I'd been told. 'It shouldn't be a huge problem,' I concluded. 'But it definitely puts us into Bigwood country.'

Chapter Seven

'This is a seriously naff idea, Chris,' was the considered Bigwood opinion, forcefully expressed the next afternoon in my little attic office. Tim shook his head. 'I know nothing about this Telfer guy but if he's a heavy hoodlum like you say then cleaning him out isn't the healthy option.'

'Which is probably why they're blackmailing us into doing it,' Annis told him.

I held the receiver out to him. 'So, would you like to tell Jill we're chickening out because it's unhealthy?'

'Hey, hey, I didn't say I'm not going to help.' Tim made dampening motions with his hands. 'I'm just having a moan, all right? I'm not in this for my health. Remind me, Chris, what am I in this for? Best not answer that. So who exactly is Telfer and who is doing the arm-twisting?'

'I've no idea who set us up. I didn't recognize the voice. But the goon was short-tempered and had skipped charm school. The voice was very distant and scratchy, which might of course have been deliberate. "Caller withheld number", as one might expect, and definitely a mobile or a satellite phone, a hint of warble. There's no way we could trace it. Even the police could have trouble doing that. I dare say they'd try but there's a waiting list and all they'd probably find is a cheap mobile in a skip somewhere. Because if you plan a caper like this then you get yourself twenty stolen mobiles and chuck each one on a passing dustcart after you've made your call, or simply drop it in the river.'

'Do you have any suspicions?'

I didn't. It came out of the blue. It could be anyone, anywhere. The boy could be long dead, the phone call could have been made from a poolside lounger of a villa on the Costa Brava for all I knew and there was little I could do except comply. I shook my head. 'Could be anyone but they're quite ruthless and they thought it out well. They obviously know all about Aqua Investigations and what kind of a rep we have. And they didn't kidnap one of us so that we'd have a full team to play with.'

Tim ran a hand over his eyes and seemed to come to some kind of conclusion. He sat up straighter. 'Okay, so who exactly is this Telfer guy?'

'We're talking about Barry here,' said Annis. 'His brother Keith got put away for aggravated this and that last spring.'

'What did he get, just out of interest?' Tim asked.

'Five years.'

'Out by Christmas,' all three of us bleated in unison.

'On the surface they're successful businessmen,' Annis continued. 'Proud, self-made men, a bit uncouth and ostentatious, a bit too loud and badly dressed in an expensive way. Bad taste in women and cars –'

'What's bad taste in cars?' I interrupted.

'Yellow.'

'Quite right.'

'Anyway, they run scrap yards and hire out heavy plant, diggers, bulldozers, rollers, etc., but they probably also hire out heavy muscle and apparently scrap cars they shouldn't, like shiny new Mercs wot don't belong to them.'

'And for committed capitalists they have a curious attitude to competition as a regulator of price: they don't seem to like it at all. That's how little brother Keith got himself nabbed, trying to stamp out the competition. With hobnail boots and a baseball bat. Brother Barry is no slouch in the casual violence department either, I hear, and he never goes anywhere without one or two heavies. No children, which is probably just as well, and last thing I heard his wife ran off with one of his bodyguards but she didn't get far and the goon was never heard of again.'

'Charming family. And we're relieving them of whatever's in their safe? I hope you bought us all open tickets to Mumbai for afters. So where does this bundle of fun keep his baubles?'

'Chez Telfer, up in Lansdown. In his safe.' I dropped the 'safe' delicately at the end. Tim often complained that I was leading him astray when he'd been going straight for years but secretly he couldn't wait to get his hands on a strongbox again. He missed it. He missed the frisson, the challenge of pitting his wits and gadgets against a safe. No gas axe or Semtex for Tim. He looked more interested already.

I walked to the map by the side of the door. The other two followed and I pointed to roughly where I remembered the house to be. 'Big place somewhere round here, overlooking Charlcombe Valley.'

'Okay, what are we waiting for then?' Tim pulled me away by the sleeve. 'Get your binoculars and take me there.'

Despite the obvious dangers of the project I couldn't help feeling the current of excitement that crackled inside Tim's car as he slowly drove his Audi TT along the narrow Charlcombe Lane. Annis had chosen the back seat and had an elbow each on the backrests of our seats. She was humming to herself. I was cradling the big binoculars and Tim was happily twiddling buttons on his modified dashboard. From the outside Tim's car appeared like any other black Audi TT but inside it had acquired a lot more dials and gadgets than were strictly necessary for the purpose of locomotion. The thing looked like it had been kitted out by Q and vertical take-off wouldn't have surprised me much.

'Stop here,' I told him as we came to a row of low white cottages on our left. We had come up the lane from the

Larkhall side and just beyond the last cottage the view opened up across the little valley. Tim pulled into the drive of the deserted-looking place and we got out. I handed him the bins and pointed up at the hill on the opposite side.

'See the large cuboid thing high above Charlcombe Manor? That's it.'

He trained the binoculars at the hillside. 'Ehm . . . quite . . . *gloomy* over there.'

I reached up and took the plastic lens caps off for him.

'Ah, much clearer like that,' he agreed. 'Oh yeah, got it. Ugly place. Mostly glass and concrete. Big, though, and the garden is massive . . . high hedges all around . . . one hell of a slope. No immediate neighbours. What's it like on the other side?'

'Much the same,' I said. 'A private little road, maybe a couple of hundred yards long between hedgerows. I've driven past the turn-off but have never been near the actual place.'

'Definitely a night job. Look at all that glass, they'd have to be blind not to see us coming. That's probably why they bought the place.' He checked his watch. 'Dark soon, we'll go and have a closer look then.'

Annis took her turn at the binoculars. 'Best way is up through the fields, I reckon. We'll have to find out what the routine is up at the house.' She handed the bins to me. 'Did you mention something about Thursday?'

'Yes, the voice said he's playing cards at the Blathwayt Arms, the pub by the race course.' I put the glasses to my eyes and had a good look at the Telfer house. Tim was right, there was an awful lot of glass, all along the ground floor, facing the garden, then the wrap-around terrace on the first floor was backed by enormous picture windows set between strips of concrete. With all that glass, how difficult could it be to get in there? The garden was very large, giving ample space around the house. There were trees and island beds and ponds, lots of places to hide but also a lot of ground to cover before you got anywhere near the house proper.

'Okay, if Thursday is a good day we'll do it Thursday. It's Sunday now, that gives us three days to get ourselves organized,' Tim suggested.

I let the glasses wander downhill from the property. A long line of hedgerow, a couple of solitary oaks, a few fences, three grey horses and a man with binoculars. Looking straight at me. A man wearing some kind of hat and a waxed jacket. Could have been a bird watcher. Could have been that the menace of this solitary figure, which transmitted itself right across the valley, was all in my mind. Yet it sent my heart hammering with sudden anxiety. I took the glasses away from my eyes to get the context. There seemed to be nobody else up there. I looked through the glasses again. By the time I found him once more he was disappearing behind a stand of trees just above the manor.

'Something stinks,' I concluded eloquently.

'You think this is a trap of some sort?' Annis asked.

'I don't know what I'm thinking yet,' I admitted. 'Just now I thought I saw a bloke watching us from the other side of the valley. The whole thing is just weird. Let's not do anything too predictable. Let's come back later.'

They grumbled but let me herd them into the car. On the way back to Mill House we bounced around ideas about how to get into Telfer's place but I had infected us all with my feelings of doom. What excitement there had been was gone. It had all turned back into the dangerous job of rescuing Jill's son, and secretly I was glad of this. We might all be a bit more careful if we had a little less fun.

Nightfall. While Annis and I changed into black clothes and trainers we wondered about the kidnapping. How did you pick a victim? Was it really random? How did he get to know about Jill and Louis in the first place? What were the criteria for a useful victim? The same as always, we decided – vulnerability, isolation, powerlessness, loneliness. Unemployed single mother was a perfect fit.

It only slightly worried me that Tim, who hadn't known what this was about when he came over, had found in the boot of his car a convenient set of black clothing to change into, including a pair of black trainers I'd never seen him wear before. It did sometimes cross my mind that I had no way of knowing just how retired a safe breaker he really was, despite his protestations that it was only me who led him astray from the path of righteousness he chose when he wrote himself a fantasy CV and started working for Bath Uni.

We set off into the dark in Tim's car. All the way there, when we spoke at all, we did so in hushed voices, as though we needed to practise stealth. This time I made Tim approach from the opposite side, up Lansdown, turn off right when the watchful spire of St Steven's suddenly loomed, and drive slowly along the narrow and unlit lane until it briefly widened near Charlcombe Manor.

We left the car squeezed against the steep bank and all got out of the driver door into the cool, dark silence. I found a few stone steps leading up the hill and in the absence of anything better stomped up those as though I knew where I was going. The slithery steps soon stopped and turned into an uneven narrow path that ended at a stile in a wooden fence. We clambered over and found ourselves in a plantation of young trees. Every nine feet in any direction stood a spindly tree tied to a stout stake. We used the stakes to pull ourselves up the steep slope into the hill fog. Once through the narrow belt of saplings we came to another barrier, this one an overgrown fence of wire strung between wooden posts. We scrambled over as best we could with as little use of our torches as possible. Thick cloud obscured the stars. The only illumination came from the reflected glow of the city beyond the hills, which allowed just enough light to see which way was up. We hadn't gone far into the meadow before the rain started its maddening dance again. I headed for the dark line of the hedgerow to my left. It ran uphill in an unsteady diagonal which I hoped would bring us within yards of Telfer's property. With the rain tap-dancing on the hood of my rainproof I led us in a puffing and squelching trudge uphill until a deeper darkness loomed in front.

I let the others catch up with their breathless leader. 'This is it. That's the hedge . . . that runs round . . . the entire property. Let's walk round to the right.'

Soon the house itself came into view above the line of vegetation, a silhouette like a decapitated pyramid. There were lights on upstairs beyond the picture windows behind what had to be enormous blinds or curtains. We moved quietly now, probing for openings in the hedge. It was impossible to make out what it consisted of in the dark but it was prickly stuff. The house was still a good forty yards uphill when Tim stopped us. 'I think I found our way in.'

I risked a brief flash from my torch. A narrow opening in the bottom of the hedge, no bigger than a foot-and-a-half in diameter. 'Rabbit tunnel. Bit small for me,' I concluded but Tim was already down there. He produced a pair of secateurs from his pockets and went to work on the opening, widening it, moving in.

'I pass the stuff back, you put it in heaps to carry away later,' he whispered.

I got the distinct feeling that Tim had done this before. Annis and I dutifully pulled away what he passed out to us and cursed quietly as thorns and prickly leaves pierced our fingers through our gloves.

Eventually Tim backed out again. 'I'm through. There was a fence in there once but most of it's rusted away. Who wants to explore?'

'You guys go,' Annis whispered. 'I'll get rid of the cuttings in the hedgerow and snuffle round the outside a bit more.'

'Okay, I'll go with Tim. If you hear any commotion, don't come in, get away,' I advised her and got down on all fours. Immediately my hands were pricked by the debris of the cuttings. As I crawled into the dark scratchiness of the hedge I tried not to think of rabbit droppings and to work out instead when I'd had my last tetanus jab. Despite Tim's pruning expertise my face was scratched by the time I got out the other side. Our tunnel opened on to a long border, five or six feet wide and full of dripping evergreens standing in mud. The house, uphill to our right, showed a diffused glow on the ground floor and the light escaping from the edges of curtains upstairs gave it the impression of a partly obscured glass lantern. Enough illumination spilled into the enormously long garden to see that the upper half had been terraced, with rectangular ponds or pools on each level. Clumps of dwarf conifers and tall grasses looked grey and dispirited, as though no one had told them they were back in fashion.

'After you, boss,' Tim invited. I waddled up the slope in a duck walk to the next island bed. Even though I had my hood down in an effort to hear something beyond the drumming of raindrops I couldn't make out anything apart from the rain slanting into the stone-bordered, weed-choked pool to my left. We made it to the next level of the garden unmolested. My biggest fear was a patrolling Dobermann or two but who would send a dog out in this? We were still at least twenty-five yards from the back of the house. I was just about to waddle on when the garden erupted into ice-bright light. I fell flat on my face and scrabbled backwards to the incomplete shelter of a stand of pampas grass. Tim was already there. 'We set off the security light,' I hissed. 'What now?'

'I don't think we did,' he hissed back. 'We weren't actually moving when it came on.'

For a moment it seemed that nothing else would happen. Then I heard faint footsteps. I lifted my head and risked a look. A bulky figure had appeared on the top terrace, pacing first one way, then the other, then it came down the first set of broad stone steps that led to the next level down. When he reached our level I could see he was a big bloke in his twenties, squinting against the rain and looking decidedly unhappy. He made straight for the water feature on the other side of the grasses we were hiding behind. I had a view from below him now as he stood by the pool just fifteen feet away from me. If he didn't spot us it would be a miracle. But then it appeared he wasn't really looking any more. 'Come on,' he chanted into the rain, rocking on his heels. 'Come oooooon.' Eventually the security light went off. 'Thank fuck for that,' he offered up fervently. In the fresh darkness I could make out his silhouette against the glimmer from the house. He bent down and fished round at the edge of the pool for a moment, then lifted out a bottle. He shook it, uncapped it, took a draught and let it plop back into the water. A noisy sniff, hawk and spit into the pond seemed to complete the ritual since he turned back towards the house, triggering the security light again as he set foot on to the steps to the next level of the garden.

I dared breathe again. 'That was close. Now what? We can't get to the house without triggering the lights and bringing one of Telfer's goons out here.'

'We don't need to. Let's check the pond life instead.'

We squatted by the side of the pool and I did the honours. The water was icy and slimy at the same time. My hand closed on the neck of a bottle and I lifted it up. It was half full. It was too dark to read the label. I unscrewed the top and sniffed. It was vodka, just as I had expected; all secret drinkers imagined that sober people couldn't smell it.

'That's our way in,' Tim assured me. 'Put it back where you found it and let's get out of here the way we came.'

I got thoroughly snagged and scratched on the way out again and was glad when I found myself back in the meadow. Annis was there, apologizing. 'Sorry about the security light, that was me. I thought I'd found an easier way in when I got to a service gate.'

'Tut. But we'd only have set it off ourselves anyway and we got away with it. Tim even thinks he knows how to get in now.'

'Yeah? How?'

'Well, it depends heavily on me not getting pneumonia so let's get back to civilization and I'll tell you.'

Next morning in my kitchen I contemplated how the things that made us feel civilized varied greatly from person to person; with Annis it was going to the theatre, in Tim's case anything with lots of mayo did the trick. What made me feel civilized was a leisurely breakfast, preferably involving hot croissant, smoked salmon, a five-minute egg and no police. One day I would manage it.

I could hear them crunch their wheels, braking hard in the yard, and knew it meant trouble. Far too early for a friendly chat. Annis hadn't put in an appearance downstairs yet and I hoped she had the sense to keep it that way. Knowing his way around the place Needham sent someone to every door but the hammering came from the front. No one knocks like the fuzz. You just can't ignore it, whether your croissants are burning in the oven or not. I did a quick mental check, remembered that my shotgun had been stolen and my handgun confiscated, and walked confidently towards my front door with the traditional 'All right all right, no need to break it down.'

Apparently there was. It flew open as a large uniformed constable shouldered through. Immediately behind him came a large Needham in Superintendent mode with a look capable of withering any gumshoe wisecracks I might have in mind. As it happened I wasn't good at that kind of thing before breakfast.

'Chris Honeysett, I'm arresting you on suspicion of murder,' he rattled off. 'You do not have to say anything but I must warn you that it may harm your defence if you do not mention when questioned something which you later rely upon in court. Anything you do say may be given in evidence. What's that smell?'

'Two "all-butter" croissants dying in the oven.'

'All right: kitchen.' He waved me on. 'You don't touch a thing,' he warned me off. 'Constable, get the damn croissants out of the oven, we don't want them catching fire.'

The constable did his bidding and left the baking tray on the top of the stove. The croissants looked just about edible, I thought, and my stomach growled in agreement.

'Right, let's go.'

I took a last hungry look at my breakfast table – cafetière of coffee, a perfectly cooked speckled egg, the smoked salmon waiting for the croissant – and let myself be pushed out of the house.

'Is this about the old geezer in my car?' We were being driven by a plain-clothed, plain-faced policeman into town.

'This is about the *murder victim* in your car. So save it. Grimshaw still your solicitor?'

'Do I really need her, Mike?'

'You've just been arrested for murder, Chris, and it's Superintendent Needham until I tell you otherwise.' Once, over a few beers, Needham had offered first-name terms and had probably regretted it ever since.

At Manvers Street police station they asked me a lot of questions they knew the answers to already, searched me half-heartedly, took my mobile away and made me wait in an overheated interview room with an elective-mute constable standing by the door. I sat and worked on changing my thirty-a-day habit into a fifty-a-day habit until the door opened and Needham and DS Sorbie turned up with their files and tapes. Sorbie scrabbled the cellophane wrapping off a new tape and did the preliminaries. When the tape recorder stopped bleeping he sat down next to Needham opposite me, told the tape who, when and what, and the ping-pong started.

'Your solicitor is on her way,' Needham said. 'But since you're happy to start without her . . .'

'What makes you suddenly think it was murder?' I asked.

'I don't suddenly think, Honeysett, the pathologist and forensics tell me. The victim did collide with your car. Whilst riding his electric bicycle. We found the crumpled remains of it hidden under some bushes beside the Lam brook, a few hundred yards from where we found your car. But Prof Meyers' report says you hit him on the head, then ran him over.'

'Prof Meyers said no such thing. Professor Earnshaw Meyers probably said something like, "The victim suffered a blow to the head prior to being involved in an accident" or some such carefully worded thing, but did he tell you what killed him? The blow to the head or the accident? Did you find any fingerprints on the bike?'

'We ask the questions, Mr Honeysett,' Sorbie suggested with forced boredom in his voice. It wasn't very convincing. Like this entire arrest thing. Needham on the other hand was a good actor. It was always difficult to unravel his ultimate motives, that's what made him such a dangerous cop if you sat on the wrong side of the table. Which is where I spent most of my time. But I had the distinct impression that Sorbie's heart wasn't really in it. Ignoring him I asked Needham: 'Have you traced the minicab driver who took me home yet?'

'Of course not, because there's no such creature.'

'There is, but he's not going to admit to picking up an illegal fare in the street without prior booking. He could get fired or lose his licence.' Memories of my way home that night were far too hazy to remember what company the cab belonged to or what the driver might have looked like. I couldn't even remember the make or colour of the car. No minicab driver, no alibi. No alibi, no croissant for breakfast. For an awfully long time. Something had to be done.

The door opened behind me and some kind of signal

was exchanged because Needham picked up his file. 'Your solicitor is here.'

As if to confirm this a clear, precise voice demanded: 'I'd like to talk to my client alone, *if* you don't mind.'

Sorbie did the 'interview suspended' palaver for the tape and followed his boss out of the room as my solicitor took a seat opposite me, setting her briefcase beside her on the floor.

There was nothing at all grim about Kate Grimshaw, in fact she was good to look at: she looked a young fifty, had a well-cut face to match her well-cut charcoal grey suit; hair dyed black, red and gold and cut very short; rather forbidding grey eyes, though. Just looking at her made me feel young again. About five, I'd say.

'All right, Honeysett, start babbling at me like an over-excited infant protesting his innocence in the face of overwhelming evidence to the contrary.'

'You misjudge me, as usual.' I lit another cigarette to dampen down the hunger that kicked about in my stomach, then I rattled off the whole story: Heather and Cairn's attempt to hire me; the mysterious men Cairn thought he'd heard threaten to let someone called Albert have an accident; how much of that I'd told Needham; what they had told me and the fact that *I had missed out on breakfast.* I might have laboured that last point a bit.

'My heart bleeds for you. Is this the story you want *them* to believe or *me* to believe?'

'It's what happened,' I protested.

'All right then. So no weapon has been found, certainly none with your prints on it. Someone stole your car and used it to run over the old dear, it happens all the time. There's nothing to link you to the victim apart from the car you reported stolen and the police have been negligent in finding your cab driver. They haven't got a snowball's chance of keeping you here. As usual I can't believe you even talked to the police without me. And for the second time! You really must like it in here. When will you learn?

73

I know you rate Superintendent Needham highly but all the same: *say nothing and call me.* How often must I tell you?' She waved my cigarette smoke away irritably.

'That's fine for you to say. Has anyone ever told you how much you charge?'

'You can pay me in paintings,' she said, dismissing my point.

'Paintings? *Tings*? *Plural*? Your fees *have* gone up.'

'A pair, forty by eighty inches, predominantly blue.'

'Predominantly blue?' I huffed. 'I don't do interior decorating.'

'And I don't do charity work. Please don't go all injured artistic soul on me, Chris, a) you can't afford it and b) I know you'd happily exchange one of your paintings for a roast turbot if one came along.'

She was right, of course. I agreed and twenty minutes later I went and collected my mobile phone from Sergeant Hayes at the desk while Grimshaw waited impatiently by the exit. The relief of getting out of there must have shown on my face.

'Don't know what you've got to smile about,' Hayes grunted as he made me sign for my phone. 'It's much safer in here than out there.'

'Yes, but the tea is lousy.'

'There is that,' he agreed and walked off to file the receipt.

Once back outside in the drizzle Grimshaw and I shook hands. 'Keep me informed of any new developments, will you? Don't wait until they pull you in again.' She pointed her key. A racing-green Jaguar in the station car park flashed its sidelights.

'What makes you think there'll be developments?'

'That hungry look on your face, it means you're off to get yourself into trouble,' she said over her shoulder.

'Talking of which, you couldn't give me a lift to trouble, could you?'

'Certainly not. There's a taxi rank around the corner.

Take some free advice, Chris,' she said as she got into her car. 'Go home. Start painting.' Then she got into her car and drove off at fifty quid a minute.

It was good advice and free and it was tempting. While I walked I got out my mobile and noted that it needed charging, which almost certainly meant some copper had played around with it while I was in there. I called Griffin's, the insurers, and asked for Haarbottle.

'Ah, Honeysett, have you nailed him?'

'Nailed him? You're watching too many cop shows. Now, I have followed Lane every waking minute over the past few days,' I lied, 'as you will see from my invoice and there's not the slightest hint that he is anything but genuine.'

'Rubbish. Keep at it. I know he's faking it, I can feel it in my waters.'

'I don't want to know about your waters. I'm standing in the rain as it is.' I was grateful I'd never felt anything in my waters. If I ever did I'd see a doctor about it. I had really hoped to rid myself of this job. With DI Deeks interested in Lane and some DC called Howell traipsing after him – and just possibly me as well – this didn't spell fun. But then there were roofers to be paid. 'Look, I don't feel right taking Griffin's money when there probably won't be a result at the end. Just how much are you prepared to fork out for this?'

'Oh no, I'm not falling for that one. I'm not allowed to tell you that, otherwise that'll be exactly the sum you'll charge us. Give it another week, then we'll call it off. Think of something. Be inventive. He has to slip up sometime. I just know it.'

'Do you realize it hasn't stopped raining since I took this job? I'm thinking of charging you extra for work in inclement weather.'

'Get a brolly,' said Haarbottle and hung up.

At the taxi rank I realized I had no money on me. Well, I'd be able to pay the driver at home.

This time I made mental notes on the make of car (Mercedes), the taxi firm (Sulis) and the back of the driver's head (square). I wedged myself into the corner of the back seat, absentmindedly took out a cigarette and lit it without even noticing I'd done so until the driver got agitated. 'Hey, there's no smoking, all right? Nuff signs everywhere.'

I apologized and chucked the cigarette out of the window with a pang of regret. I'd be smoking in my sleep soon. When we splashed into the yard at Mill House I asked him to wait so I could get enough money to pay the extortionate fare. I ran through the rain to the front door. It was locked. I felt for my keys and remembered I hadn't brought them, so I gave the bell-pull a workout despite the fact that Annis's Land Rover was missing. I just didn't want to believe the way the day was going. I made apologetic gestures towards the cab driver and walked round to the kitchen door. Locked. When I got back to the front the driver had got out of the car. Cab drivers hate getting out of the car. 'Problems?' he asked.

'Didn't bring my keys,' I explained. 'I expected someone to be in.'

'Oh yeah?'

'It's no problem though.' If a mere constable could do it then so could I. I took a short run at it and rammed the door open with my shoulder. Just like in the movies, except in the movies no one ever hopped about afterwards rubbing their sore shoulder and cursing like their Tourette's had just kicked in. Right then ... money. I hunted round in a couple of jackets without result.

The driver was standing in the door, eyeing me doubtfully. 'You do live here, right?'

In the end I had to pay him in small change scraped together from a gherkin jar full of silver and copper coins I kept on top of the fridge and he was not a happy man when he drove off. At least, should anyone else have got themselves bumped off in the meantime, he would definitely remember driving me home.

76

In the kitchen I opened the bread bin: empty. There was no sign of my abandoned breakfast. I opened the fridge: no smoked salmon left. There was a note from Annis by the kettle.

Gone shopping, there isn't a thing to eat in the house.

Chapter Eight

When Annis came back she noisily unpacked the shopping on the kitchen table. While I attacked the groceries armed with a loaded butter knife she slapped down several ominous items. 'Bleach, toilet cleaner, cream cleanser, Marigolds, Hoover bags.'

'*Hoover bags*,' I repeated in awe. We hadn't had Hoover bags for months. Our perennial problem was that the somewhat relaxed attitude to housework and the chaotic habits of two painters combined unfavourably with Tim's eating procedures. There were probably enough crisps and salted nuts down the back of the furniture to see the squirrels and us through the winter. Despite the considerable size of the barn we used for a studio, 'stuff' tended to drift down to the house – canvas samples, whole paintings, drawings, sketch books, paint-stained art books, oil pastels and bits of string. It was usually Annis who capitulated first and started making spring-clean noises, having a slightly lower yuk-threshold than me.

I fled on the Norton into the hill fog that crept down the sides of the valley, then crossed over into Swainswick via Bailbrook Lane. Over here visibility was even worse. Once I'd taken to the narrow lanes that snaked through the Lam Valley the fog made orientation difficult. My poor abused DS had of course long been removed to the police compound where forensic technicians went over it with things a lot finer than the proverbial, yet even if the fog hadn't obscured the opposite hillside I'd have found it hard to make out which field exactly it and the dead body had been found in. The smashed gate would give it away of course but I was on the wrong side of the Lam brook and the further I rode into the valley the less I could see. The lane I cautiously puttered along was at least tarmacked and gently rose and fell but was taking me nowhere near the place. I realized I had probably driven past the turn-off in the mist and was just slowing to turn back when a cluster of farm buildings hove darkly into view.

It was mid-afternoon yet the daylight could not have been described as broad. The buildings were substantial and satisfyingly old, apart from a huge modern brick and corrugated asbestos shed that, judging by the smell, was home to a large number of poultry. A no-nonsense wooden sign, hand-painted in black letters, proclaimed this to be Spring Farm. The big metal gates were open on a cluttered yard containing enough old farm machinery to start a museum of agriculture but mercifully there were no dogs in evidence (did I mention I was terrified of dogs?) so I rode straight in. The unusual exhaust note of the Norton served as a bell. A bulky bloke in black jumper, filthy yellow plastic dungarees and black wellies appeared from the far end of the shed, holding what looked like a broad broom devoid of bristles. I left the bike next to a square concrete tank of some sort and walked the twenty yards to the waiting man. At first, judging by his way of moving and the tightly curled hair, he appeared to be youngish but every yard I covered put a year on him until I came to stop before a man in his fifties. His square face was badly let down by a thin irregular nose and a small disapproving mouth. He lent on his muck-scraper and barked his greeting. 'Yeah?' He somehow managed to make the word sound like 'Get back on your bike and ride out of here while you still can.' Or perhaps it was just the fog getting to me.

I explained who I was and began by asking about the Citroën in the field but he interrupted me. 'Ask the farmer.'

This was accompanied by a jerk of the head towards the farmhouse proper.

'You're not the farmer?'

'He's in the house.'

'Okay. Did you by any chance see –'

'Ask the farmer.'

'Okay, thank you so much.'

He waited until I was halfway towards what I took to be the front door, then called after me.

'He's busy!'

I turned but he was already disappearing round the corner of the shed. I knocked at the iron-shod door of the farmhouse and waited. For a while nothing happened. I knocked again. In mid-knock the door was snatched wide open by a man somewhere in his forties, who stepped forward and filled the old doorframe completely with his broad shoulders. He actually had to stoop to get out, where he straightened up and sniffed as though the all-pervading smell of chicken shit was somehow a new phenomenon. His face was pale and unshaven and could have done with some sleep. About a week's worth. His checked shirt and cords had seen better days.

I pointed over my shoulder. 'The man said –'

'Brian? Where is the bastard?'

'He's gone round that –'

'Who are you, anyway?'

I introduced myself. 'I'm a private investigator, and I wondered if I could ask –'

'Ha!' It was more a challenge than a laugh. Challenge to what, I didn't know. He turned round and disappeared inside again but left the door open. 'Private investigator. Yeah, just what I need,' he grumbled over his shoulder.

I followed him through a wide corridor, its floor darkly tiled and cluttered with boots and wellies, into a big, cold, dysfunctional kitchen.

'Private secretary is what I need, actually.' His sweeping arm gesture invited me to appreciate the chaos of paperwork on the table, the chairs and the floor. An old-fashioned electric typewriter and a big-buttoned calculator stood half-buried amongst the papers, books and booklets, lists, maps and notepads. Adding to the chaos were the teetering piles of dinner plates and other crockery waiting to be washed everywhere and the stacks of used pots and pans. Some of those had also found space on the chairs and floor. More than anything he needed a housekeeper. It was my turn to sniff: there was more than a hint of decay here and someone had been hitting the bottle.

'You any good with paperwork? Perhaps you could investigate this little lot for me. It's certainly criminal. Thought up by the evil geniuses in Brussels, I've no doubt. Care for a drink? Hope you don't mind if I do,' he said when I shook my head. 'Not that I really give a shit. About anything much.' He picked up a bottle of supermarket gin from under the table and poured himself a generous measure into a glass blind with grime. Then he waggled the bottle towards me in a way that was meant to be tempting.

'No thanks, really, I'm driving.'

'No shit. I thought you came in a biplane. You look like a barnstorming stunt pilot in that get-up.' He let himself drop heavily on to the only chair that wasn't covered in paperwork or dirty kitchenware. 'Siddown, make some space for yourself and call me Jack 'cause that's my name. Jack Fryer. Small fry. Cheers.' He raised his glass in salute. Here was a man who had been drinking steadily for hours and handled it with a depressing and frightening tautness that balanced precariously on top of a barely suppressed rage.

I carefully cleared a chair for myself and gestured at the papers festooning the table. 'So, what's all this?' I asked. Anyone can make a mistake.

'This is called a SUBSIDY APPLICATION FORM,' he said in capital letters. 'The *new* subsidy, of course.'

'I see.'

81

'Do you, fuck! But hey, let me enlighten you. Used to be that we received payments based on the number of animals we reared. Aha? Made sense? No more. From now on subsidies will be based on number of acres farmed, no matter how many animals on them. What could be simpler? Suicide, that's what. Let me show you. These,' he flung them in the air one by one, 'are the ex . . . plana . . . tory . . . booklets. Two, three, five . . . about ten of them. And then there are the maps. And the lists. Every acre needs to be registered with the Rural Payments Agency and they manage to miss half of your fields off the lists and if you call their fucking helpline you get some twelve-year-old twit telling you the payments have been put back by three months. The bank's already said they won't play ball any more which means I could easily lose the farm. And even if I don't, the new subsidies will amount to only half of what we used to get which means we'll no longer make any profit at all. I don't know why I bother with this fucking crap. If I had the money I'd sue the minister for agriculture for destroying my livelihood. And driving me to drink. Are you sorry you asked yet?'

'No, not at all.'

'Well, that makes you a right weirdo. So what do you want? If you can't calculate acreage or repair dishwashers then you're no fucking use to me at all.' He waved a hand at the piles of furry dishes in and around the sink.

'You can wash these things by hand, you know?'

'Bollocks. I tried it once. It can't be done. Did you say private investigator? What might you be investigating on my farm?'

Botulism, I nearly said, looking at spoons stuck in half-eaten tins of food, but asked about my DS instead. Had he noticed it across the valley?

'Of course I did. And the police already asked me a lot of dumb questions about it on Sunday.'

'What kind of dumb questions?' I was hoping to get the answers without having to ask dumb questions myself.

Jack obliged. 'When had I first noticed there was a black car in the middle of the field? I noticed it when I looked out the window Thursday morning. Why didn't I report it then? Because it's not my bloody field, that's why.'

'Whose bloody field is it?'

'Tony bloody Blackfield's bloody field. Bought it for Lane End Farm some ten years ago from the Fairchilds. And Blackfield's just the kind of bloke to leave an old wreck in it, if only to piss everybody off. Either that or bloody joyriders dumped it there, I thought at the time. Then they told me about the dead guy in the car. Was anyone missing, did I know anyone fitting the description? What, a bloke with half his brain seeping from his ears? No, can't say I do, officer. And so it went on. Did I know someone called Honeysomething?'

'Honeysett.'

'That's the one. What a stupid name. I'd never heard of him.'

'I'm Honeysett.'

'Thought that's what you said.'

'It was my car you saw, but I didn't drive it there. Neither did I stick a dead body in the back. But I'd like to know who did.'

'That's understandable, but why ask me?'

'Got to start somewhere. Where can I find the farmer who owns the field?'

He snorted his contempt. 'Blackfield? Some farmer. Keep on down the lane, take the first turn to the left, cross the Lam via the bridge, then keep going north, ignoring all else until you see a big ugly mess. And that's just his face. Ha! You can't miss it, his place is a shambles. Though what kind of reception you'll get I can't say.'

'You don't think much of him, then? As a farmer, I mean.'

'I don't think much of him in any capacity. He's not doing much farming though, that's for sure.'

'Then what does he do?'

Jack Fryer pulled his unshaven face into the caricature of a grin. 'That's a damn good question and you should definitely ask him that. And please come back and let me know what his answer was.' This thought seemed to produce some genuine mirth for a moment, then his smile vanished without a trace. 'Now if that's all, I'd like to get on with this shit here.'

'Sure. I'll see myself out.'

On my way to the front door, while searching in my pockets for matches to light a much-needed Camel, I came across a crumpled piece of paper. I unfolded it. It turned out to be the so-called map Cairn had given me at the Rose and Crown. The thing was hand-drawn in black biro in a shaky and spidery line, and the tiny writing on it was so illegible it took me a moment to decide which way was up. I turned round and walked back into the rancid kitchen. 'One more thing . . .'

'Yes, Mr Columbo.'

'This is supposed to be a map of the area. Show me where I am.'

'You're back in my kitchen which is . . .' He smoothed the map on the table and squinted at it. 'Here. That squiggle is Spring Farm.'

'Do you know someone called Albert?'

He shook his head.

I felt stupid but I had to ask it. 'Do you know of any witches around here?'

'Can never find one when you need one, right? Are you as weird as you appear or is this gin faulty?'

'Just stuff some kids told me about a witch living in the valley.'

'Kids? Oh, I think I know who they mean, the Stone woman. Stupid brats. It's like you've stepped into the Middle Ages when you set foot in the valley. People are as superstitious as ever. Hardly surprising with a whole new generation of New Age brats desperate to believe in any kind of crap as long as it's different from the crap their parents believed in.'

'Stone woman?'

'Yes. That's her name. She's not as stony as all that. I suppose she's a target for that kind of thing. Calling her a witch, I mean. She grows herbs down at Grumpy Hollow.'

'*Grumpy Hollow*? Are you serious?'

'That's what the place is called. Always has been. No idea why. When we were kids we'd go and play at the Hollow, there's a couple of springs down there and we found it quite spooky but perhaps it was just because it had a weird name.'

'Is it near here? Can you show me on this map?'

'Yeah, it's right there, it's marked even, see it?' He pointed to another squiggle and some writing that I had thought spelled Guppy Horror, which wouldn't have surprised me one bit, this being Somerset after all. I folded the map back into my pocket. 'Right, thanks. This time I'm really out of here, promise.'

'Glad to hear it.'

Once outside again I finally got a cigarette lit and took it as an excuse to wander about in the yard. You can't really ride a motorbike and smoke at the same time so it was plausible that I'd hang about for a bit longer. Not that I knew what I was looking for but I thought I'd recognize it when I saw it. That's how I had always worked in the past – hung around, made a nuisance of myself, stuck my nose in. The mist had thickened even further, which gave me the irrational feeling that the valley itself was trying to make things difficult for me, though Jack Fryer had been helpful enough. I sauntered further towards the back of the long chicken shed where a steel-grey double door turned out to be locked when I tried to open it. A couple of paces further along and the square-faced man suddenly swung round the corner again, still carrying his shit scraper. 'Did the farmer say you can come round here?'

'He didn't say I couldn't,' I suggested. 'I'm just having a fag before getting back on the bike.'

He simply stared hard with disapproving eyes and gave me the distinct impression that he considered me another bit of shit to be scraped out of the yard.

I ignored it. 'What's that Stone woman like down at Grumpy Hollow?' I asked, hooking a thumb in the general direction the map had indicated.

His eyes widened and he gripped the scraper's handle harder. 'Stay away from there if I was you.'

'Why's that?'

'S'not a good place, it's a witchy place. And the Stone woman, I'm not saying she's a witch but you can't help but wonder. Stuff you hear.'

'What kind of stuff?'

'Strangers coming and going. Weird stuff she grows.' He shrugged. 'I heard someone say down the Surgery that half the stuff she grows is poisonous. Stuff like that.'

'At the surgery?'

'Brains Surgery.'

'Brain surgery?'

'It's a pub in Larkhall, Brains Surgery,' he said slowly. 'Brains, it's a beer.'

'Poison? I wouldn't have thought there was that big a market for it.'

He shrugged again. 'You don't know, do you?' He turned and walked away, once more rounding the corner of the shed in pursuit of avian excrement. I didn't follow him. Whether he meant that I didn't know or one never knows I wasn't certain, but if someone told me there was a witchy place full of poison then I considered it my duty to go there and be scared.

As I walked towards the Norton I could just make out Jack Fryer's face through the grimy kitchen window behind his stacks of mouldy dishes, watching me. I gave a cheery wave with the hand that held the cigarette, hoping it might explain why I was still there, then took a last puff, flicked the butt into the weeds by the gate and kick-started the bike. It took a few goes, the Norton never did like murk.

By now I could see no more than a hundred yards in any direction. It was a stupid idea to ride deeper into this valley which I didn't know at all. If the fog got any thicker I'd have trouble finding my way around. The complete absence of signposting made me wonder whether the signs that were taken down in 1940 to confuse an invading Jerry had ever gone up again. The lanes were just wide enough for a tractor around here so I pootled slowly along, having no desire to become embedded in the back of some farm machinery. After a while a turn-off came into view on the left, an unmade road that led downhill and looked slippery. It was. But the Norton coped admirably with the wet, rutted track that curved down steeply between hedgerows. I only caught glimpses of sheep in the fields on either side, sitting about in dripping, dispirited huddles. I didn't want to depress them any further so refrained from shouting the traditional 'Mint sauce!' at them. I was too busy trying to keep the bike steady anyway. When I finally reached the bottom I was confronted by a stand of trees, a stream and no bridge. The lane disappeared into the stream and reappeared on the other side. In other words, a ford. It wasn't exactly a raging torrent but after a week of nearly solid rainfall this was no babbling brook either. There was no easy way of telling how deep it was at the centre without walking right in. Fallen leaves from the mixed bit of woodland the stream bisected here had been churned into slippery mush by heavy tyres. That was the trouble with the countryside: most of it was built with four-wheel-drives in mind. I had one-wheel-drive but just didn't fancy turning round so I pointed the Norton at a likely-looking spot in the brook, put it in first and opened the throttle wide. The rear wheel raced, eventually found some grip and propelled the bike forward. Before I knew it I was completely drenched in icy water and plastered with mud.

The engine sputtered and died on reaching the other side of the stream, probably feeling it had done enough by getting me across. I wheeled the bike to a tree where I could leave it leaning and draining, feeling quite a bit like leaning and draining myself. I knew it would be hopeless trying to restart the engine straight away. Having stuck my helmet on the handlebars I set off on foot. If the scribbly map was right then the path that led through this narrow band of trees would lead directly to Grumpy Hollow and 'the Stone woman', as Jack Fryer put it.

With no engine running the sudden noise reduction made me aware of the many sounds that are drowned by motorized transport: the rushing of the stream over its stony bed; the dripping of moisture from the fog-laden trees; the odd dispirited moan of a sheep or lowing of a cow in the distance; the squelching of water inside my boots and the growling of my stomach. I stomped along what was now just a muddy track, though the water-filled ruts showed that cars did come down here. The track lost the stream after a while and the trees were thinning out. It became even quieter. Another fifty yards and the track widened into a rutted quagmire. Bits of assorted fencing were ineffectually leaning this way and that. What had once been a wooden five-bar gate was mouldering in the weeds. A square sign tied with garden twine to the one surviving and otherwise unoccupied gatepost read PRIVATE KEEP OUT. A smaller, handwritten sign underneath proclaimed DANGER, POISONOUS PLANTS. This just had to be the entrance to Grumpy Hollow. Here the land fell away to a shallow bowl into which the mist had settled – or was this where they made the stuff? – and out of it rose solitary trees and the roofs of various structures. This then was Stone's herb farm, although 'farm' seemed too grand a word for such a ramshackle affair. I couldn't see a living soul. It was far too foggy and boggy and wet. I was hungry and thirsty. And wet and muddy. And just how poisonous were these plants anyway? I took a few unenthusiastic steps through what remained of the gate and sniffed the stagnant air. Something came flying out of the gloom. It missed my head by a few inches and slammed into the mud somewhere behind me. I turned around to see what it might have been when another missile sailed past, close enough for me to feel the air move. I looked all round but in the gloom and mist couldn't see anyone. A scarecrow poked its unmoving head out of the mist, there were muck-heaps, water tanks, sheds and all sorts. Another missile landed near me. 'Hey, stop that!' I protested ineffectively in a to-whom-it-may-concern fashion. Ineffectively, since the next missile hit me squarely on the right knee. 'Ow! All right already, I get the message!' Rubbing my knee with one hand and waving the other in surrender I hobbled back through the gate. A last vindictive missile landed near me. I picked it up. It was a small apple. Not exactly lethal but a hard enough object when thrown with enough force. When I got back to the ford I washed the mud off it and took a bite. Not only was it hard enough to threaten my dental work but it was so sour it made me shudder. My assailant hadn't wasted any dessert apples on me. I spat it out, plonked the helmet back on my head and for five minutes worked up a sweat pumping the kick-starter on the Norton. When it finally fired up I thought it a very cheerful sound. This time I managed to cross the stream without drowning the engine and I rode out of the valley before the fog could swallow me up.

Chapter Nine

A good cook always starts by putting the kettle on. Anyone hoping to be a good cook should also first grapple with mud-encrusted laces, drop squelching boots in the hall, hang leather jacket over a chair near the stove, stuff wet and filthy jeans into the washing machine, divest himself of any remaining items of clothing, letting them drop to the floor en route to the bathroom, then stand under a hot and generous shower groaning and spluttering until the General Decrepitude Index sinks back to acceptable levels. Next, dry off leisurely in a warm and draught-free room. Clothing self in comfortable and well-cut attire, freshly laundered and ironed, preferably by someone else, nicely rounds off the process. Now fully restored, cook should re-enter the steamy kitchen where by now the kettle has boiled completely dry and sits crackling and growling like an evil thing on the stove.

A good cook refills white-hot kettle at the sink, accompanied by much banging and steam, yet a minimum of burns and swearing, then returns it to the heat. A good cook is now ready for a drink. More than ready.

From the kitchen window I could see that up in the studio the lights were on, which probably meant that Annis was still whirling about there. The sitting room, I noticed with relief, was as messy as ever. I banked up the fire and went to tackle the current famine.

Something simple. I quickly chopped an onion, a few sticks of celery and a red pepper, chucked them in a pot and covered them with a ladle of stock. While that was bubbling I furnished myself with a bottle of Pilsner Urquell; my Existential Fear Factor responded nicely by dropping a few notches. My Accumulated Guilt Quotient on the other hand remained dangerously high. It had hardly been an afternoon of great achievements. My riding about in Lam Valley had been little more than a diversion. It had certainly contributed nothing towards freeing Jill's son and I had dug up no great revelations concerning Dead Guy Albert in the back of my DS. That there was some despair amongst farmers after BSE and the disastrously handled Foot and Mouth 'crisis' was hardly news to me either. Jack Fryer's kitchen had given a fair impression of a pit of despair but unless Albert turned out to be an employee of the Rural Payments Agency I couldn't see any connection. Yet I had no choice. I had to find an explanation of how the body got into my car. I couldn't help Jill while in police custody.

Grumpy Hollow had been more of a surprise. It had probably just been local kids, feeling safely hidden in the mist, taking a few pot shots at a stranger. Either that or the Stone woman was the silent violent type. Yet since I'd clearly been trespassing, a few well-aimed apples lobbed through the mist wasn't exactly a disproportionate reaction either. Airborne fruit or not, I would have to go back there. Preferably on a day when I could see it coming.

The stock had reduced by now so I added chopped tomatoes, tomato purée, a pinch of sugar and some torn basil leaves from a plant that clung to life in a pot on the windowsill. I seasoned the sauce and left it to simmer while I put on the water for the pasta.

As for getting some paintings done ... I tried not to think about it. The only time I didn't feel guilty about not painting enough was while I was painting. Our forthcoming burglary worried me. Tim had assured me that he had a plan and everything would work just fine. Although I had been known to climb through the odd window and could if necessary open a door with picklocks – as long as I remembered to bring sandwiches and had no other engagements that day – I had come to rely heavily on Tim's expertise in that area. It wasn't so much the break-in itself but the consequences that worried me. Not that I had the least fear that we might get trouble from the law. If Telfer, after discovering the burglary, called the police at all then the statistics said we had a pretty good chance of never getting fingered for it. It was more Telfer's reaction I was worried about. That and what we might find.

The water in the big pan was seething. I poured in half a packet of conchiglie pasta shells, stirred a drained can of tuna and some capers into the sauce and went to fetch Annis. The path our feet had carved through the meadow over the years was slippery and the mist lay thick and unmoving in our valley. The grass was too high again, I noticed as it brushed against my legs, and would soon need its last cut of the year. There was no sign of Annis in the studio. The door was open – neither of us ever remembered to lock it – and the daylight bulbs were on, but not a soul inside. The painting on her easel looked good. It also looked finished, though Annis would probably find a million minute things to change before she was happy with it. She'd dropped a brush in front of the easel. I picked it up, wiped it and dropped it into a jar of white spirit. There was nothing curious about any of this, I told myself as I turned out the light and closed the door behind me. We sometimes forgot to switch the lights off or simply didn't go back up to the studio when we had thought we would. Yet I had been so convinced that she was busy painting that I felt a little unnerved at not finding her there. I slithered back to the house and climbed the stairs to her room. Perhaps she had fallen asleep. I slowly and quietly opened her door. The bedside lamp was on, lending the room a warm amber glow. Propped up on her pillows Annis was lying naked on the bed, looking up at me with large green eyes and chewing on her lower lip. Beside her Tim's naked form was asleep, his woolly head on her stomach, one hand resting on her breast. There were empty takeaway cartons on the floor. The room smelled of Chinese food, of cigarettes and wine and lovemaking.

'Sorry,' I said quietly.

'Sorry,' Annis mouthed silently and crinkled her forehead with worry lines.

I closed the door gently, then clomped down the stairs to the kitchen. I grabbed the bottle of Urquell, emptied it, opened another from the fridge. I lit a cigarette and puffed at it, standing by the stove, looking at nothing in particular.

This had never happened before. The triangle that was Tim, Annis and myself had lasted for . . . was it three years already? But we had been what I liked to think of as discreet about it. Annis lived with me but from time to time stayed the night at Tim's place. No one counted the nights and we never talked about it. Normally Annis and I slept in my large bedroom with the big windows at the front; only when Tim stayed over did she sleep in her own room and Tim on a sofa downstairs . . . We had never discussed this, yet an unspoken rule had just been broken. Only, when I thought about it, this seemed rather petty. A 'not under this roof' rule could surely only be there so I might conveniently forget that I was sharing Annis's sexual favours with Tim and had done so right from the start. Then why was I so . . . I was looking for the right word and was surprised when I found it . . . bloody upset about it?

Behind me Annis padded barefoot into the kitchen. I didn't turn around. Listened to her light a cigarette from the packet on the table and inhale. 'You want to talk?' she asked quietly.

I turned round then. She was wearing jeans, a crumpled black T-shirt and electrified hair. 'What's to talk about?'

She sat down at the table. 'Then why make me feel like I've done something really bad? You're unhappy, so let's talk about it.'

'No, it's just . . .it's just it never happened before. I thought you and Tim wouldn't . . . I don't know. Where's his bloody car?'

'He'd been drinking, came by cab.'

'But you don't normally . . .' I stubbed out the cigarette and fumbled for another one.

'Sleep with him here? Not usually, no. It just happened like that today.'

Having got the cigarette lit I sucked hard on it, then nearly choked on the smoke trying to talk through it. 'And it was really important that you . . . shagged him this minute? It couldn't have waited? I didn't know things between you were so passionate, so urgent.'

'It wasn't like that, Chris. Tim was feeling down, he wanted to see me. He said he needed me and I told him to come over.'

'So next time you're at his place and I'm down and I need you you're going to invite me round Tim's for a shag while he's out getting you a takeaway, is that it?'

'No, of course not, but then it would never happen anyway.' She twirled the glass ashtray around in front of her with a sudden, sharp movement.

'What? What wouldn't?'

'You calling me and saying you need me.'

I was confounded by this. 'But I do need you.'

'Do you.' It wasn't a question, it was a flat statement of doubt.

'Of course I need you, I love you,' I protested.

Annis smoked silently for a while and chased a spent match round the ashtray with her cigarette. 'You never said.'

'What do you mean, of course I did, I must have done, I mean . . . Didn't I?' I sank into a chair opposite her.

'Believe me, Chris, I'd remember.'

'But you know, don't you? You do know I love you.'

She seemed to think about it for a moment. She looked sad all of a sudden, and tired. She gave a tiny shrug. 'I know you're fond of me, I mean we've lived here together for years now and . . . But then we lived here for two years before we ever slept with each other. And if it hadn't been for me climbing into the bath with you we probably never would have. And you didn't object when you found out I was sleeping with Tim then.'

'That's hardly fair, I think your exact words were, "If you two are going to make a big deal out of this I won't sleep with either of you again," so what did you expect us to do? Specifically what was I supposed to do that I didn't?'

'I don't know. But whatever it was you didn't do it.'

'We'd only just started going to bed together, I didn't know then that . . . how . . . I was going to feel about you later, how could I, and then everything seemed to run along fine. It was you who made the rules, anyway. Tim and I had no say in it. *You* decided.'

'You didn't have to accept it, Chris. If I told you to jump in the mill race you wouldn't do that.' In a quieter tone she said: 'Tim finds it hard. Tim *always* found it hard to share me. And you think it's all on my terms but I find it hard to share me sometimes. This isn't normal, you know, what we're doing.'

'You started it.'

'Will you stop saying that? As though it made any difference! It's got nothing to do with what's happening now!'

'What *is* happening now?' I was suddenly scared. I was more scared than I had been for a long time.

'I don't know that anything is. Perhaps there should be, I really don't know. You're the grown-up. You're nearly twice my age, I always thought you'd know all this stuff. I didn't plan this, I didn't go out of my way to create this kind of life for myself, it just happened and it happened because I was here and *you* were here. Getting it on with both you and Tim was just me in a weird mood then. I never thought about it for the long term, I never thought it through at all. As you said, it had only just started. And I didn't do it so you could fight about me, either. But neither of you did, you just seemed to think it was all right

95

that we had this triangle. It seemed quite hip, somehow, I was impressed. With myself as well.'

'And now?'

'I keep telling you, I don't know. Your supper's burning, I think.'

At that moment I could smell it too. I shot up out of my chair and pushed the pots off the heat. The pasta was just boiling dry and the sauce was nothing but a sizzling dribble at the bottom of the pan. This was becoming a habit.

I turned to Annis who was already at the door. She paused. 'When did you first realize?'

'What?'

'That you loved me?'

I thought back, trying to remember.

Annis slipped out of the door.

Chapter Ten

There was no sign of Tim next day when I carefully carried my hangover downstairs, in the middle of the morning, following the smell of coffee into the kitchen. I lowered myself slowly on to a chair. Annis was there at the stove, insinuating long strips of bacon into a pan of sizzling oil.

'Want some?' she asked. 'Speak now or forever hold your peace.'

'No thanks, I'm feeling a bit ... delicate. Where's that coffee I can smell?'

She poured me a mug from the cafetière and shoved it in front of me, then unsuccessfully tried to run her hand through my tangled hair.

'Is your hair part of the Make Space for Wildlife initiative?'

'My hair hurts, I can't possibly brush it.'

'I thought Pilsner didn't give you a hangover?'

'It does if you try and drink all of it.'

'Ah.' She rummaged around in a drawer and found a squashed carton of painkillers. So that's where they lived. She doled out two pills into my eager hand. 'Eejit.'

I looked round the kitchen. Annis followed my gaze in silent triumph. The place was spotless and sparkled, despite the gloom of the day. She hadn't just cleaned the place, she had burnished it.

'Talking of filth ...' I told Annis my muddy tale while she sat down and attacked a couple of eggs, a mountain of fried mushrooms and a pile of crispy bacon. 'Is that break-fast?' I asked.

'Second breakfast. I've been up for *hours*. You want to borrow the Landy then.'

I hid my surprise behind a gulp of coffee. 'Yes, please.'

'No problem.' She dug out the keys from her jeans pocket and put them on the table, halfway between us; Annis's most treasured possession – apart from her brushes, perhaps – and not a bribe in sight. As I tried to casually palm the keys she covered my hand with hers. She speared a mushroom and offered it up to my mouth. I closed my lips around the fragrant fungus, chewed and swallowed. She gave me a smile that barely registered before it vanished again, released my hand and returned to her breakfast. 'Okay, you can go now.'

I climbed into the Landy's cab and fiddled with the igni-tion. I wasn't sure about the moon phase but hoped that the old diesel was oblivious to the dank weather. It was grey and damp but there was no fog this morning and the radio had promised dramatic improvements for later in the day. I didn't share their optimism. The engine caught and the ancient contraption vibrated into life, belching a black cloud of pollution out the back. I would have another go at Grumpy Hollow, hoping somehow to get ahead of Avon and Somerset. They had the annoying habit of jump-ing out at me from unusual places and right now that was the last thing I needed.

As I pulled away I caught a glimpse of movement behind the hall window and raised a hand in salute. I felt guilty about my reaction last night when I found Tim in Annis's bed and yet more guilt for being so inarticulate about loving the woman. I felt guilty for having allowed Jill's son to be used as a lever to make me do someone's dirty work for him. In fact my Accumulated Guilt Quotient was so high that smoking on an empty stomach hardly registered, though I was acutely aware of the stupidity of it while I fought to light a cigarette single-handedly with my temperamental lighter whilst coughing all the way up the track to the lane. Dark thoughts about how every lungful ate into my life expectancy helped to take my mind off things until I got to Lam Valley. I rattled past Chickenshit Farm, where I hoped Jack Fryer had managed some sleep, not to mention washing up, and after a couple of wrong turns found the track that led steeply down to the ford across the stream and on to Grumpy Hollow. I passed the tree where yesterday I had left the bike and ground on slowly through the mud.

In the churned-up area in front of the missing gate to the little herb farm I abandoned the Landy and walked from there. A length of rope had been strung from gatepost to gatepost, surely a purely psychological measure to reinforce the warnings on the signs to keep out. I ducked under it and walked on. Here the mists still lingered and being mindful of yesterday's welcome I advanced cautiously. There were plenty of hiding places around here. The place was shambolic in a curiously attractive way. It had an air that reminded me of the charm of picturesque neglect the outbuildings at Mill House had acquired, though there was no sign of idleness here, quite the opposite; I'd never seen a place more densely worked and cultivated. Every corner appeared to be crammed with plants, many sheltered from the weather by bits of glass and grimy sheets of builders' polythene. There appeared to be a couple of figures watching me from the middle of a small field of bright green foliage to my left. I waved and called hello. The figures didn't move or answer and as I got closer I realized I'd been trying to converse with scarecrows. Very realistic ones. I was wondering if they were meant to scare more than just the birds. As I carefully advanced downhill past a zinc trough full of scummy green water, plants growing in rows of beds bordered with flimsy wooden boards, barrels, muck heaps and all kinds of junk, the structures at the centre of all this took on more definite shapes. An ancient-looking Volvo estate – it was *beige*, and when did they stop making cars that colour? – stood with its nose pointing uphill. Near a couple of pollarded willows sat an old-fashioned hump-backed caravan. Five feet away and at right angles to that stood a pale blue and weathered old shepherd's hut, its wheels disappearing into the muddy grass. Connecting the two and shielding the space in between from the worst of the weather hung a home-made porch consisting of bits of wood, canvas and tarpaulin. Nests of bottles, presumably empty, had accrued beside the hut; wine bottles, beer bottles, water bottles, gas bottles. Behind the caravan stood a greenhouse, botched together from sash windows and, by the look of it, old shower cubicles, and beyond that stretched the grey caterpillar of a polytunnel far into the plantation. A couple of sheds, knocked together from old pallets and tar-paper, completed the picture. Thin wisps of grey smoke escaped from the lum-hatted stove pipe protruding at a drunken angle from the roof of the hut. Apart from the smell of wetness, of mud and dank vegetation, there was the undeniable aroma of country cooking in the air. My stomach rumbled loudly. A dim light showed in the little window of the shepherd's hut. I splashed towards it, intending to knock on the side.

'Hold it right there.'

I held it right there. It was a commanding female voice and it came from behind me. I turned round. She was pointing a rifle at me from the corner of the caravan. It had to be the Stone woman but it was me who felt petrified.

'Don't point that thing at me, there's no need for that,' I said in my friendliest I'm-just-a-harmless-detective voice. 'You must be,' I opted for neutral ground, 'Ms Stone.'

'Right first time. Now up the hill and back where you came from. I've had enough of people creeping round my place.' She motioned with the rifle. 'Go on.'

By now I'd had time to take a closer look. She was covered in several layers of the kind of washed-out olive drab and used-to-be-blue stuff people working in the country always seemed to wear but her feet were trendily clad in pink wellies. Ms Stone tried hard to sound and look fierce, squinting along the barrel of her gun and lowering her voice, but that couldn't disguise the fact that even in all this dripping murk she looked somehow . . . sunny. Cheerful. There was sandy beach-blonde hair escaping from her multicoloured knitted hat, the unsquinting eye was a clear sea blue and her tanned face was strikingly devoid of hairy warts and other witchy accessories.

'I'm harmless, honestly. And that's an air rifle you're pointing at me. It's hardly a deadly weapon.'

'At sixteen pounds per square inch it would certainly ruin your day if I pulled the trigger, I can promise you that much.' But she lowered it nevertheless and pointed it at my mud-caked boots instead. 'Start walking then.'

'I just want to talk. I'm a private investigator.'

'Don't care.' She shrugged her shoulders. 'There's enough signs up there telling you people to keep out but you just keep coming.'

'It's true, I did see the signs and ignored them but then there wasn't a bell to ring or anything,' I complained. 'So if one doesn't walk past the signs how does one get to see you?'

'One gets invited. You one didn't invite. So get lost, will you?' A note of tiredness had crept into her voice. 'I've had enough visitors to last me the rest of the year. Perhaps longer.'

'The police?'

'Yes, them too, though they were a joy compared with some of my other callers.'

I took out my packet of cigarettes, shook one out and lit it, mainly to buy some time. Her eyes followed my every move, as though mesmerized. I offered her one. She closed the fifteen feet of space between us and yanked a cigarette out of the packet. She had it lit so fast with her own lighter, produced from a trouser pocket, there could be no doubt that I was watching a true addict suffering from extreme nicotine deprivation.

She sucked greedily at her cigarette, the gun comfortably cradled in the crook of her arm, then let the smoke out slowly. 'I'm trying to give up. Why aren't you walking yet?' But her shoulders slumped in relaxation as she took another puff and exhaled with a sigh of contentment.

'I'm sorry, I didn't mean to sabotage your efforts to give up smoking. I know how difficult it is.'

'Ah, bollocks, I just can't really afford to buy any, that's all. And tobacco is the one thing I don't grow down here, far too much hassle.'

'What is it you *are* growing down here? Herbs, someone said.'

'Herbs mainly, but I try and grow most of my own food as well.'

'And you live here?' I failed to keep the astonishment out of my voice.

'Yeah, anything wrong with that?'

'No, not at all, it's very . . .' I was looking for a word that wouldn't wake up her trigger finger. '. . . romantic,' I said.

'Romantic, my arse. Not when half your crop's keeling over from botrytis in this damn weather, blight has got your spuds, the rabbits have had your carrots, the badgers your sweetcorn and the pigeons the rest.'

The aroma of cooking intensified in the air and I suddenly identified the smell. I nodded towards the shepherd's hut. 'I think I can smell pigeon now.'

'Oh, shit.' She rushed past me, up the three steps and through the door into the hut. 'If it's ruined then it'll be your bloody fault,' she cried.

I followed her. The inside of the hut, which was no more than six by twelve feet, was a cosy affair, lit by a couple of low voltage lamps. On the left under the window were a table and chair, both covered in books. There was a small leather armchair in one corner and the squat wood-burning stove in the other. She had taken the casserole off the stove with a pair of gardening gloves and put it on the floor, where she was examining it, cigarette dangling from her lips. She grabbed hold of a wooden spoon.

'If it's stuck to the bottom it's best to decant it into a fresh pot without stirring it,' I warned.

She gave me an exasperated look, then pushed past me out of the door, leaving her gun leaning against the wall. A moment later she returned carrying a fire-blackened cast-iron casserole dish with an ancient-looking dog following at her heels. I shrank against the wall but the tired mongrel only sniffed perfunctorily in my direction, then flopped down near the stove. 'Don't mind Taxi, he's too tired to bite.' The Stone woman tumbled deep red sauce and pigeons into the clean casserole dish. 'It's all right, it was only just catching at the bottom.' She took a swig from an open bottle of red, added a good slug to the dish and stirred it in. With the casserole returned to the stove top she let herself fall into the battered red armchair. 'You can cook, huh? Dropped in to give me a cooking lesson, that it? Or perhaps you just have a lot of experience burning stuff? Who are you anyway? You look slightly less menacing without your goggles. That was you yesterday, wasn't it? Persistent, aren't you? And you're a private investigator?'

'Do you always ask half a dozen questions in one breath? Yes, no, yes and yes, it was and I am. I think that covers it. My name's Chris Honeysett. So, was it you who tried to scare me off with airborne top-fruit?'

'Tried to? Worked pretty well, I thought. I'm Gemma Stone. Most people call me Gem.'

'Gem Stone, I get it.'

'Very astute, only I'm not the precious type. So what do you want from me? You're also less muddy today. Did you crawl here yesterday?'

'I came by bike yesterday but the engine conked out at the ford.'

'So that's what I heard. I wondered why the engine sound didn't come any nearer. Made me suspicious. People with legitimate business know to sound their horn at the gate and wait.'

'Ex-gate.' I felt it was only fair to point this out. 'I was unsure of the etiquette. And at the time quite hornless, I assure you. My normal conveyance, by the way, is a black Citroën DS21.'

Her mouth formed a silent 'oh' and she nodded sagely. 'So that was yours, was it?'

'Did you see it?'

She pointed for me to sit on the wooden chair. 'Just chuck the books on the table.'

I did. All of them were about aspects of horticulture and herbalism.

'No, didn't see it but the police told me about it. I'm afraid I couldn't help them either. I haven't been up that way for ages, too busy down here. They said there was a dead bloke in the back. You didn't have anything to do with that then, presumably.'

'Nothing at all. My car was stolen from a car park in Larkhall and found in that field with a dead body in the back.'

The dog closed his eyes and sighed. 'And what exactly made you come to me with this story?'

The answer to that was easy. Cairn had overheard two men talking about a guy called Albert and 'the old witch', though here in the light I guessed Gemma was still comfortably in her thirties. 'For a while the police thought I had killed the guy. Perhaps they still do. Thought I might do a bit of investigating myself. I'm asking everybody.'

'The police already asked me. Sorry, no idea.'

'And you're not missing anyone, obviously.'

Her eyes were resting on a gardening calendar pinned to the wall by the table. 'No, can't say I do. It's a one woman show, this,' she said but a note of doubt had crept into her voice.

'I think the dead man's name was Albert Something.'

'Oh? The police didn't mention that.' She frowned, then smiled brightly and rose. 'Sorry, can't help,' she said with determination. 'Now, if you don't mind, I've got things to do.'

'Oh, all right.' I got up and went outside into the brightening afternoon. Gaps had appeared in the cloud and the mists were burning away fast. 'So what kind of herbs are you growing? Poisonous ones? I saw the sign.'

'Nah, that's just to scare off the kids. Not that it's working too well. Somehow the place is a magnet for bored children, nutters, vandals and prowlers. And of course private detectives, the police, drunk neighbours and all the other wildlife Somerset has to offer. I'm thinking of getting a noisier gun. Yeah, I grow all kinds of herbs, medicinal as well as culinary,' she explained. She was walking me back to the broken gate to make sure I really left.

'And you're making a living that way?'

'I'm still here, aren't I?' she said sharply. I guessed this wasn't a favourite topic.

Just then I noticed that now there appeared to be only one scarecrow standing guard. I pointed at it. 'Ehm . . .'

'Yes, I can stand very still if need be. You learn that when you're hunting for pigeons with an air gun.'

At the gate I offered her a cigarette as a parting gift. She took two, gave me a lopsided grin that died on her face even before she had turned round, then trotted back towards her muddy camp.

The Land Rover started straight away as though eager to get out of the place. As I negotiated the muddy track and the even muddier ford I couldn't help thinking that Gem had looked just a little worried ever since I mentioned the name Albert, though she had ploughed on bravely enough through the rest of our conversation. If she really was as worried as I thought then it was only a matter of time until she made some kind of move – if only to find some more cigarettes to calm herself down. In which case it was a private detective's duty to wait round the corner and follow her. I turned left along the lane, since I presumed she'd go right towards the nearest spot of civilization, found a passing place wide enough to turn the Landy around in and point it the right way, then waited.

And waited. The stuttering engine sound of a microlight plane crossing the valley did nothing to convince me that this was a sport I should rush to get into, though I envied whoever was up there the freedom to buzz across the countryside without having to follow the roads. It was quite pleasant sitting there with the windows open while the sun went in and out of the cloud breaks. But after a while it got tedious, so to pass the time I started worrying about things: about Jill's son, locked up somewhere, terrified of what might happen to him; about me and Annis; about Tim and Annis; about the dead guy in my car, despite Grimshaw's assurances; about Thursday's break-in, despite Tim's assurances.

I could hear the surge of the Volvo's old engine long before it gained the track, so had plenty of time to start my own car and wonder how I was going to follow the woman without her spotting me behind her in an empty, if winding, country lane. When I first caught a glimpse of the Volvo ahead of me my worries disappeared. Not only was the rear window of the estate blind with mud and obscured by who-knows-what junk in the back but half the glass was missing from her only wing mirror. Nevertheless I let her get a couple of bends ahead to be on the safe side. The speed at which she pushed her old banger along confirmed to me that this was one worried woman – or one with one hell of a tobacco craving. As if to confirm the latter she stopped her car on a double yellow line in Larkhall, jumped out and disappeared into a convenience store. Two minutes later she came out with a copy of the *Bath Chronicle* and two packets of cigarettes and dived back into her car. A moment later a white puff of smoke appeared from the driver window, a black puff of smoke from the car's exhaust and we were off again. She turned sharp left, crossed a couple of main roads and headed west into the country again. For a while we were more or less following the Kennet and Avon canal then the Volvo slowed and without indicating turned into a narrow tree-lined track between empty fields. As the track curved around into a slight depression crowded with more trees a police constable by the side of the road gave me the first indication that the circus was in town but by then it was far too late. The Volvo had already stopped on the track in front and Gem had got out, looking back at me without apparent surprise. I'd have to work on my shadowing technique. Beyond, a patrol car, a big grey Ford and a technicians' van were crowded into the small gravelled space in front of a tiny crumbling bungalow. It looked like a post-war prefab that had managed to survive into the twenty-first century by hiding under a clump of trees in the countryside.

The constable put his face to the driver window. 'Would you mind switching your engine off, sir? And could you tell me what you are doing here, please?'

'Nothing, really. I think I must have taken a wrong turning, I'll just back out again, shall I?'

'I don't think so, sir.' He reached in through the open window and snatched the keys so quickly I didn't get a chance to bite his hand. He pointed invitingly towards the bungalow. If I was where I thought I was then this could spell serious trouble. In my humble opinion Gem, who obviously knew a lot more about the expired gent in my car than she let on, had driven straight to Mr Albert Something's house to check on his general well-being or more specifically his continued existence which, judging by the assembled police troupe, was now in serious doubt. And since I had vigorously denied all knowledge of the dead man's identity I might find my own presence here hard to explain away. Gem was walking quickly ahead of me towards the bungalow where a multi-tasking uniformed constable moved across to intercept her while holding on to a cat and talking into her radio at the same time. I followed more warily and couldn't stifle a groan when Detective Inspector Deeks popped out of the front door like an evil jack-in-the-box. He seemed to react with surprise at seeing Gem and with anger at seeing me. To my own surprise he charged along the few algae-green flag-stones in front of the house, straight past Gem and the WPC to confront me.

He brought his face close and spoke in a low voice charged with fury. 'What the hell are you doing here, Honeysett?'

'I was just following her,' I said, pointing at Gem who appeared to have instantly bonded with the WPC over the cat.

'Why were you following Gem Stone?'

'It's a detective thing, you wouldn't understand.'

'Stop clowning around. You know whose shack this is? Was?'

'Albert Whatsit's who expired in my car. I'm only guessing, of course.'

'You must be bloody psychic. Yes, Albert Barrington. The woman who drops round his free-range bleedin' eggs once a week got worried. No one else seems to have missed him. Except you and Gemma Stone obviously suddenly decided that you did. Did you know all along who the stiff was? You're a mad fuck, Honeysett, and I loathe the sight of you, you know that? I want you out of here, pronto, so I can forget I saw you here. Now get back into your . . . *thing* and drive it away.'

Did I know the *stiff*? Now what kind of language was that for a police officer? The deceased, surely. 'Gosh, that's a *gorgeous* animal,' I said loudly and ducked from under his incinerating gaze to join Gem Stone and the WPC who were busy ear-scratching the confused and mewing cat the policewoman was holding. The cat's fur was a marbled grey and black but the downy fluff on his stomach flamed in autumnal gold. Until that very moment I had never shown even the remotest interest in pets of any kind but Deeks probably didn't know that. I was just getting a little confused by his attitude and wanted to buy myself some time to work it out. After all, he'd spent the last few years trying to make my life a misery whenever the chance presented itself and now he wanted to just forget I'd been here? 'He really is cute,' I said to Gem. 'Was he Albert's?' The cat wriggled in the policewoman's arms and sniffed at me.

'You like cats then?' Gem asked with just a hint of suspicion.

'Yeah, I'm quite potty about cats,' I lied. 'Though I don't have one myself at the moment.'

'Yes, I suppose he's Al's, technically, though he'd only just appeared out of nowhere a short while ago, as they do. Al wasn't sure he should keep him. He wasn't very well, you know. He wasn't even sure that he could afford to keep him ... cat food, flea collars, worming tablets, vet bills ...'

'Do you know the cat's name then?' the constable asked Gem. She was obviously a cat lover herself and oblivious to the fact that her uniform had already collected enough cat hair for her to knit her own moggy.

'He didn't want to give him a name until he'd made a decision about whether to keep him, he thought it would make it more difficult to let him go. What's going to happen to him?'

The constable pulled a pained face. 'Normally, in these cases, unless someone comes forward to claim the animal, like a relative, for instance, then he would have to be put down –'

'Put down?' Gem echoed, horrified. 'As far as I know Al didn't have any relatives.'

'How about you then?' The policewoman smiled invitingly and held the cat out to her.

'I can't. I've got a dog who wouldn't take kindly to introducing a cat. Anyway, herb beds and cats don't really mix.'

Deeks appeared by my side and just stared at me as though he couldn't believe what he was seeing. Perhaps he couldn't. I tried to ignore him.

'How about you, Mr . . .?' The constable proffered the wriggling thing.

'I really can't. My place is . . . ehm . . .'

'Huge,' Deeks completed. 'A cat is exactly what you need. Thank you, constable.' He relieved her of the cat and shoved him at me, where he clawed his way up my leather jacket so he could stare at me with enormous eyes.

'Hang on . . . I'm not sure I can afford to take on a cat, you know? Vet bills, worming collars, flea tablets –'

'Rubbish, the moggy's yours. Now beat it.'

'Hey, just wait a second –'

'You've run out of seconds.' He grabbed me by the arm and dragged me along to the Landy. 'You're getting out of here and I don't want to see you again near here or Gem Stone's or anywhere, actually.' He opened the door for me. 'Get in there before Needham turns up and hauls your arse down the station again.'

I deposited the cat beside me. The first constable supplied my keys. I backed the Landy up as fast as I could. I knew when I wasn't wanted and despite my curiosity the mention of Needham had convinced me I'd better figure this one out from a distance. When I glanced back towards the bungalow I saw Deeks talking intensely to the constable while keeping an avuncular arm around her shoulder, the constable nodding, nodding, nodding. The cat jumped into the footwell. He looked panicked by the sudden turn of events. I'd have to get rid of the animal at the first opportunity or I'd end up like one of those private eyes who discuss their cases with their moggy and take them down the pub for a beer. At least we'd achieved a stay of execution for the thing. At the moment I had plenty of other worries. We needed to get Jill's son back and for that we would break into Telfer's house and rob his safe. But I now had new stuff to worry about: for a start,

110

Deeks obviously knew Gemma Stone. He didn't seem at all surprised to see her there, nor did he object to her presence. Me however he couldn't wait to get rid of. And since in the past few years he'd never missed an opportunity to drag me into Manvers Street under the flimsiest of pretexts this new attitude of wanting to keep me *out* of the interview room worried me not a little. Now I had an animal to look after, at least until I could find someone to foist it on. While rattling back towards Mill House through a fresh offering of drizzle from the man upstairs I couldn't help marvelling at how, since answering that dreaded phone call from Griffin's on that stormy morning, when I had nothing more hectic planned than squeezing a tube of cobalt blue, my life had suddenly become rather crowded. Sometimes though you just couldn't back out or delegate. Serenity lay at the other end of burglary and – I was getting to know myself – a certain amount of mayhem.

I parked the Landy in the puddle-pocked yard close to the door and got out, walked round to the other side and opened the door for the cat to jump out. He looked at me with almond-shaped eyes of palest green, then looked past me left and right, sniffed, meowed and didn't budge. 'It's just a bit of rain,' I chided, 'don't be pathetic.' He retreated into the furthest corner. I grabbed him. He scrabbled and clawed up my jacket and meowed. I carried him like a squirming baby indoors and set him down on the stone-flagged floor of the hall. He began sniffing around at once and cautiously inspected every nook and cranny. If he was going to give the whole of Mill House this kind of treatment he'd be a very busy cat for a few days. Annis appeared from the direction of the kitchen, having heard me suggest to the cat he may go ahead and spray my carpets if he was tired of life, and then started making exactly the same noises Gem and the constable had made. It had to be a genetic thing.

'What's his name? Kittykittykitty.'

'He hasn't got one and he won't need one since he's not staying. He's just a refugee. He used to belong to the dead guy.'

'Poor thing, lost your daddy.'

I rolled my eyes. 'Look at this as a transit camp,' I told the cat as I squeezed past the mutual admiration society. '*A clearing house.*'

'How can you be so cruel? You could call him Tiddles.'

'No chance!' Last thing I saw when I slipped round the corner was Annis hugging him to her chest and examining his bits. As if I didn't have enough competition already. I had nearly made it to the kitchen when she called me back.

'Did you bring any cat food?'

I walked back warily. '*Cat* food?'

'Cat – meow – hunger – food. Cat food.'

'Can't he eat what we're having?'

'Pumpkin, sweet potato and banana curry?'

'Ah.'

'So then you'd better go and get some. I think he's hungry.' The cat looked at me from the safety of her arms and meowed his agreement.

It had started.

Chapter Eleven

'If it's Thursday then it must be burglary,' Annis murmured, wrapping her warm limbs tighter around me and snuggling her face deeper into my shoulder. It was still early, judging by the thin quality of the light, and I was wondering whether it was time for breakfast yet when I heard a scrabbling noise at the door. I saw the brass door handle move a little, then stop, then silence. Interesting. Not interesting enough to let go of the woman in my arms – not many things were – but still noteworthy that the nameless cat could stretch that high. More scrabbling. The door handle dipped, the door opened a few inches. I briefly saw the cat hang from his front paws on the handle, then drop out of sight. The door closed. Seconds later the thing had jumped on the bed and was walking confidently all over us.

'Annis, the cat can open doors,' I said in alarm.

'Great. We could call him Paws.'

'No chance.'

'Let's try and teach him to warm croissants then . . .'

It was over a breakfast of said croissants, heated in the oven without feline help, that I sought once more to simplify my life. I called Giles Haarbottle at Griffin's and told him again that I was now convinced Lane was kosher.

'All right, if you say so, but I don't believe a word of it. Ah well, you can't win them all. Sometimes that's just how the cookie crumbles, you win some, you lose some.'

'Mr Haarbottle, there are only so many clichés I can handle at breakfast time . . .'

'Breakfast time? I've been at work for hours,' he complained. 'It's the early bird that catches the worm, you know?'

'But it's the early worm that gets caught. And remember, it's the second mouse that gets the cheese: I'll send you my invoice.'

As soon as I cut the connection the phone rang. It was Sergeant Hayes. 'Good news, Honeysett. They released what's left of your car. What's more they delivered it back here, which was kind of them, but we want you to pick it up pronto. Before traffic decide it's not roadworthy, which I'm sure it isn't.'

'I'm on my way,' I promised, not entirely truthfully, since it suddenly dawned on me that the keys hadn't been in the ignition when it was found and I didn't have the foggiest where the spare set might be.

It took nearly an hour and several upended drawers to locate them. They were hiding in a little wooden box along with a book of matches from a Turkish seaside restaurant, a champagne cork with lipstick marks and a dead beetle. If there was a story behind this then I didn't remember it. By the time I got back downstairs, triumphantly waving the keys and expecting a lift to the station, Annis had gone out.

Another expensive taxi ride later and I was reunited with the DS. The bonnet was crinkled and one headlight smashed, the driver side was scratched and dented, and there was a star-shaped crack in the windscreen but I greeted the poor thing like an old friend. Miraculously the CD player was still there and not a single disc was missing. The rest of my possessions, Dictaphone, camcorder, my lightweight binoculars, were handed to me in a clear plastic bag. Nothing had been stolen. Nothing had even been touched. The car had been cleaned by the technicians, on the inside only, with some stuff that possibly smelled worse than death but faint stains still remained on the upholstery. I drove home with all windows open, with Radiohead at a satisfying volume level, wondering if anyone might deign to let me know who Albert really was and how he ended up in my car. I would go and ask Gemma Stone again, who obviously knew more about it then she let on, but not today. Needham and Deeks seemed to have decided I had nothing to do with it and anyway I had to cook supper for three, then commit burglary. Now, what was appropriate food for a break-in? Something light – you won't feel much like climbing through windows after a three course meal that includes treacle tart – but at the same time sustaining – you don't want your stomach to start growling halfway through. Raiding Telfer's fridge really wasn't part of the deal. It would be bad enough to come home and find your safe had been cleaned out.

I stood in the open kitchen door, watching the rain drown what was once a thriving herb garden, and called Jill. We had spoken every day, during which time she had shown a heartbreaking composure. 'It's tonight, isn't it? I never wished anyone luck for a burglary before but there it is, good luck, Chris.'

I promised to call again as soon as there was any news.

Once we were all assembled in the kitchen, Tim already dressed in black and Annis with her hair in a tight plait, I went to work. Cooking in the face of adversity. I reckoned the wok was as hot as it would go and the water in the large saucepan was seething. I dropped a bundle of egg noodles into it. Then I poured oil into the wok, quickly followed by shredded spring onion, ginger and garlic. Keeping everything moving round in the pan I threw in shitake mushrooms dusted with corn flour and pak choi stalks. A good slug of rice wine and a few squirts of soy, then the torn leaves of the pak choi and some chili sauce. By the time the leaves had wilted to a glossy dark green it was ready to serve. In and out in three minutes like a good burglar. We slurped the noodles and chased what Tim insisted on calling shit-ache mushroom with chopsticks until we had finished every bit of it.

Tim dispelled my last-minute doubts. 'It should be so hard. If Telfer goes playing cards at the Blathwayt Arms tonight like the man promised then we'll be all right. It's just a house with a safe, not the Royal Mint.'

Unless of course he had left it well guarded or installed some bizarrely sophisticated alarm system or had filled the house with trained attack dogs or kept a pet leopard or . . . I just couldn't help fretting while Annis and I drove to the Blathwayt Arms high on Lansdown after dark. Tim had gone ahead to the Telfer house alone. I stopped the car by the side of the road a hundred yards or so from the pub so it wouldn't attract attention.

'I'll just check he's really here and looks like he's enjoying himself, then we'll zoom down and join Tim.'

'I'll come with you,' Annis said quickly. 'This car smells bad, it needs a clean. Also a new headlight, windscreen replaced, the bonnet straightened out and the side resprayed.'

'Tell me something I don't know.'

'You've got soy sauce on your shirt.'

The Blathwayt was a large out-of-town pub with an over-ambitious car park and catered mainly to racecourse punters and golfers. It had recently left exotic 1970s fare like prawn cocktail and surf 'n' turf-style nonsense behind and had gone down the 'pan fried' scallop/braised lamb with 'mint jus' road. I vaguely knew what Telfer looked like from seeing his picture in the papers but unfortunately had no idea what car he drove, which would have been helpful. There were three yellow cars parked outside. We pushed through the door and into the warm and cosily lit bar and dining room. There was a large fire burning in the grate. Several tables were taken by couples and families; none of them looked like gangsters. If Telfer was there to

116

play cards and money was changing hands then the game would take place away from the public area in a room upstairs. Just when I was wondering how to go about this a waiter made for the stairs with a large tray full of a variety of drinks, all of them extremely blokish-looking, i.e. there wasn't a slice of lemon or paper parasol in sight. I intercepted him at the foot of the stairs.

'Has the Telfer party arrived yet?'

'Yes, a few minutes ago.'

'Mr Telfer himself, too?'

'Naturally. May I ask . . .' He looked at me with badly disguised irritation; the tray had to weigh a ton. I counted eighteen drinks. Rather a large number for a card game, I thought, until I realized that there were probably three of everything – they ordered ahead to be undisturbed for a while.

'I had hoped to catch Mr Telfer before the game started but I really wouldn't want to disturb him. When do they normally finish?'

'It's a private party so they can go on as long as they like but they usually finish around midnight.'

I thanked him and we left. There'd be plenty of time then. I called Tim on his mobile and told him the news he'd been waiting for. 'It's just as well, I've set the train in motion. You know where to find me.'

I did. After parking the DS in Charlcombe Lane we climbed up to Telfer's property the way we had come when we recced the place and caught up with Tim by the hole in the hedge. It was dark and our legs were damp from the grass but for once it wasn't raining. Worryingly there were lights showing all over the house.

'Do you think there's someone in or is it just for show?' I asked.

'Oh, there's someone in, I always figured he would leave someone here. It's the same slob we encountered last time. We'll have no problems tonight.'

'I wish I shared your optimism. So what kind of train were you talking about?' I whispered.

'What?'

'The one you said you'd set in motion.'

'Oh that. Well, I think it's best I demonstrate. Let's go tunnelling,' he said, picking up a small black leather bag that contained his gear.

I had brought a zip-up canvas bag myself to carry away whatever we found in the safe. This time I'd also brought decent leather gloves. I slipped them on and followed Tim and Annis through the autumnal hedge.

'You guys take cover down there where the security lights won't catch you,' Tim instructed us. 'Keep an eye on the goon's favourite pond. I'll go and trigger the lights.'

'Bigwood knows best,' I murmured to myself and squeezed with Annis into the soot-black shadow of a trio of not-so-dwarf conifers. Moments later the acid glare of the security lights flooded the upper part of the garden and Tim came skidding down the grass in a hurry to join us. We each found a gap in the vegetation to peer through. It was a short wait. The same big guy we had seen at our last visit pushed open the verandah doors and practically fell through them. He carried a pool cue like a club. His gait appeared more than a little uncertain as he negotiated the steps, down one level where he paused for a shuffle to steady himself, then another level to the pond where his vodka bottle was hidden. He was talking to himself in a happy slurring voice but being much further away this time I couldn't make out the words.

'The guy is three sheets to the wind,' I concluded.

'More than that,' Tim corrected me confidently. 'I'd say at least four sheets. I know someone at the chemistry department up at the uni. He's working on a new drug in his spare time. Strictly recreational, you understand, and he let me have a small sample, which I dropped into this bozo's bottle of booze since he seems to reward himself with a drink each time he has to investigate why the

118

security lights come on. He's had a good swig already. The next one should finish him off.'

'Finish him off how?' I said in alarm. The bozo in question was kneeling by the pond's edge, leaning heavily on his cue and fishing around for his bottle in the murky water. 'What effect does the drug have?'

'You get extremely blissed out and it creates the impression that you know everything there is to know in the world.'

The goon had found the bottle, cackled and straightened up.

'Taken at the right dosage it makes you feel as though any second now you'll understand all the secrets of the universe.'

The goon took a swig from the bottle, corked it and keeled over on to the grass like a felled tree.

'Unfortunately it abruptly sends you to sleep just before you do,' Tim said in a normal voice and got up. 'Needs more work.'

While we carried the limp and heavy body up two flights of stone steps and through the verandah door the goon began to snore. We deposited him on the nearest sofa. There were three of those in the spacious and dimly lit room, arranged around a freestanding faux fireplace with an excessive amount of wrought iron, hammered copper and snowy sheepskins around its base. In one corner a bar with four stools sported enough optics to start a pub. Dotted all over the place were imitation coconut palms in large pots, complete with plastic coconuts, and on one wall hung a TV screen so enormous it took a while to walk past it.

I'd brought the pool cue. 'Let's make sure he's not got a game going with some mates, shall we?' I suggested in a low voice. I crossed the room, passed the broad sweep of the open-sided staircase, into a wide area with several doors off and a wall of glass bricks at the end beyond which I suspected lay the entrance hall. One door on the left was ajar and showed light. I listened but didn't hear a sound. I pushed the door open with the cue: a games room, dominated by a pool table. Half the balls were scattered on the immaculate green baize but the black appeared to be missing. A cigarette still smouldered in an ashtray on a side table that also supported an open backgammon set. I put the cigarette out and returned the cue to the rack which already held half a dozen others.

Tim and Annis had quickly inspected the other rooms on this floor: dining room, kitchen and a bathroom. The safe had to be on the next floor. Just as we began padding up the stairs the imitation grandfather clock round the corner chimed: ten o'clock. Upstairs a hall with more plastic palms had five doors leading off it. One was ajar and turned out to be another bathroom. I tried the next one; a sparsely furnished bedroom with a very large window. It reminded me of a hospital room. Annis had opened the door opposite. 'Bingo,' she announced softly. Tim and I were both moving towards it when a door at the end of the hall opened a few inches and a female voice shouted: 'Darren? Bring me another drink, will you? And go easy on the tonic, no matter what my husband told you, all right? Dar-*ren*?'

We'd all frozen as soon as we heard the voice but playing dead in the middle of the hall was clearly not going to work. We crept quietly into the office Annis had found. I left the door open a tiny crack so I could see what, if anything, was happening outside. Only seconds passed before a woman swished past. The unexpected Mrs Telfer brought with her a cloud of flowery perfume. Her head was a black helmet of shoulder-length lifeless hair and she wore a dressing gown that shimmered lime green in the twilight. She called the goon's name again from the top before slippering downstairs.

'Is the safe in here?' I asked.

Tim snapped on his tiny torch. 'Fifty quid says it's behind that yucky painting.' The yucky painting was a

Renoir print of a garden scene in a gold frame, hung at an awkward height that just screamed wall safe.

'Then get to it, I'll keep an eye out for the thirsty lady.' I tiptoed into the hall and stood at the top of the stairs. From here I could see Darren the goon still comatose on the sofa. Clinking of glass was followed by the swish of silk. Mrs Telfer appeared carrying a fresh drink and stood beside the blissed-out sleeper. 'I can't believe you managed to get rat-arsed so quickly.' His limbs were splayed wide, one leg resting on the floor. She gave it a half-hearted prod with a slippered foot. 'You better get your act together by the time Barry comes back. He'll expect me drunk but he'll expect you sober.'

I withdrew sharpish as she turned towards the stairs. I closed the office door behind me and hushed Tim, who froze. When I heard the bedroom door close at the end of the hall I signalled to him to continue. As my eyes got accustomed to the dark again I could make out Annis leaning against a filing cabinet, her arms crossed in front of her. The Renoir print had indeed swung back on hidden hinges like a door. Behind it was a disappointingly small grey door with one combination dial and one handle. Tim had the safe wired up with electronic gadgets like a patient having his physical. He was wearing headphones, listening to the innards of the mechanism. One gadget showed a glimmer of red numbers in the dark. Tim spun the dial this way and that, then stowed all his gear in his bag before laying a hand on the handle. If there were unexpected alarm bells to go off then this was the moment. I could hear him take a short breath and hold it. Then he pulled. With a satisfying little click the door opened. I was by his side with my Maglite torch in my mouth. There was no time to sort through the content. Take everything, the voice had said. I emptied it into my bag: a fat, gaping envelope stuffed with fifties; a heavy box file; some slim plastic folders; a lady's mink fur hat and a small, blue jewellery box. I checked there was nothing left in the darkest recess, then zipped up my bag while Tim closed the safe and swung the painting back into place. The rest was easy. We tiptoed out of the place like comic strip burglars, past the sleeping Darren and down to the pond where Tim took the time to empty and rinse the vodka bottle, leaving it floating in the pond. There was every chance Darren might be found queuing at the Jobcentre tomorrow.

We parted company on the other side of the hedge.

'I'll go back in Tim's car, if you don't mind,' Annis said. 'For purely olfactory reasons of course.'

Okay, I'd definitely have to do something about the smell in my car. While Annis and Tim, who had parked in a side street off Lansdown hill, walked up I walked down through the tufty grass, climbed the by now familiar fence, crossed the little plantation of trees without the aid of a torch and slithered into Charlcombe Lane only a few yards from where the DS was parked. Not bad for a cloudy, moonless night, I told myself.

Annis's absence in the car allowed me to play a tape of Turkish pop music, which she detested, at nosebleed volume. It was small compensation though and an acidic stab of jealousy marred the satisfaction I should have felt at having the wherewithal to free Louis in a holdall on the seat next to me. I could hardly curb my curiosity as to what on earth, besides the money, could have been so important but sensibly drove off immediately. The money would come to about six grand, I guessed, not an amount to commit kidnap and risk life imprisonment for. The real reason had to lie in the files, unless the little jewellery box contained a very rare bauble indeed. My hand crept towards the bag but headlights appeared over the rise ahead and passing in this narrow lane took some negotiating. I dipped my headlights and slowed, looking for a passing place. The other car's headlights remained on full beam and it zoomed close so fast I had no choice but to stop completely. Smelling a rat I quickly locked my driver door but by the time I reached over to the passenger door it was being yanked open. Even if the guy in the balaclava hadn't brandished a nail-studded baseball bat there was little I could have done to stop him snatching the bag, it happened so fast. He slammed the door shut and vanished into the dark. Having all my doors locked would probably only have resulted in having all my windows smashed, since another guy, also dressed in combat jacket, jeans and balaclava and identically armed, appeared between the lights and my car. I checked behind me. Another vehicle with only sidelights showing lurked not far behind. The second guy swung his baseball bat at my near-side front wheel, puncturing it with a nail, then took out my last remaining headlight with an almost casual swipe of the bat. The whole operation was over in seconds. The car in front reversed at speed until it slew around where the lane briefly widened. With the headlights facing away at last I had the fleeting impression of a dark blue car, a Golf or one of its rival clones. The one behind me seemed to have vanished into the night.

For a while I just sat, muttered short and useful words and thumped the steering wheel. What had the voice said? 'When you've pulled it off, we'll know. We'll be in touch.' They'd just been in touch and I had done the one thing I had promised Jill not to do: let the ransom go without seeing her boy safely back first. How was I going to explain this? I was glad now that Annis hadn't been with me since she might have tried to put herself between the bag and the baseball bat.

When my heart finally stopped hammering against my rib cage I got out and inspected the damage. One very deflated tyre. I dug out my torch and went looking for the car jack and the spare in the boot. There was no car jack. I vaguely remembered using it to prise open a chained-up door a while back . . . My breakdown service had recently sent me a polite letter suggesting I invest in a new car, better servicing or try someone else entirely next time since I had relied rather heavily on their assistance recently.

There was only one thing to do: I called Jake. After he had roundly cursed and insulted me and my piece of effing French junk he promised to pick me and the DS up asap. Then I called Tim's mobile. He answered on the second ring.

'What's up, Honeypot? Where are you? We just got in.'

I told him.

'You're shitting me. Sorry, obviously not. Are you all right? Did they say anything? Sure they didn't leave the kid somewhere in the lane?'

'Not where I can see but then that doesn't mean much since there's no street lighting up here. If they had meant to hand over the boy they wouldn't have snatched the loot armed with clubs but you never can tell. I'll check the lane while I'm waiting to be picked up.'

'Perhaps they just wanted to make sure we didn't have time to study the stuff too closely. Perhaps they'll just let him go now.'

'Perhaps. Or perhaps we'll never hear from them again and Louis never comes back. Because he's dead already.'

'But why would they kill him?'

'Because they don't want to be identified? Because the kid saw their faces? Because kidnap and murder carry the same penalty anyway? Because they're arseholes? How would I know?' There was silence at the other end. 'I'm sorry. Look, I'll have a recce up here while I wait for Jake to pick up this wreck. It'll give me time to think about how I'll explain this to Jill.'

'Do you want us to call her?' Tim offered.

'No. No, I'll go round there myself later.'

'Oh, okay.' I could hear the relief in Tim's voice, which made me appreciate his offer even more. I terminated the call and walked up the lane. My little torch that seemed so appropriate in the confines of a room to be burgled sent only a feeble glow into the vast darkness of the night. I walked as far as the row of little white cottages, then walked all the way back past my car and as far as the next house a few hundred yards along. I was half hoping, half fearing to find the boy, tied up and gagged, perhaps, and waiting to be found and released, but there was nobody, there was nothing. When I could hear the big diesel engine of Jake's truck I jogged back. Jake was the long-suffering mechanic who had kept the DS running all these years. He worked out of what used to be a small farm between Bath and Chippenham and specialized in restoring classic cars – classic *British* cars, as he never stopped reminding me – and without him the old Citroën would long have gone to the scrapheap.

'Which is where this thing belongs, Chris,' he reminded me as he attached the cable to the front under the unkind glare of a massive light fixed to the cab of his truck. 'It's a wreck, a disgrace. You think this has street cred? It had ten years ago perhaps when you could still recognize it as a motor vehicle. If you were hoping for the Withnail-and-I look I'm afraid I have to tell you: the missing headlight's a nice touch but otherwise you really overdid it. Now it's just junk.' He engaged the winch and the DS creaked slowly up the ramps.

I really didn't want to deal with this but it served as a welcome distraction from the other monumental failure of the day. 'It's only a flat tyre,' I whined.

'Nonsense,' he contradicted. 'It's everything. You don't think you could drive around in *daylight* with this, do you? The police would have you pulled over in no time.'

'Can't you straighten that out? It's just cosmetic, really . . .'

He put the chocks in place and tightened the straps that secured the DS on the flat bed of the truck. 'Cosmetic? I would need to use embalming fluid. The bodywork was nine-tenths filler anyway. I can't go on giving you dodgy MOTs because someone's going to die in this if it stays on the road.'

If the car restoration business was ever a bit slack he could always try clairvoyance. He pulled his baseball cap

125

off, baring his bald head in mock reverence. 'It's had it, Chris. You couldn't afford to have this restored and I don't want to restore it. Start thinking about a replacement. Come on, I'll drop you off at your place.' He slapped the cap back on his head.

I climbed into the messy cab strewn with pork pie wrappers and empty fag packets and wedged myself into the corner like a sulking kid. The fact that I had just messed up the handover of the ransom sat so heavily on me I could not bring myself to grieve much over the final demise of my DS21. I would have to use the Norton for a cold and windy while and unless I could lay my hands on a useful amount of money soon it might be rather a long while, too. Roofers had to be paid. I owed half of my troubles to one stormy day.

And the other half? There was a hollow where my stomach should be and somewhere in that hollow sat a hard ball of fear, the size of a child's fist. There couldn't be even the slightest pretence now that I was still in control of the situation. A woman whose son's life depended on me was waiting to hear my explanation of how I intended to get him back with nothing to bargain with; the roofs of my house and studio had large plastic-covered holes in them; I had a show coming up and no paintings to enter and a love relationship, the triangular nature of which seemed to be shifting and distorting. To top it all off I just had my means of transport declared as unfit for use as I appeared to be myself.

Jake hustled the big truck along the deserted lane, flaying the hedgerows in the process. 'And how's things, apart from car trouble?'

Chapter Twelve

As the hours drained away like molasses from a leaky tin the atmosphere at Mill House became stifled, stale and desperate. No phone call, no message. I gave myself until the morning to abdicate from detective work for ever.

Annis and I had delivered the bad news to Jill at her place in Harley Street in person. There were no tears and no recrimination, just hollow-eyed quiet fear.

She remained implacably opposed to calling the police. 'I'm too scared. But I'll call my sister now.'

Back at Mill House nobody slept much. Tim dozed in one corner of the sofa, I haunted the other while Annis stayed curled up in the big blue armchair, the one my father had killed himself in. Ashtrays were full and the sour taste of too much coffee and cigarettes complemented the grinding headache behind my forehead. All night the blustery wind had thrown rain against the blind windows like handfuls of grit. When dawn finally came it was barely an improvement. Dirty clouds rolled low over the valley and the light was feeble. I started the morning rituals of breakfast for form's sake. It helped me mark the end of the night, the end, I hoped, of our helpless waiting around. Decisions would be made today – one way or another – and we would be released from limbo. Handing round tea and toast felt like the first positive thing I'd done for a long time. It was acknowledged by grunts and mumbled thanks and restored some life into the deadly tableau of the last few hours, yet nobody found anything new to say. A few remarks about the dreadfulness of the weather soon dried up. Everything else had been discussed to death.

It was nine o'clock exactly when the cordless phone that had been lying in the middle of the coffee table like a dead thing gave its electronic warble. All three of us jumped and made some kind of involuntary sound. I grabbed the handset, took a deep breath and answered.

'You've got the stuff then, all of it?' The voice sounded thin and far away.

Instant sweat formed on my hands. 'What do you mean? You got it all.'

'Don't fuck about, Honeysett. Take down these directions. Bring the stuff, all of it, mind, wrapped in several carrier bags, and take –'

'Hold it. I don't have the stuff.'

'What the fuck do you mean, you don't have it? I know you cleaned out his safe, the grapevine's buzzing with it.'

'And two blokes with balaclavas and baseball bats mugged me for it in Charlcombe Lane five minutes later. I presumed that was you. You're telling me it wasn't?'

'Of course it fucking wasn't, we had a deal, why should I have to mug you for the stuff? You handed it over? You didn't even put up a fight?'

'How do you know I didn't put up a fight?' I protested.

'Because you're not talking from a hospital bed, you arsehole. You totally fucked this up.'

'Where is Louis? We kept our side of the bargain, we emptied Telfer's safe. Someone obviously knew that was going down and only you could have told them, we certainly didn't. So return the boy. Keep your side of –'

'Shut up, Honeysett. Do you think I'm going to all the trouble of snatching the kid and feeding him baked beans and Hula Hoops and listen to him whining all week just so I can give him back for nothing? I can't believe you fucked this up. If I find out you are trying to pull a fast one I'll make you regret it.'

'I'm not. I was held up. Baseball bats studded with nails. I wouldn't do anything to put the boy in danger.'

'Shut up, now, let me think.' There was a brief pause. 'All right, Honeysett. I'll find something else for you to do. Until you deliver, the boy stays where he is.' The line clicked dead.

'Verdict?' Annis asked after a moment of intense silence.

'He said it wasn't him, or them, that held me up in Charlcombe Lane. Someone else knows what's happening here, but whoever has Telfer's stuff now isn't connected with the kidnapping. Something seriously weird is going on here.' I thought of the man in the hat watching us through binoculars. 'This all smells somehow of a turf war between rival gangs, everyone ripping off everyone else, with us smack in the middle. The worst thing about it is he won't hand over the boy until we've pulled some other stunt for him.'

'Did he say what he wants?' Tim asked, looking worried now.

'No.'

'I know you don't want to hear this, Chris,' Annis said, 'but I think it's time we went to the police. We're completely at this guy's mercy and Jill has had about all she can take, not to mention the boy's –'

'Save your breath, I agree.' It seemed obvious now. I had felt defeated ever since I had lost the ransom loot in Charlcombe.

'You do?'

'I do.' It was more than just the logical conclusion of an operation gone so wrong that it could no longer be expected to work out well and it was more than fear for the boy's well-being. It was a leaden tiredness and a sudden and complete loss of faith in my own abilities. Standing in the middle of the room, uselessly holding on to the phone, with two pairs of expectant eyes on me, I felt like running away. I'm only a painter, I felt like saying, this isn't my kind of job. Had I volunteered for this? Must have done. Whatever for? Did I really need this much excitement? 'I'll take it straight to Needham, personally, no phone calls, it's safer that way.' I chucked the phone on to the sofa.

'You want us there?' Tim asked.

'No, you lot stay here.'

Half an hour later I was riding the Norton through blustery wind and rain into town, nearly blinded by the moisture on my goggles. The rain stung my face. I was on my surreptitious way to the police station where I would explain to Superintendent Needham how I had got myself into the biggest mess of my less-than-illustrious career as a private eye. It would not count as betraying a client's confidence since Jill was by no means a client but it was without doubt an admission of total failure. And trust. What if I was laying Louis open to reprisals? I was no longer sure whether I had to take the death threat seriously. Surely that was just something kidnappers said to frighten you?

Halfway down the London Road I got a bad case of the jitters. I began to feel as though I was caught in the cross hairs in a madman's rifle sights. I was getting more paranoid by the minute. I checked over my shoulder – the Norton had no mirrors – every few seconds, not knowing what I was looking for.

I parked the bike in the motorcycle bay in North Parade Passage, locked up the helmet and stuffed gloves and goggles into my pocket. I'd try and see Needham privately. I had to arrange for us to talk outside the station where we couldn't be overheard. I'd make sure though that someone heard me say that it had to do with the Albert Barrington murder, not that I thought that was any guarantee that our kidnapper, if he had an ear in the station, wouldn't somehow suspect foul play. Foul play ... Who was I playing foul? The kidnapper? Hardly. But was I breaking a promise to Jill for 'her own good' or the boy's or for my own peace of mind? Did I simply want to abdicate responsibility because I'd had enough? I couldn't deny that

130

I was planning to heave a deep sigh of relief and hide in my studio for the foreseeable future from the moment the police took charge of this mess.

I was walking along Manvers Street on the opposite side from the police station and slowed down now to check the cars in the car park in front of it. Needham's big grey saloon was in its reserved space. Traffic was steady. Just as I got ready to dodge across between two buses a voice behind me piped up. 'Sir?'

'What!' I turned around and found myself looking at a young man of perhaps twenty. It was hard to tell because only the small tanned oval of his face was visible as he peered out through rain-blinded glasses from the enormous hooded plastic poncho that covered him and what for his sake I hoped was a rucksack.

'I'm supposed to give you this.' He breathlessly held out a folded piece of paper. His accent was antipodean and he might have sprinted from the backpackers' hostel a few doors down.

It was a lined piece of paper from a notepad, folded into a small rectangle and already damp. I opened it up. It was written in biro in hastily scribbled capitals.

HOPE YOU'RE NOT THINKING OF TALKING TO THE POLICE. TOLD YOU I'D KNOW. TOLD YOU WHAT WILL HAPPEN. WAIT TO BE CONTACTED.

'Who gave you this?'

'Some guy.' He gestured over his shoulder.

'Where? What did he look like?'

'I don't know, only saw him for a moment. Back there at the corner. He wore a hat. Gave me a fiver to catch you up.' He was already moving on, towards the station.

'Wait a second, I need a better description than that.' I tried to hold him back by the arm but he shook himself loose.

'Look, mate, I can't stop, I gotta make the fuckin' train to Heathrow. I'm outa here, your weather's turned to shit, mate, in case you hadn't noticed.'

131

I trotted beside him. 'What kind of a man was he? I mean was he young, old, tall, short, fat, slim?'

'Just normal, like. He wore a hat. I only saw him for a second and I can't see much through wet specs anyway. Rain's always a pain in the ass.' He peered at me over his wet glasses.

'What else was he wearing?'

'Jeez, if I'd known you'd give me the third degree I'd have told him to forget it. Some coat I guess, nothing so it'd stick in your mind, all right?'

That always depended on the mind, I thought, and let him get on. I watched him weave his way through the traffic between bus and railway station. I looked around, behind me, along Manvers Street, scanned the pavements full of pedestrians pushing hurriedly through the rain in both directions. Where was the dark sinister stranger in a hat watching from a street corner? Where was the threatening soundtrack that always helped TV detectives to know when they were being watched with ill intent? The rain stopped abruptly. A long row of faces in a passing tourist coach looked up; I followed their gaze. The dark clouds were being rolled back by a high wind and bright, broken cloud followed from the west. By the time I had squelched my way back to the Norton the sun had made an appearance. Good, my jeans might dry off eventually. I used my sleeve to wipe the water off the seat, started the engine and rode off towards the unfamiliar sunshine.

There was not much else I could do. I had to be seen to be leaving. Nothing could have better reinforced the paranoid feeling that I was constantly being kept tabs on than the note that seemed to burn acidly in my pocket. *Told you what will happen.* Go here, don't go there. Stop, start, fetch. *Wait to be contacted.* The impersonal phrase did nothing to hide the very personal nature of the relationship: I've got you by the balls and you will do my bidding. His bidding, his robbing. A man in a hat.

132

How long would I let myself be blackmailed? Wasn't it in the nature of blackmail that it never stopped, that the blackmailer never went away? Would it be all over, would Louis have been reunited with his mother by now, if I hadn't let myself be mugged of the ransom? Who had held me up in the lane after the burglary? All three of us had sworn blind that we hadn't told a soul. That almost certainly meant that either the kidnapper himself had bragged about it in the pub or he had himself staged the mugging. I was not in a position to steal it back, whichever scenario held true, because I didn't have the first idea who I was dealing with and I had the distinct impression that shouting 'Who are you?' down the phone might not make him give me his name, address and National Insurance number. It was beginning to dawn on me that not only did I have Louis's abductor on my back but very likely a third party that knew what I was doing and when I was doing it (one which might soon be joined by Mr Disappointed of Lansdown demanding his stuff back, possibly with menaces).

While I was furiously chewing this over and without giving it much thought I'd hustled the bike up Lansdown Road and turned into Charlcombe Lane. I didn't know what I was hoping to find as I rumbled past the scene of my humiliation and indeed I didn't see anything that might be of use. But not so much further on stood a cast-iron signpost pointing towards the village of Woolley and the Lam valley where I had strange and unfinished business. I slowed to a less ferocious pace, took the turn and began to enjoy the sun as it dodged in and out of clouds as though desperate to dry the steaming land below. I passed small orderly farms, fields of grazing cows and sheep, yards full of scratching chickens and a herd of alpacas eyeing me as curiously as I did them. In the tiny village of Woolley the Norton's growl brought children out into the single track lane that connected the small community with the outside world. I turned a corner and immediately a steep descent brought me down to the bottom of the valley where I crossed the Lam brook via a narrow bridge near the old gunpowder mill. Following the undulating lanes I soon reached Spring Farm where I'd met Jack Fryer struggling with his subsidy application. The gate to the yard was firmly closed and there was no sign of life. But the unmistakable smell of several thousand chickens reassured me that he hadn't yet packed it all in. I shunned the muddy turn-off towards Grumpy Hollow and Gemma Stone's ramshackle herb farm and rode on along the deserted lane. A horse poked its head over a hedge and snorted. I rode on until I came to a fork in the road and instinctively took the left; it was narrower and the road surface was nearly worn away. After I had passed a long and dilapidated structure made mainly from corrugated metal and girders, the tree-lined road lazily rose and fell for a quarter of a mile. Then it suddenly climbed steeply before broadening out as I approached what simply had to be Lane End Farm. One minor clue of course was the fact that the lane ended here at a high and substantial modern gate set into a chain link fence topped with barbed wire. The fence ran up the side of the hill to my left where it disappeared into the trees. A sign fastened to the chain link advertised the fact that there was *24 hour Security*, illustrated with the drawing of an uncommonly ferocious-looking dog. To the right the fencing seemed to run across the entire end of the valley, which was much narrower here. The other clue, keeping in mind what Jack Fryer had said, was that beyond the fence lay what looked like a mix between junk yard and building site.

Beside the insubstantial and neglected-looking farmhouse and the few outbuildings I could make out, there stood a mass of shipping containers, by the looks of it simply plonked into the muddy grass of the field, perhaps a hundred and fifty yards from the fence. Many were blue, some white, but most of them were rusty. They seemed to have grown up there like a small hideous village around the L-shaped farmhouse's grey and utilitarian shape. I glimpsed one or two Portakabins and a blue Portaloo among the containers. It was a depressing sight. Lane End Farm occupied nearly the entire end of the valley and as far as I could see nobody farmed it. The containers, apart from being ugly in themselves, looked out of place in a field many miles from the nearest port. To the left the hillside was covered in what looked like the remains of ancient woodland. Far to the right of the 'farm' snaked the other fork of the lane, disappearing into the distance. There was no farming machinery to be seen but a large van was driving along a track on the far end of the property and beside the furthest container a mobile crane stretched its telescopic arm skywards in a mute salute. I dismounted and leant the bike against the fence. After giving the gate, which was topped with razor-sharp spikes, a futile pull I decided to do a little exploring on foot. Judging by the path worn alongside the fence to the left I wasn't the first to take this route up into the wood, in fact there was evidence that someone walked here quite regularly. I just hoped it wasn't a patrol of dogs. The place looked like it should have guard dogs tethered to overhead wires patrolling the perimeter, then all it needed was a watchtower to make the stalag impression complete.

The fence curved sharply away and I left it behind for a while, just enjoying my walk. It wasn't much of a climb from the gate before I stood on the crest of the hill. The woodland was dense here but wind and rain had done their bit to thin out the autumn foliage. I could see below me that the fence skirted the edge of the wood for a while, running east while it did. I made my way downhill again through the pathless strip of woodland. Halfway down I nearly slithered into something on the damp leaf litter: a dead dog. It was Taxi, Gem Stone's old mongrel. There wasn't even a second's hesitation before pronouncing him dead, his head was such a bloody mess. Had I found him on the road I'd have assumed he'd been run over but here, in the middle of the strip of woodland? I knelt down and forced myself to take a closer look. I'd have made a bad crime scene technician, or one that threw up a lot over the evidence.

The blood was dried and there were ants crawling all over the beast's fur. It quickly became obvious that his skull had been bashed in, even without the spatter of blood on the surrounding leaf litter. All that told me was that it happened right here.

I thought I could smell death too, despite the strong breeze that pulled the last leaves off the trees and sent them dancing around me.

I slithered further down the hill until I reached the fence. It cut at an angle here which brought me closer to the containers, allowing me to get a better view of the set-up. Walking on I kept close to the fence, which turned out to be a mistake. A gravelled track ran north out of what was really quite a small farm, through another gate and then disappeared over the rise where it would eventually connect to the Lansdown Road. A large van in the unmistakable red livery of the postal service made its way towards the gate. At the same time a skinhead on a quad bike appeared from between the rows of containers and took a fast and bumpy ride straight towards me. Who said there was never one around when you needed one? Pretending not to have noticed him I walked on along the fence.

'Oi, you!' He started shouting from twenty yards away. I kept walking.

'Hey! Get away from there.' He caught up with me and kept jerkily apace with me on the noisy quad. He was about thirty, dressed in faded black combat trousers, camouflage jacket and army boots. He had a broad, round-featured face and made the quad bike look puny. I was quite glad we had a fence between us. 'Are you deaf or something?'

'Is this Tony Blackfield's place?' I asked.

'What if it is? Are you from the *Chronicle*? We've got planning permission for this so you can shove it.'

'I can? And what is "this"?'

'Storage units. Secure storage units is what they are.'

'They look like clapped-out shipping containers to me.'

'That's what they were, now they're storage units for rent. Secure storage units and I'm security. So piss off from our fence. You're trespassing.' He gave the throttle an angry twist and jerked ahead a few yards, then stopped the bike and got off.

I stopped too. 'I'm trespassing? I presumed the farm started on that side of the fence.'

'Well, it doesn't. Lane End includes the woodland and we'd be obliged if people kept the fuck out of it.'

'Right. Perhaps you should have run the fence around it then.'

'Oh yeah? Have you got any idea how much fencing costs?'

'Not this attractive kind, no.' I stroked the chain link.

'Well, it costs a fucking fortune. Now are you going or do I have to remove you?' he said, jangling a bunch of keys clipped to his belt. I had felt quite safe and smug on this side of the fence, but now I noticed a small door set into it a few yards further down.

I changed my tune. 'Fine, I'm going. I see the Royal Mail use your units as well?'

'Yes, because we're cheap. They don't tell us what they store here but I suspect it's second class mail,' he said unsmilingly and probably meant it. He got back on his bike. 'Don't be fucking ages about it. Go back to the road by the shortest route.' Then he grabbed a handful of throttle and bumped back towards the container park.

Secure storage. Not such a daft idea, really, apart from the traffic it engendered and the sheer hideousness of it all.

Now that I knew it was there I could just make out the dead dog on the slope to my right. I gave it a wide berth on my way back. At the gate I wheeled the Norton about, sat astride it, and was fastening my helmet strap when the sound of a motorcycle engine approached from downhill. At first I presumed it to be the skinhead on his quad, wanting more words; instead it was a figure on a muddy trail bike that appeared at the bottom of the rise where it came to an abrupt and squelching stop. The rider wore jeans, heavy boots, a red and white jacket and a helmet with blue-tinted goggles; more I couldn't make out before he jerked his bike around in a ragged turn, while keeping an eye on me. Perhaps he was turning because he realized the lane ended here but I had the distinct feeling the sight of me at the top of the lane was unexpected and had spooked him. One way to find out. I worked the kick-starter. To my immense surprise the engine fired instantly and I shot down the hill in pursuit. If I was wrong about it I would soon know. With my momentary downhill advantage the distance between us quickly closed to only eight or ten yards so that I could easily have read his number plate if there'd been one. No doubt it was hearing the old-fashioned roar of the Norton's twin peashooter pipes that made him glance over his shoulder. I saw him twist his throttle and he pulled away. I dropped a gear, followed suit and squeezed the last ounce of torque out of the Norton. The ancient technology responded bravely and I kept up with him while we flew past the corrugated iron barn, but as the bend approached I realized that I'd be unable to compete not just with the dirt tyres and modern engine but with the apparent willingness of the rider to risk going arse over tit in order to shake me off. Spattering mud and stones and skating with one foot on the ground, he took the corner at an impressive speed and then sped off in a power slide. By the time I had negotiated the muddy bend and got to the crossroads only the sound of his engine gave away that he had tuned right, towards Spring Farm. Now back on decent tarmac I accelerated with a bit more confidence in my tyres and took the next three bends idiotically fast. It was only the plume of black exhaust the enormous tractor sent skyward as it pulled out of a gate into the lane that stopped me from ploughing into it. Too late to brake. I squeezed myself into the opposite side of the lane, foliage whipping my helmet, and shot past the giant machine screaming, with inches to spare. Driving the monster was Jack Fryer.

By the time my heart and I had slowed down again there was no sign of the other rider and all I could hear was the puttering of the Norton and the surge of the tractor's big diesel. I pootled on in true geriatric style, narked by my idiotic little chase, giving myself an earful of abuse. My Accumulated Guilt Quotient was running high enough; crumpling the Norton and booking myself into hospital would have sent it into orbit.

Without even thinking about it I took the turn to Gemma's place, crossed the stream without drowning the engine and once more left the bike under the tree. The track from here on in had been so churned up it was quite pointless trying to carefully pick my way between the bogs and puddles. I just squelched and splashed through regardless, in a temper with myself, the weather, the world. The rope was still across the entrance; I ducked under it. The woman's car was there and a thin thread of smoke rose from the shepherd's hut. The nights were getting colder now and I tried not to imagine what it must be like to spend a cold and wet winter in a clapped-out caravan. And coming to that, why didn't I ask her? Along with a few other irritable questions I had on my back burner.

The hut was closed up and, as I could see through the window, unoccupied. The door to the caravan was ajar, an invitation to snoop if ever I saw one. When I pushed it open with two fingers it creaked ominously on its hinges; served me right. Now would have been the last opportunity for any pretence of polite behaviour, like a hearty call of 'Hello, anybody home?', but I was in Grumpy Detective Mode and just walked in. Not very far because there wasn't far to go. It was truly tiny. Everything inside appeared to have been shrunk, too. The gas cooker had only two rings and the sink was full, giving room to a single cauliflower. Cupboards were built into every nook and cranny. At the back was an unruly bed disgorging blankets and cushions over the side, a narrow table cluttered with the remains of a breakfast that had included a boiled egg, and in front of that a short upholstered bench. There was an ashtray crammed with the butts of hand-rolled cigarettes and two empty bottles of Bulgarian table wine. But it was also quite homely: a chilli plant in a pot bearing bright yellow fruit on the table by the window; blue and red cushions with star and moon motifs; a heavy midnight-blue curtain still covering the larger back window; postcards, some of the seaside but mainly of the cutesy dog variety, pinned and Blu-Tacked to every surface. There were several photos of Taxi, looking younger. I opened a cupboard to the left of the cooker: jar upon jar of dried herbs, bottled fruit and pickled roots. Next to the sink an opaque sliding door revealed a claustrophobically narrow shower cubicle housing a mop and bucket.

I stepped outside again. There was less wind at the bottom of the Hollow but up in the sky the clouds still raced, producing a painter's nightmare of sudden lights and darks. I walked around the side of the caravan between the sheds and the trees. The home-made greenhouse sheltered some broad-leafed plants I didn't recognize. Walking over duckboards made from old wooden pallets I passed a stone trough gently overflowing with water that welled up from below; one of the springs, no doubt. The ground around here looked spongy, hence the duckboards. To the left, the wooden double doors of a large polytunnel stood wide open. Despite that, the difference in atmosphere as I stepped inside was remarkable. It was several degrees warmer, there was no wind and the earthy and verdant smell reminded me of warmer climates, of spring in the Mediterranean. The tunnel was about

140

eighteen feet wide and seemed to stretch on for ever. The centre was taken up with an endless length of staging full of plants in black plastic pots as well as old tins, buckets and washing-up bowls. On either side in the ground, stretching into infinity it seemed, grew a jungle of plants. I took the right-hand path down the tunnel. Some of this jungle I recognized. There were ragged-looking tomato plants and some kind of spiky cucumber, then a multitude of lettuces.

I walked on right to the end where, near a set of closed doors under several lemon trees laden with small jewel-like fruit, Gemma huddled with her legs drawn up in a decrepit cane chair. A knitted hat, pointed and with ear flaps, gave her a vaguely Tibetan air. She was smoking an elegant, long-stemmed pipe, sending clouds of smoke, fragrant with cannabis, my way. By her side a tea chest supported a mug of tea and smoking paraphernalia.

'Wondered when you would turn up,' she said, her speech somewhat impeded by her bruised, swollen and torn lips. Dried blood scabbed the splits. One eye, too, was blackening and almost swollen shut.

'About now,' I said, distracted by her abused face. I looked around. Hers was the only chair. This wasn't a place where Gemma Stone entertained. It was a place to rest from work, or perhaps it was her refuge from the world; a violent world, by the looks of it. The light at the end of this tunnel came filtered through the foliage of the potted lemon grove. I found an empty bucket nearby, turned it over and sat. She ignored me, looking straight past me into the jungle.

Some of my grumpy detective mood had evaporated in the warmth of concern but I couldn't just sit there and get stoned from passive smoking, which was quite possible considering the liveliness of Gemma's pipe. I lit one of my less entertaining cigarettes and added my smoke to the heavy atmosphere.

'You want to talk about it?' I said at last.

'What?'

I raised an eyebrow.

'You mean this?' She pointed the stem of her pipe at the blackened eye. 'Nothing to tell, I fell.'

'Right,' I said with less than full conviction.

'Look, it's really none of your business but if I'd been in a fight I'd say so, okay, it's hardly a big deal. I got drunk, I slipped, I fell, end of story.'

It was always possible, I'd seen the empty bottles. 'That wasn't what I meant,' I lied.

'Oh, Albert. Yes.' She returned her attention to the pipe.

'So he was one of your clients? Why didn't you say so?'

'Who do you think you are?' she said sharply. 'The police are bad enough, then you turn up, uninvited, asking me questions. Every other day, I might add. I don't have to tell *you* anything.' Shooting me a resentful look was difficult with only one working eye but she managed it quite well. 'Yes, he bought herbal remedies from me, he was a regular customer.'

'But you didn't tell the police that either.'

'How much d'you think I want police traipsing all over this place, looking for murderers under the flowerpots?'

'Not a lot,' I agreed.

'Too right. I don't pay tax much, I'm not a trained herbalist, and anyway, no one is licensed to dispense the kind of herb I was supplying to Al. He had bad arthritis and smoking pot alleviates the symptoms. Everyone knows that but it's illegal nevertheless.'

'I'm aware of it.'

'Well then. Nearly a third of this tunnel is given over to growing cannabis. Harvest is over now,' she gestured down the tunnel, 'but there's enough evidence around the place to put me away any time.'

'So Albert had been here the day he was murdered to buy a supply of pot?'

'No. Never got here.'

'But you were expecting him?'

142

'He hadn't made an appointment or anything. He'd just turn up on his electric bike at fairly regular intervals. I did think he was due around that time, that day or the next.'

'I thought you didn't like people just turning up.'

'People like *you*. But Al was all right. We met at the Bath flower show, I had a stall there selling herbs one year.'

'And you'd been to his place.'

'Once or twice when he was too bad to even use the electric bike. He'd send word through the chicken lady who brings him eggs that he couldn't come, which meant he was more desperate than ever, so I'd go round, see what I could do for him. When you mentioned Albert I got worried and drove over.'

Chicken Lady, Pot Lady . . . Perhaps it was worth finding out what other ladies there might have been in his life and if they too had reasons not to come forward. 'Okay, so far so good. Now explain why you seem to be completely invisible to DI Deeks. It's a trick I would pay money to learn.'

'Deeks is an arsehole,' she said flatly. 'You'd do well to stay away from him.'

'That's common knowledge but not an explanation.'

'I've known him for years. He picked me up for possession once, ages ago. We came to an understanding. He has a pretty good idea of what goes on down here at Grumpy Hollow. Too good an idea.' She put down her pipe which had gone out, then picked up her mug of tea and took a sip, which she instantly spat out again in an arc across the path. 'Eargh, cold tea. Yuch.' She got up and walked off down the path. 'I'll need to make some fresh.'

'Hey, wait a second.' I went after her. 'You mean to say you managed to bribe Deeks into turning a blind eye?'

'Managed to?' Stopping beside a cucumber plant she produced a curved pruning knife, liberated one of the fruits and carried on. 'You don't have to try hard with Deeks, he's as corrupt as they come.' She walked up to me and tapped my chest with the smooth-skinned cucumber.

'Now *I've* got a question: how come you knew it was Al who'd died in your car when the police didn't?'

'I was coming to that.' And not before time. 'A couple of kids had told me they thought they'd overheard two men threaten to arrange a little accident for someone called Albert.'

'Oh? Did those kids happen to say who made the threat?'

'No. It was dark and they didn't see who it was.'

'And you think –'

'Wait, there was more. In the same breath they also mentioned something similar might happen to *the old witch snooping around at night.*'

'So . . .?' She managed to put considerable challenge into the one syllable.

I squirmed around. 'Ehm, well, I thought that perhaps, you know, they might have been referring to you, in which case you might be in consid—'

'The old witch? The *old* witch? And you think they were talking about me? I'm thirty-eight! Ouch!' She dabbed her lips; one of her cuts had torn open. 'Well okay, I feel a hundred and eight today but really!' She flashed me a one-eyed rebuke. 'Do *you* think I look like an old witch?'

Always the hard questions. I wisely ignored this one. 'You're not taking this seriously,' I said instead.

'*This is serious*. Just because I work up to my neck in muck half the time in the aptly named Grumpy Hollow doesn't mean I'm completely beyond caring. So?'

'Of course not.'

'Course not what?'

'Of course you don't look like an old witch. Though you appear to have inherited your wardrobe from one.' It just slipped out, you know how it goes.

She took a slow deep breath. 'Says the bloke who rides around dressed like a crashed Spitfire pilot. Ha. Now I *really* need more tea.'

I followed her back to the caravan. 'And you're not worried?'

144

'For the old witch?' She shrugged. 'Perhaps. But look around you, what would you have me do? If someone wants to hurt me who's going to stop them?' When we reached the caravan she squinted at the bottom hinge of the door. 'Had a good look around inside then, did you?'

'How can you tell?'

'I left a dried lentil behind the hinge, it's on the ground now. No matter. Come in, I might even make you a mug of tea.'

I sat at the table while Gemma lit the gas under a whistling kettle on the stove and cleared away her breakfast debris. 'You know how they say it's a small world? Well, you've no idea how small until you've tried living in a caravan. Now, let's see.' She stood on tiptoe to rummage in a cupboard fitted into the curve of the roof above the bed. From there she produced a shoe box, set it opened on to the table and almost reverentially folded back the tissue paper to reveal a pair of tiny, shiny, insubstantial-looking shoes, black, strappy, open-toed with three-inch heels. She lifted them out and placed them on the table, then turned them until they pointed accusingly at me. 'And how far do you think I'd get in those? I wouldn't even make it to the car. No, no, no, wait.' Another dive into the cupboard above my head. This time she produced a bundle wrapped in tissue paper. She opened it and let the content unwind in front of her: a little black dress, bias-cut, black beads shimmering around the neckline. 'Do you know when I last wore that?' She rolled it up again, quickly, angrily. 'I don't. Can't even remember. Oh, yes I can, Christmas two years ago. Jack Fryer had invited me for Christmas dinner at Spring Farm. When I got there it turned out I was the only guest. He had too much Christmas cheer and lunged at me over the roast chicken. I stuck a fork in one of his paws and drove myself home. Ever since then, usually around the full moon when he's had a skinful, he comes round here to apologize and tries to *make it up to me*, if you know what I mean. I keep a special fork for him in my

145

drawer,' she concluded and carefully put away the shoes before seeing to the kettle which had begun to whistle like a steam train.

'Couldn't you get a more aggressive dog to help guard this place?' I suggested tactlessly when two mugs of tea steamed between us.

She shook her head. 'Not while Taxi is around,' she said, looking out of the window.

'I have bad news, I'm afraid.'

Gemma put her mug down. She understood instantly. 'Oh. Poor Taxi. I had him for ever, it seemed. He went walkabouts some time yesterday. I was afraid that in this weather . . . Where did you find him?'

'Just a bit further up the valley.'

'You mean near Blackfield's place?'

I nodded.

'Any sign of how he died?'

'Not really. Hard to tell, I'm not a vet, you know.'

'So he wasn't run over or anything obvious like that. Probably old age, he was ancient, and the weather has been lousy. But I always hoped he'd just lie down by the stove and fade away, not out in the cold. But he always liked to roam. Come on, drink up, show me.'

'I'm not sure that's such a good idea . . .'

'Rubbish. Can't let him just lie there. I thought you loved animals. We'll go and bury him.' She walked out, leaving me little choice but to gulp my scalding hot tea and follow her. With spade over her shoulder, pointy hat and scabbed and bruised face, she appeared to have stepped out of some medieval tapestry, the kind where people lie about with arrows stuck in their eyes. She chucked the spade into the cluttered back of the Volvo and we got in.

'How's Al's cat settling in with you?' she asked as she propelled the car up the slope.

'Oh, he's fine, still sniffing out the place. He can open doors, did you know that?'

Gemma stopped so I could get out and remove the rope

from across the entrance. 'Have you decided what to call him yet?' she asked when I got back in.

'Not yet.'

'He's a cute cat. You could call him Widget.'

'No chance.'

'Suit yourself.' She took the ford of the brook as though it was open road, just briefly flicking the windscreen wipers on and off. Once up in the lane she cranked the big Zeppelin of a car round the corners in grim, high speed silence and eventually powered it up the hill so fast I thought she was going to drive smack through the locked gate on to Blackfield's land. Instead she stopped a couple of inches short of the chain link, jumped out and got the spade.

'Go on, show us.'

'Actually, I think he did have some kind of accident. It looked as if . . . someone might have hit him.'

'Hit him,' she repeated flatly.

I risked a glance over my shoulder. Her face was set in a rigid scowl. We walked on in silence. It didn't take long to reach the point where I had turned down the hill. I slithered through the leaf litter with Gemma at my heels and found Taxi's corpse easily.

Gemma stood motionless in front of it, gripping the spade like a weapon. 'The bastards. They didn't have to do that.'

She obviously had some idea of the who and why but an odd rasp in her voice made me think that this wasn't the moment to quiz her about it. My own list of suspects was very short. Eventually she dragged her eyes away, sniffed. 'I changed my mind, I don't want to bury him here,' she said, looking towards the fence. 'I'll bury him at the Hollow. Can you give me a hand? He's quite heavy.'

Despite the cold, flies buzzed as we lifted the cold body. Gemma carried the front of the animal, oblivious to the blood and gore of the broken skull. We walked awkwardly up the slope, nearly fell twice. My mobile chimed as we reached the top. I shifted the weight on to my left arm and answered it.

It was Annis. 'At last, I've been trying to get hold of you for ages but it said your mobile was unavailable. What's going on, where are you, what are you doing?'

I sighed. There was some kind of liquid draining from the dead dog on to my clothes. I could feel ants crawl up my sleeves. A fat fly buzzed insanely around my head. 'I'll explain later.'

'Sooner rather than later. He called again and he seems furious, demanded to speak to you. He has another job for us but he wants you on the phone when he calls again at . . . well, in less than an hour from now. Can you get here?'

'I'll be there,' I said simply and rang off.

We found space among the crates, buckets and tools in the crowded back for the dog and I closed the door with all the reverence I could muster. When I got in myself I noticed several bluebottles had made it into the car. Gemma reversed down the hill like she'd been driving backwards all her life, stuffed the back half of the car into the track-side weeds by the barn at the bottom and cranked the wheel around with furious efficiency before propelling us back towards the Hollow.

Digging a hole large and deep enough to bury the dog turned out to be surprisingly hard work. We dug the grave on the side of the slope, away from the springs, taking turns with the only spade. The ground was wet and heavy. When we had laid the dead animal at the bottom Gemma picked up the spade and without ceremony began the task of backfilling. I went off to wash my hands at the spring. By the time I got back she had nearly finished.

'Thanks for doing that. Can you go now, please?' she asked without looking at me.

I ignored the request. 'Do you ever go to those woods?'

'Of course I do. I go mushroom picking there for a start.'

'But it's private property? Blackfield owns it?'

'Yeah, they own it, so what. Blackfield's a complete

148

bastard and wants no one near his property, he doesn't give a shit for the few mushrooms I take away. Perhaps he got a few threatening letters or something when he started up that business with the containers and that's what turned him into a paranoid antisocial bastard, that's my most charitable theory anyway. We had words about me collecting wild herbs and mushrooms around there before he started with the containers though.'

'And you do that at night?' I was thinking about 'the old witch snooping at night'.

'Yes, some plants are best collected after nightfall. Or so it says in some of my old herbals and I have no reason to doubt it. Anyway, I like walking at night, it's peaceful.'

Albert Barrington hadn't found it so peaceful, though you could argue he'd found peace in the end. 'Blackfield, is he the big guy with a shaved head? Dresses like a Hollywood mercenary?'

'That's Tony's son Jim. I think you'll find it's him who's in charge now. He went off for a few years, no interest in farming whatsoever. Can't blame him, he saw his parents work themselves into the ground for no reward. Mind you, if he'd stayed they wouldn't have been so shorthanded in the first place. Small mixed farm. Mad Cow Disease, Foot and Mouth, it doesn't take much, the margins are so small. Then Tony's wife died, cancer I think, not sure, the Big C's still only whispered around here. Jim came back, took over, got rid of the last animals. I think Blackfield senior never recovered from losing his wife. Apparently he still keeps three chickens and only talks to them. Sounds like depression if you ask me. And when he looks out the window he sees a sea of containers rusting in his fields. Cheerful. You met his son then.'

'Yes. He's a charmer. Do you think he's the one who killed your dog?'

'Don't know. Probably. Didn't I ask you to go a while back?' She looked a tired pointy-hatted pixie now, gazing past me, unfocused.

'All right. Look, I'll leave you my number.' I made her accept one of my cards. Then I looked around. 'You've got a phone, I take it?'

She snorted. 'Dream on. They refused to give me a land line since none of this,' she waved her arms in an irritable gesture, 'amounts to a *permanent abode*. And you can't get a mobile signal down here.'

That explained why Annis had had trouble getting hold of me. 'How do you conduct business?'

'Look, I get by, okay? Perhaps we could discuss my communication problems at some other point in the future? The *distant* future?'

'Right. Take care.' I didn't want to leave, even though I wasn't wanted, even though I was very much wanted elsewhere. 'Perhaps you really should get a noisier gun.'

As I rode back towards Larkhall and the London Road I thought I could hear another motorcycle engine behind me but I didn't see any vehicles, though I kept looking over my shoulder. Then the sound was drowned out by the drone of a microlight plane flying lazy circles under the clouds.

Chapter Thirteen

I stared at the cordless handset I had carried round the house since my arrival, waiting for the hated electronic warble that would announce the dreaded call.

'Am I failing Jill? And Louis? Am I doing it all wrong?' I asked Annis.

She buried her hands deep in the pockets of her jeans and shrugged heavily. 'If he managed to intercept you before you even got to the police station then you were right, he knows what you're doing and probably has you watched. I'm not sure we can do much about it. You can try and give your tail the slip but that doesn't mean you can keep police involvement hidden from him. The police might cock it up just as easily as we could and he might kill the boy in revenge or to avoid detection. If Louis has seen his face he's probably doomed anyway. He's not going to be allowed to give the police a detailed description of his kidnapper after he's released. And you have to consider the possibility that he's dead already.' She patted me on the arm in a gesture that was meant to be sympathetic but made me feel worse. There, there. 'I'll make us a nice pot of tea, how about that?' she said in a creaky Miss Marple parody, but I had to admit that the British panacea for all ills and crises was just what I wanted right now. I never got it.

Just as soon as Annis had left the room the phone trilled in my hand and my stomach muscles contracted into an aching mess.

'Honeysett.'

'I'm disappointed in the kind of service you run, Honeysett. I expect more when I hire staff. So listen closely, shithead, and don't interrupt, here's how you can make good your earlier cock-up, though I'm still not completely convinced you aren't trying to pull a fast one. But then again, I can't believe you would jeopardize a boy's health like that.' His distorted, tinny voice sounded as inhuman and robotic as ever. I found it impossible to picture Louis's kidnapper; he remained a shadow attached to a sound that emanated from this piece of plastic I held against my ear.

'How is the boy, how is Louis?'

'Bored and whining and annoying as fuck but he'll be all right if you do what you're told. So listen carefully. Write this down because I won't tell you again: Rufus Connabear, at Restharrow, near Monkton Farleigh.'

'Hang on, I need to find a pen.'

'Don't fuck about, I haven't got time to spell it for you!' he shouted down the phone as I scrabbled around for a biro. 'Connabear. Retired businessman, and very comfortably retired he must be. He has to have more dosh than sense because he spent an awful lot of it on rare stamps. And I have it on good authority that he owns something very rare indeed, a Penny Black. The world's first ever stamp. Worth an absolute fucking fortune and he keeps it at home instead of the bank where it belongs, so you can see he's a nerd, an anorak, a stamp-collecting loser who deserves what's coming to him. Which is you. Because you shall relieve old Rufus of the Penny Black.'

Even I had heard of the famous stamp. After all, it was from Bath that the first ever postage stamp, printed in black ink and then costing one penny, was sent in 1840, every school kid probably knew that. I wondered just how many shiny pennies it was worth now.

'You have three days, Honeysett, and no fuck-ups this time, I won't believe another disaster. I'll be keeping a close eye on you, just to make sure.'

I was going to protest that three days didn't leave me much time to plan the robbery when engine sounds made me rush to the window. I recognized Superintendent Needham's big grey saloon barrelling self-importantly through the gate. 'I'll do my best. Got to hang up now, unexpected visitors.' I cut the connection. My head was buzzing. When did I sign up for this much excitement? Perhaps retired stamp collectors had entirely the right idea. I stepped away from the window so I could spy on Needham unobserved for a minute. I could see he was using DS Sorbie as a driver. And as though a visit from Needham wasn't bad enough, no sooner had he squeezed out of his car than DI Deeks made an appearance, driving himself and even more self-importantly blocking the exit with his big ugly Ford.

'Shit. That's all we needed.' Annis joined me by the window. 'What does the bastard want this time?'

'Needham, he'll –'

'No, Louis's kidnapper.'

'Another burglary. Stamp collector's house. He wants us to steal the Penny Black.'

'Is that all?'

Outside the three officers had a quick pow-wow, then the besuited Needham and leather-jacketed Sorbie moved towards the house while Deeks, wearing his horrible rain-proof, settled on the bonnet of his car, arms folded.

'Hard to pull off?' Annis asked.

'Won't know until we've taken a look but he's only given us three days. Do you see what I see?'

'The new boy is carrying what will no doubt be Needham's search warrant.'

'Yup, with the ink still wet.'

The doorbell jingled loudly and the door was being rapped in typical police fashion. I opened it before some-one decided to kick it in again.

'Honeysett, this is DS Sorbie and he has a search war-rant. Show the man,' he encouraged him as he hefted past me. I barely glanced at the paper, looking instead over Sorbie's shoulder to check on Deeks, but he no longer adorned the bonnet of his car and was nowhere to be seen, which was a bit worrying.

'After you.' Sorbie made an inviting gesture down the hall with his warrant.

I had little choice. Needham had already disappeared right towards the kitchen. I hurried after him. 'Keep an eye on Sorbie, there's something weird about this,' I managed to murmur to Annis as I passed her. Needham was already half-heartedly furtling about in the kitchen, opening cupboards without bothering to search them, letting his left hand trail over objects as though he was thinking with his fleshy fingers. I decided to play it by ear. The kettle was already quietly singing on the back of the stove.

'Coffee?' I knew Needham loved real coffee while his life was plagued by the ersatz brew his underlings invariably brought him, mostly in plastic cups.

'And why not,' he conceded without hesitation and disappeared into the pantry, where he inspected the shelves with his head gently cocked to one side and his hands behind his back. I had the distinct feeling that, perhaps unlike Deeks and Sorbie, he was here on a culinary search but I didn't think this was the time to ask him how his diet was going. I could hear Sorbie rummaging in the cupboard under the stairs. I suddenly broke into a sweat. If Sorbie demanded the key for the gun locker and found my shotgun missing some awkward questions might be asked, since I had never reported the thing stolen. I knew who had it and still harboured hopes of retrieving it. But the question never came and I could soon hear him moving upstairs, shadowed by a vigilant Annis.

Watched by an appreciative Superintendent I spun out the ritual of coffee making, ground the beans finely in the noisy little mill, transferred the fragrant grounds to a cafetière, splashed recently boiled water on it, depressed the plunger and decanted the resulting brew into a warmed coffee pot. The cat appeared as if from nowhere, swished around Needham's legs and gave his polished shoes a deep sniffing.

'Didn't know you had a cat.'

'He's just passing through.'

'What's his name?' He bent down and scratched the cat's ears.

'He hasn't got one.'

'You could call him Mackerel.'

'Not a chance.' Eventually I poured two cups and handed one to Needham, who accepted it with only the faintest hint of a smile and let himself sink on to a chair with a little grunt. 'You're a damn nuisance, Chris, but at least you're a civilized nuisance. You wouldn't have any sweetener of course?' he asked while tumbling sugar cubes into his cup.

'What are you after, Mike?' Something about this visit was decidedly odd. 'You're not looking for blunt instruments, are you? What's the latest on Barrington's death? You must know by now it wasn't me, so why keep harassing me?'

'Harassing? You feel harassed? You really shouldn't. Relax,' he said with an expansive sweep of his arms. 'It's all routine. You know the drill.'

I patted my pockets in search of cigarettes and came up with nothing. I made to get some but he was well ahead of me.

'Sit down, Honeypot, have one of mine.' He slithered a packet of Camel across the table.

'But you don't smoke,' I protested while I peeled the cellophane off the brand new pack.

'Took them off an underage kid earlier.'

'Who happened to smoke my brand.' Why did I get the feeling he didn't want me to leave the kitchen while his minions rummaged around my place?

'You don't smoke anything else, do you?' he asked casually.

'You know I don't. It bores me.'

'Well, Albert Barrington didn't find it boring, that's for sure. And at his age. Pot-head pensioners, that's all we need now. Where do our senior citizens go to score these days, what do you reckon? Do dealers hang around their minibuses outside the bingo halls? Or do they grow the stuff down the allotment? A new category for the show bench, I dare say . . .' Needham appeared to be talking to himself and between occasional sips of coffee kept up a leisurely stream of whimsical observations about the changing nature of drug crime on his patch. There didn't seem to be anything he wanted from me. Though if he really didn't know who Barrington used to buy his blow from then he and Deeks had to have had a complete communication breakdown. I began to wonder just how good a deal Gem Stone had struck with him that he managed to keep her out of a murder inquiry. The longer we sat around the more fidgety I became, with Deeks and Sorbie crawling all over my place. I lit another cigarette with the stub of the first and poured more coffee. Through the half-glazed kitchen door I saw Deeks trundling past across the meadow, returning from the studio no doubt. I trusted Needham, as a due-process-by-the-book-god-honest copper, but Sorbie was still an unknown quantity and I did now know that Deeks was bent, which made his traipsing round the property without an escort rather nerve-racking. My skin tingled with sweat. Needham didn't comment but probably hadn't made Detective Superintendent without having a nose for other people's fear. At the same time as luxuriating in his coffee break and wittering on about Policing the City of Bath (you could hear the capital letters) as though he was addressing a committee of concerned citizens he seemed to be listening not to my answers but to the house around him.

'This is just a formality, Honeysett, we must be seen never to leave a tern unstoned, as they say.' He chuckled to himself. I just hate it when he chuckles. 'A pensioner getting murdered excites the press for some reason and then the press go and excite the pensioners. Old people feel the most vulnerable to violent crime, even though in reality they're the least likely to suffer from it. Or any other crime, for that matter. The group most likely to be victims of crime are the fifteen to twenty-five-year-olds, which is the very group that scares the pensioners. But statistics mean nothing and perception is everything.'

'Oh, quite.' I didn't find it easy to join in with this drivel, whether it was true or not. 'Did you ever find a weapon?'

'The Good Old Blunt Instrument? No. But we have a notion it might have been a cricket bat that rendered him senseless. Your car then finished him off. Shame you didn't report it missing earlier, you'd be completely in the clear now.' He shrugged it off as though it was of little real importance.

'Cricket bat, how very British,' I observed.

'Well, believe it or not our hoodlum fraternity have started trading in their American ash for English willow recently. Ever since prosecutors started asking defendants – who just happened to have baseball bats in their cars at the time of their arrest – to explain the finer details of the game for the benefit of the court. Long faces all round of course, it's like asking a kid from the Bronx to explain the rules of cricket. Personally I believe as a weapon the cricket bat has the edge. You play at all? Ah, here comes the faithful Sorbie,' he said, drained his cup and rose. 'Thanks for the coffee, Honeysett, we shan't bother you any longer. For now.' He silently directed DI Sorbie out of the house. 'Miss Jordan,' Sorbie said flatly in farewell to Annis. Deeks already stood by his car. We watched as doors slammed and the drivers sorted themselves out, turning their ugly big saloons around in my potholed yard. I was so relieved I barely managed to suppress the impulse to give them a cheery wave as they surged out of the gate.

'Phew,' I observed eloquently.

Annis let out a deep breath with puffed-out cheeks. 'What did they want?'

I shrugged. 'What could they have been looking for?'

'Sorbie didn't say. He didn't answer any of my questions and never volunteered a word. I annoyed the shit out of him for sure.'

'Did you see at all what Deeks was up to outside?'

'No, I couldn't keep an eye on both. Nothing much to find, though, is there?'

'That's not necessarily what I'm worried about.'

'You don't think Deeks would plant stuff on us? You're getting paranoid, Chris.'

'You're right. Nevertheless, I'll have a wander about, see what Deeks saw.'

I pulled on my jacket and made myself walk slowly all over my little realm; I kicked at things rusting and mouldering in the outbuildings, got my trouser legs damp crossing the meadow, stood by the mill pond reflecting the dull lead of the sky. The feeling of being watched was growing all the time and I began to imagine eyes and ears in every shadow. Indeed, if Needham was half as clever as I suspected him to be then he had come here to stir things up so he could watch what happened next.

I made doubly sure that no one was hanging around among the hedgerows. The more I thought about it the less sense the last twenty minutes made. I had seen police searches before and they'd been protracted, painstaking affairs involving many officers and technicians, not a couple of CID types wandering about the place with their hands in their pockets while their superior officer took coffee in the kitchen. But when I found no sign of them anywhere I was just too relieved to worry about it for long.

'It's out near Monkton Farleigh,' I explained to Annis while I topped up the Norton's tank from a jerry can. 'Rufus Connabear, at Restharrow.'

'Hairy, evil-smelling dwarf –'

'You know him?' I interrupted in astonishment.

'No, restharrow, you twit! It's a dwarf shrub, grows like a weed all over the place near my parents' house in Devon, and it stinks. Strange name to give your house but I guess it takes all sorts.'

'I've come to that conclusion myself recently.'

Monkton Farleigh was a pretty one-eyed village roughly halfway between Bath and Bradford-on-Avon. As soon as I'd reached the top of Bathford Hill and the road emerged from the woodland I turned left. After barely a mile I came to a row of three cottages on my left where a tall blonde woman cheerfully herded a clutch of kids into her front garden. I resisted the temptation to ask directions to Restharrow. People would surely remember a man on a vintage motorcycle asking questions once the famous Penny Black had disappeared. Instead I simply rattled along, past church, high street, pub and manor, and before I knew it I was out the other side, leaving the village behind. It took me a while, pottering along various narrow lanes bound by hedgerows, until I found what I was looking for. I was lucky that the place announced itself as Restharrow in faded gilt lettering on a rustic wooden sign stuck to the stone wall that faced the lane. It was not what I had expected. I had been certain a wealthy – even if retired – stamp collector would live in a grander place but quickly reminded myself that any period cottage within a certain radius of Bath was now considered to be worth a small fortune. It was a substantial enough place though and somehow dark, almost sinister, standing alone at a fork in the tree-shaded lane, surrounded by a stone wall just high enough to keep livestock out and sheltered by hedges to the north and west at the back. Two enormous walnut trees teeming with squirrels overshadowed house and garden. There was no garage but a covered car port containing a gleaming blue Jaguar.

Apparently all we had was three days. That didn't leave much time to establish what the man's routines were, who else might be living here or coming and going on a regular basis. I allowed myself less than a minute in front of the house with the engine idling, pretending to be answering a text message while snapping pictures of the place with my phone. The front garden was lushly overgrown in the kind of extreme laissez-faire style of horticulture I approved of. I was just about to pull away when a man appeared from the passage between the house and the car port. He was a lean man in his late sixties, had sparse silver hair and wore mustard-coloured trousers, a collarless white shirt and bright yellow Marigolds. He was dragging a bulging green refuse bag behind him.

I put away my mobile. It was that movement rather than the sound of the engine which made him look across. Perhaps I could still have ridden off but the way he adjusted his thin gold spectacles on his nose to scrutinize me made me decide it might look suspicious. Instead I pulled in closer to the open double gate on the drive and parked the bike. He let his bag drop now and surveyed my appearance and the motorbike, screwing up his face with the intensity of a man who has missed several eye-tests. The iron gate was the same height as the wall, about four feet and therefore largely symbolic.

'I'm a bit lost, I'm afraid,' I ventured.

He didn't immediately answer, instead he came towards me and after nodding at my tattered jacket rather than me began inspecting the bike. 'Norton, thought so,' he said with the croaky voice of someone who hasn't spoken a word all day. He elaborately cleared his throat.

'Yes, she's recently been restored after a crash. They did a beautiful job,' I explained.

'Sorry, you have to speak up, I'm afraid I didn't put my deaf-aids in this morning.' He tapped both his ears in explanation.

'Recently restored,' I repeated loudly.

160

'I remember when they first started making this model. I had an Ariel at the time, the 600 cc side-valve.'

'The side-valve, right . . .' Fortunately nothing more seemed to be required of me. Otherwise I'd have been forced to admit that where you stuck your valves on a bike was a matter of supreme indifference to me.

After spending a few minutes in the golden age of motorcycling he eventually came back to the present. 'Was there something you wanted?'

'Just directions, really. I was looking for a scenic route to Melksham and got lost.'

'Ah, well, you're not so very lost. I have a map of the area, I'll show you.'

I followed him to his front door. He snapped off the Marigolds. 'I try and keep the garden going but I find it a bit of a struggle. My wife used to look after that side of things of course. I'm not green-fingered at all, I'm afraid.'

'You could perhaps get a gardener to look after it for you . . .?'

'I suppose I could at that,' he said as though the thought had never occurred to him before. 'Right, if you wait a minute I'll get the map.' He slapped the Marigolds on to the newel post and left me standing by a painted milk urn full of walking sticks while he went upstairs, one hand firmly on the banister. I looked around the gloomy hall. I thought I could detect the so-called female touch in the choice of coloured wallpaper and framed botanical drawings but also sensed a certain edge of neglect in the dirt trodden into the expensive carpet, the layer of dust on everything and even of time slowly running down in the sedate ticking of the longcase clock at the foot of the stairs. Rufus Connabear lived alone and didn't employ a cleaner or a gardener, I concluded. I tiptoed into the kitchen. This was quite clean and tidy with a simple wooden table playing host to neat piles of letters and other papers, weighted down with clean coffee mugs. Through the window above the sink I could see into the shady garden with its overcrowded beds and overgrown hedge. The old-fashioned back door, I noted with satisfaction, had no security features beyond a simple lock and key.

Back in the hall, while listening for footsteps from above, I peered through the open door into the sitting room. Too many pieces of furniture had been crammed in here; an olive-green three-piece suite, a separate large armchair in a similar colour that nevertheless didn't quite match. There were underemployed bookshelves on two walls. A sideboard, a small table and several plant stands featuring pots minus the plants completed the clutter. The room had windows back and front, though the back windows were almost completely blocked against the light by the dense foliage of some kind of evergreen outside, making the overstuffed room more gloomy than necessary. Still no sound of footsteps. Now or never. I took a deep breath, crossed the room to the back windows and unlatched the nearest one without actually opening it. Just then I could hear movement above and gained the hall in a hectic bit of tiptoe work around the plant stands as Connabear's legs appeared on the stairs.

'Sorry it took so long,' he said as he descended in a careful fashion. 'I was sure I could lay my hands on it easily but it proved not to be where I thought it was. I found it in the end, though. Come through,' he added. In the kitchen he spread out his Ordnance Survey map of the area and pointed out where we were and my best route to Melksham from his front door. It was quite ludicrously simple which made me suspect he had fetched the map simply for something to do, or for a moment of company. Soon he was back on our first subject, telling me more about the development of Ariel and Norton motorcycles than I could possibly hope to remember and laying a papery hand on my arm whenever I made a move towards the door. It was another fifteen minutes until I was allowed outside to mount the Norton again and even then one of his hands remained firmly on the handlebar while he

lamented the number of cars on the roads and the dis-
courtesy of today's drivers. Even though I vigorously
agreed with him on this last point I could hardly wait to
get out there amongst them once more.

Eventually he let me go and I gave him a cheery wave
as I rumbled away down the lane. I would report what
little I had found out to Tim and trust to his expertise to
get at the stamp, though I hoped I had made things easier
for us by opening the latch on the downstairs window.
Thanks to Connabear's directions I was soon back on the
A363, returning to Bath. When I drew into the yard at Mill
House, however, I could see from Annis's face as she stood
in the door, nodding at what was being said to her on the
cordless phone, that we had fresh problems. She handed
me the phone.

Tim was at the other end of the line, sounding unusually
troubled. 'I'm being followed. Absolutely everywhere. Go
turn your confuser on, I'll mail the guys to you.'

Up in my attic office I cranked up my computer, then
checked my mail. He had sent me three pictures he had
taken that day; one, a grainy image probably taken on his
mobile of two men, casually dressed, late twenties, early
thirties. The location looked like the university car park.
The other two pictures were taken with a better camera
from Tim's sitting-room window. They showed the same
men on the other side of Tim's street, about fifty yards to
the left. In the first they were sitting in a blue Vauxhall, the
passenger with his arm out of the window, adjusting
the wing mirror. Both had sharp haircuts and looked wide
awake. In the second picture one of them was just returning to the car with a shopping bag from the nearby Co-op.

'I don't recognize them,' said Annis, looking over my
shoulder.

I called Tim back. 'Yeah, I got them but we don't know
them. When did you pick them up?'

'Oh, they were here when I drove to work but of course
I didn't suspect anything then. When I spotted them again

at my lunch break I started to take notice, and when I had to cross the campus in the middle of the afternoon and they were there, waiting, I got suspicious. Took a picture of them on the phone. They followed me home, though to give them their dues I didn't spot their car behind me, so they know how to follow people. They're still down there, still sitting in the car, eating. Man, you know you've landed a shit job when all your food is triangular and your drinks come in plastic bottles.'

'Don't tell them that. Did you see them talking into phones or radios?'

'No. And they seem to have run out of things to say to each other. Most of the time they're just sitting there.'

'Are they trying to be discreet or do they want you to know they are there?'

'Oh no, they're pretending not to be there.'

'They're probably fuzz-balls then,' I concluded rashly. 'There's two ways to go about it. You can pretend you haven't noticed and then give them the slip or you go out there and confront them.' I couldn't see any other possibilities because right now I wanted Tim here at Mill House so we could make a move towards getting at the Penny Black.

'I don't think that's such a good idea, Chris.' Tim spoke slowly, still thinking. 'If they're fuzz then they could only be here for two things, the break-in at Telfer's house or something I pulled off a very long time ago. The best thing is to pretend I haven't noticed them and do nothing suspicious at all. I'm just an IT guy at Bath Uni, doing my normal day-to-day stuff and I've got nothing to hide.'

'Did Annis tell you about the new job the bastard has lined up for us?'

'She did.'

'Well, then you know I need you here right now. There's not much time. Try and give them the slip.'

'I don't like it, Chris. I thought I'd lost them on the way home and yet they reappeared.'

'That's because they know where you live, dummy.'

'And do you think they don't know we're mates and where *you* live? If we go breaking into the stamp-man's place together it'll be like bringing my own arresting officers with me. We can't risk that. You'll have to do it yourself.'

'But I'm rubbish at that kind of thing.' Eloquent silence at Tim's end. 'Feel free to contradict me at any point. And he's bound to have the thing in a safe.'

'You won't know that until you've been looking. But even if he has . . .' He hesitated. 'I could perhaps lend you my gear, show you how to work it . . . but I think it's best we don't have direct contact at the moment. You had a look at the house, did he seem to have lots of security?'

'None, as far as I could see,' I admitted. Rufus Connabear didn't even have double glazing to shut the draught out, let alone locks on the windows to keep out burglars.

'There you go. You can have a stab at it then. A kid could do the place over. Only be careful, just because you can't see security doesn't always mean there isn't any, though most people make it obvious to discourage you from even trying. How many people live in the house?'

'I think the guy lives alone. He's retirement age and a bit deaf.'

'There you go, if it's in a safe you can use dynamite. Just kidding. You'll have no problems, mate, it'll be a doddle . . .'

Tim was right of course but breaking into people's houses, even though I'd done it before, all in a good cause, you understand, wasn't a task I relished.

'I'll come with you if you like,' Annis offered. 'As long as we don't have to climb up ladders or go up drainpipes.' Annis was fearless at sea level but couldn't stand heights.

'No, there's no point. The fewer bodies on this journey the better.' Especially with someone as accident prone as me at the helm. 'I'll do it by myself and I'll do it tonight.'

165

Chapter Fourteen

The feeble beam of the Norton's headlamp was half drowned by the downpour and illuminated nothing but ten yards of rain bouncing hard off the slickened tarmac on the nightblack lane. I approached the house from the other side, that way I could avoid going through Monkton Farleigh; the otherworldly exhaust note of the machine might stick in the minds of light sleepers in the village. Despite having pored over a map earlier I had no exact idea how far away from Restharrow I was, but when at last I spotted a passing place in the lane that wasn't filled with several inches of water I gratefully parked the bike, stuffed my gloves into the helmet and hung it on the handlebars. The rain had returned at midnight and had fallen relentlessly out of black skies since then, yet I had eschewed Annis's offer of the Landy. It was much easier to find a place for stashing the bike than a bulky Land Rover. The drawbacks of using two wheels however became quickly obvious: I was wet, very, very wet. I shivered inside my rain-heavy, sodden gear and set off. My left boot had sprung a leak and before long I had managed to step into a good-sized puddle with it and was miserably squelching along in near total darkness. I had hoped to negotiate my way to the house by starlight but with a hundred per cent cloud cover and pouring rain I was soon forced to use the Mini Maglite I had brought. After five minutes of trudging along the undulating lane I realized I had parked too far from the house. A couple of minutes later I was wondering whether to go back and move the Norton when Restharrow appeared as if out of nowhere, looming darker in the darkness on my right. I killed the light and stood in the big, cold, wet darkness for a while. It yielded nothing. No light was showing at the house. In fact there was no light anywhere and I couldn't hear a thing beyond the relentless rain. I wondered how weather affected the burglary figures but not for long because this burglary couldn't wait for a balmy summer's evening. The only good thing about the heavy rain was that it might help to mask little sounds, like me squelching off the road and walking painfully into a fence I hadn't seen. I clicked the torch on at short intervals to get my bearings then tried to battle on without it but the darkness out here seemed complete. After slipping and falling once, bumping my knee against the stone wall twice and repeatedly getting my jacket caught on invisible snags I'd had enough and turned on the torch for good. I was bound to make less noise that way.

I managed to scramble over the wall – a child would have done it in half the time – towards the back of the garden and dropped into a muddy flowerbed on the other side. Something hard and thorny travelled up my trouser leg as I did and sliced my calf open as I came down. Before I could stop myself I had informed the darkness in pithy, monosyllabic words of what I thought about this development.

Well, Rufus Connabear was either still asleep or he wasn't. If he was awake and looking out of his windows then he'd be calling the police about now, if not then I had the smallest chance of getting away with this lunatic effort. I had to keep the torch on all the time now just to avoid big pots full of dead-looking plants everywhere and some concrete bunny rabbits with scary, knowing smiles. At last I got to the back of the cottage and the dense evergreen shrubs that obscured the window I had unlocked on my previous visit. I had to crouch low and come up close to the wall to get through there at all. The windows opened outwards. I put the Maglite in my mouth and got my fingernails under the frame and pulled. Nothing. I pulled harder. More nothing. I got out my keys and used one as a lever. It bent. I trained the torch beam higher to where the latch was. It *looked* open. Of course when I'd unfastened the latch earlier I hadn't had time to try whether the window actually opened. For all I knew it had been painted shut three generations ago. I fought my way out of the wet and scratchy shrub and decided I was already thoroughly cheesed off with the way my night was panning out. Having squeezed under the tiny ornamental porch of the back door for some shelter I fumbled with muddy hands for a cigarette that was already drooping with dampness when I prised it out of the packet. Miraculously I got it lit. For a brief moment I stood there, pressed against the kitchen door, and enjoyed the illusion of warmth my smoke provided until a large and well-aimed drop of rain extinguished the glow with a hiss. Disgusted, I flicked the wet thing into the darkness; one for the forensic boys.

Plan B: I pulled on a pair of latex gloves and tried the door handle. The door was locked, but it was always worth a try.

Plan C then: I shone my torch through the little glass pane closest to the lock. Sure enough, the key was in the door. I got the glass cutters out and one of those hooks with suction nipples we used for hanging tea towels from. I stuck the nipple on to the pane, gave it a tug to test it was on, then cut a triangle out of the glass. Holding on to the hook with one hand I gave it a tap with the cutter's handle and it snapped loose. I eased it out and let it fall into the nearest flowerpot. Through the resulting hole I could now easily reach the key. I turned it very slowly, then tried the door handle again. The lock was disengaged but the door still didn't want to open. There had to be a bolt somewhere. At the top? At the bottom? Both? The bottom one would hold me up for at least five minutes but most people

168

stopped bothering with it after a while because it meant bending down, so made do with the one at the top. Or they installed a cat flap, which rendered the bolt meaningless, as anyone could simply reach through.

I engaged the cutter again at the top pane of glass and it snapped out as easily as the first. Reaching through I found the bolt and wriggled it back, a fraction of an inch at a time, until the door eased open. I looked down. Sure enough, there was an identical bolt at the bottom which had not been engaged. I slipped inside and gently clicked the door shut behind me. The noise of the rain fell away. Standing still in the kitchen I listened: water dripping off me on to the floor; a fridge-freezer humming near the door. The workings of the grandfather clock in the hall seemed monstrously loud. I crept forward and was appalled at the squelching sound my left boot produced. Putting weight only on to the heel stopped the noise but didn't exactly make me feel sure-footed. First I investigated the sitting room. I had a strong feeling the stamp collection would be upstairs but would feel like an idiot if I had braved the stairs and the whole of the first floor with Connabear asleep only to later find what I was looking for downstairs. Some of the bookshelves had drawers at the bottom. At first I thought I'd hit pay dirt when I found fat albums wedged into one but they turned out to be full of deckle-edged black and white prints of people taking cycling holidays. I closed the heavy drawer carefully, straightened up, turned and swept an ornament off the shelf with the little black rucksack I'd forgotten I was carrying. It hit the thick carpet with a horribly loud thump but didn't break. I put it back where I thought it had been. It was another bunny rabbit and seemed to have the same evil smile as its larger cousins in the garden. After having managed to squeeze around the sofas, armchairs, tables and plant stands without knocking anything else over I started on the dreaded stairs. I just knew they would creak at some point, no matter how lightly I trod, and sure enough, the last but one groaned loudly as I stood on it. I froze. My breath seemed so loud I was sure it could be heard for miles around. I waited, ready for flight should I hear the slightest sound, but nothing happened. Eventually I gathered the nerve to take the last two steps. I stood in the thickly carpeted upstairs corridor, carefully playing the torch beam about. There were five doors, all of them closed apart from the one at the end. From there vitreous china sparkled in the torch beam, which made it a safe bet for being a bathroom. This still left a bewildering choice of doors. At all times while thinking about the break-in I had firmly held in my mind an image of one closed door – with Connabear comfortably and noisily snoring behind it – and the others open for me to wander in and out of until I'd located the Penny Black.

I crept along the corridor and listened at each door in turn for Rufus Connabear's breathing or perhaps a helpful little snuffle. Not a sound behind any of them. It suddenly struck me that I hadn't bothered to check whether his car was sheltering in the port, so for all I knew Connabear and his Jag might be miles away, heading for France on a cross-Channel ferry, let's say. Dream on.

There was no easy solution, I simply had to open one of the doors and see what I'd find. Obviously I had a one in four chance of getting it right first time, though, not being a betting man, how the odds changed after that was a bit hazy in my mind. Anyway, I told myself as I turned the first brass door knob, my chances sounded pretty good to my non-mathematical brain. Pointing the torch down the hall so that only reflected light would fall into the room I opened the door very slowly. I could make out a kind of padded seat and then the bottom of a bed. Was the bed occupied? I strained my hearing but couldn't be sure. I stuck my head through the gap. The bed was empty and I remembered to breathe again. Widening the crack I padded inside to have a look around. I could use the torch quite freely now. There were no signs of recent occupation but for a spare room it had some character, with more books on shelves and tiny framed watercolours on the walls, and the ill-judged addition of a rabbit ornament here and there. I went through the chest of drawers to the left of the window – it was full of linen. Under the bed were lengths of curved tubular aluminium, perhaps part of an exercise machine, and fluff. The place smelled unused and dusty. Not bothering to close the door I moved to the next. Even putting my ear right against it I heard nothing above the rain that the wind flung against the blind window in the corridor. It suddenly occurred to me that now I had a one in three chance of opening the wrong door. How had that happened? How had the odds turned so dramatically against me? Perhaps it was simply a 'glass half-full/half-empty' situation? Or should that be quarter-empty, I really wasn't sure . . .

Telling myself to get a grip I turned the brass knob and opened the door a fraction. All I could make out was an ornate secretaire and chair by the uncurtained window but my nose told me that this room had to be occupied. The moist and stale fug of sleep hung unmistakably in the air, together with the sound of my hammering heart. Connabear's bedroom. With him in it. Was the Penny Black there too? I didn't want to admit to that possibility yet. Creeping about in his bedroom while the man was asleep had to be the absolute last resort. Needing hearing aids to communicate easily with people was different from being profoundly deaf. I was sure sooner or later he'd hear me rummaging so close to him. Anyway, it was pitch dark, I'd have to use my torch and if nothing else surely that would wake him. If he woke up the shock of finding me there might give him a heart attack. Or me.

The next door seemed different. There was just not enough wall space on either side for it to be anything but a walk-in cupboard or another bathroom perhaps. I moved on to the last door. To make sure, I listened again, in case I had been wrong about the man living by himself. This

171

was it. This just had to be the room where he kept his pet cobras and poisonous jumping spiders. I took even longer turning the knob and easing the door open since I'd been too scared to close the bedroom door again and I felt sure the tiniest squeak might wake him. As soon as the gap was wide enough I squeezed through and gratefully closed the door behind me. I found the light switch and flicked it on. After creeping around by torchlight it seemed insanely bright and scary but would speed up my search. It would probably show under the door so I had to be quick; didn't old people get up to go to the loo a lot at night?

I was standing in a fair-sized study, the main feature of which was a mahogany desk and dark leather chair. On the tidy desk sat phone, blotter, brass lamp and leather picture frame holding a small black and white photo. Either side of the window stood wooden filing cabinets that matched the wood of the desk, and two bookshelves to my right completed the furnishings. They were stuffed with what looked like reference books and at least one complete encyclopedia. On the wall behind the desk hung a framed landscape painting, done with more enthusiasm than skill in oily impasto. I made straight for it as the likeliest place to hide a safe and lifted it off the wall. No wall safe, I was glad to see. I hadn't really meant to lift the picture completely off the hook and now I found it hard to marry the hook and nail again. I rested it on the floor, rolled the chair closer to the wall, then picked up the painting again and climbed gingerly up. Then I stopped. What was I doing? I was a burglar, there was no need to clear up after myself, the main thing was to find the daft stamp and get the hell out again. But since I was already up there ... Before I managed to get the framed horror back on the nail the door flew open, making me scream with surprise and nearly lose my balance.

'Don't move, you bastard! Put that down!' Even in his black pyjamas Connabear looked wide awake. He was wearing both his hearing aids and pointing both barrels of his shotgun at me. And he looked furious. As for his contradictory demands I chose not moving as the safer option. 'It's you,' he said next. The disappointment in his croaky voice was obvious but he seemed to shrug it off quickly. 'Put that painting back on the wall.'

'Okay, just don't do anything rash with that gun.' I fumbled some more with the hook and at last caught the nail.

'Now put your hands up and get your filthy boots off my chair.'

I stepped down with my hands up. Something in the way he held the gun convinced me that it was loaded and that old Rufus had experience in handling it.

He nodded his head up at the daub. 'You weren't really going to steal that, were you? My wife painted that.'

Now I noticed the initials in the bottom-right corner, P.C. 'Well, ehm, it's rather nice,' I lied. 'I'm a painter myself, so I have an eye for these things.'

'Oh yeah? No wonder you have to resort to robbing people if you think that's a nice painting. It's a horrible mess, my wife had no talent for art whatsoever. I'm keeping it for my daughter's sake who is similarly afflicted, though I always make sure I'm sitting with my back to it. Right, move around to the window, but slowly, and keep your hands up. You scum, you thought I was just a doddery old codger. You thought you could turn the place over and probably just clout me one if I woke up . . .'

'No, of course not,' I protested.

'I thought you were a nice young man yesterday. Really did. Nicely spoken, too. And to think I even let you in the house. You make one false move and I'll happily shoot you.'

'You can't mean that,' I suggested, lowering my hands.

He tightened his grip on the weapon. 'Oh yeah? You just try it.'

'Make an awful mess,' I suggested.

'*I look forward to it,*' he said and looked like he meant it.

'The last guy who shot a burglar with a shotgun, you know, that farmer, he spent years in prison.'

'Ah, but he shot him from behind, I'll shoot you from the front,' he said conversationally. 'Actually he's out now. And anyway, didn't they change the law on defending your property? I think we're allowed to shoot you now.'

My arms were already tired from manoeuvring the heavily framed daub about and keeping them in the air was surprisingly hard work. How to get out of this one? As usual, I'd have to talk myself out of it. The really disconcerting thing was that he seemed so much more awake than me, but then I'd heard it said that old people needed less sleep. I felt suddenly exhausted and thought I could easily nod off with my hands in the air.

He moved behind the desk and sat in the chair, then propelled himself forward with his slippered feet until he could rest the gun barrels on the desk and keep the weapon trained on me with one hand. Then he reached for the phone.

'No, please, don't call the police.' Of all the things that might happen, getting arrested had never figured in any scenarios I had imagined. Unmoved, he dialled 999.

Last chance now. 'I am being blackmailed into breaking into your house, it's not what I normally do, there's a boy's life at stake, in fact I'm a private eye and a client's son has been kidnapped and breaking in here and stealing the Penny Black is part of the ransom, you have to believe me.' I rattled it all off quickly before he'd get through to the police.

He paused and gave me a contemptuous look. 'That's the most pathetic cock and bull story I have heard for a long time.'

'Honestly. I wish there was a less fantastical explanation but that's the situation I'm in.'

He shook his head and waggled the receiver at me. 'Did you cut the phone line?'

'No, didn't think of that. Should've, I suppose. Why, is it not working?'

'No, must be the weather. It happens. Joys of country living.' He replaced the receiver and gripped the gun with both hands again. 'So you're trying to tell me someone went to the trouble of kidnapping a boy – which carries a mandatory life sentence if I'm not mistaken – to make you steal my Penny Black?' He shook his head. 'That's a very unlikely story, Mr Burglar.'

'Why? Drugs, money, art, diamonds, rare stamps, it's all currency in criminal circles.'

He nodded. 'True. Do you have any idea how much money we are talking about here?'

'Not really.'

'About two-fifty.'

'Quarter of a million?' I whistled.

'No, you saphead. Pounds. Two hundred and fifty pounds will buy you a fair example.'

'There must be some mistake. It must be worth more than that. I thought it being the first ever stamp and . . .' I faltered, faced with the pitiful look he gave me.

'Do you know how many of them were issued?' he asked, frowning disapprovingly at my ignorance. 'More than sixty million of them. Even an unused one in mint condition wouldn't exactly break the bank.'

'So they got it completely wrong . . .' A thin silver lining stole into my mind, looking for a cloud.

'It's a common misconception,' he explained happily. 'Now if we were talking about, let's say, the Blue Mauritius, then a million dollars would be a good starting price, and the Treskilling Yellow sold for over a couple of million a while back.'

'But you don't have any of those . . .?'

'No, never had, either. I offloaded most of my collection long ago, and just in time too. Others got badly burnt when the bottom fell out of the stamp market in the eighties but I saw it coming. And it's about to happen again, I might add.' He lifted his nose as though he could sniff the imminent collapse of the stamp market in this very room. 'I kept the Penny Blacks though. Out of sentimentality, mainly. I remember being very excited when I was able to add a copy to my collection when I was a young man. I don't remember what I paid for it but it seemed a fair bit of money to me then. And then there's the historical connection of course. They were issued in Bath after all.'

'Yes, I know about that part. Did you say Penny *Blacks*? Plural?'

'Yes, I have three examples. One is right here, see?' He turned the picture frame on the desk around and proffered it up for my inspection. Without thinking I walked up to the desk and took it – and noticed in passing that I didn't get shot. What earlier I had taken to be a small black and white photograph was in fact the famous stamp. It had the head of a young Queen Victoria on it and bore the legend *Postage, One Penny*. In the bottom left-hand corner was a Q and in the bottom right a G.

'What do those letters mean?' I enquired.

'Oh, they give the exact position of the stamp on the sheet. They were printed in sheets of two hundred and forty, you see, twenty rows of twelve, so this example came from the seventeenth row, Q, and the seventh position, G.'

I handed him the frame and he set it back in its place on his desk. There were no other pictures, no photographs of his wife, for example, I noted. Perhaps he had fonder memories of the stamp than of the dearly departed dauber. 'So the man who forced me to break in here to steal that stamp is labouring under a serious misconception, i.e. that the thing is worth a fortune.'

'So it appears. Are you being serious about this kidnapped boy story then? Surely you could have simply gone to the police. Should have, I should add.'

'It's the mother's decision. *No police*. Who am I to make that decision for her? I feel guilty enough as it is. The kidnappers told her to get in touch with me so they could use her son to make me do their bidding. This isn't the first burglary they forced me into, but the last one went wrong. Then they came up with this scheme and here I am looking down the barrels of . . . a rather fine shotgun, I can't help noticing.'

'Yes, it is rather fine, and it does you credit to have noticed it. You're a better judge of guns than paintings perhaps. It's a James Purdey, engraved by Stephen Kelly, one of a pair. Probably the most expensive items in the house, that's what you should have gone for,' he said, giving me a schoolmasterly look over the top of his gold spectacles.

'Look, I'm really not a habitual house-breaker. I'm a private investigator, as well as a painter . . .' I started rummaging in my jacket pockets for a business card while Connabear tightened his bony grip on the polished walnut stock of the gun. When at last I managed to fish one out it was damp and dog-eared and looked like I'd found it in the street somewhere.

He took the proffered card reluctantly but the expression on his face brightened as he looked at it. 'Honeysett. You're the chap who found that woman who was imprisoned in the old railway station, that made national news, Nikki Somebody or other. I remember seeing your picture.'

'Nikki Reid.'

'That's her. Worked for an estate agency. So . . . this story you told me is really true? About the boy?'

'I'm afraid it is. I messed up the first burglary they asked me to do, well, the burglary went all right but then I got mugged on the way home . . .'

'Nowhere is safe . . .'

'So it seems. And . . . so they changed their demands. They gave me your name and address and told me to steal that stamp and now I messed up this burglary too.'

'I'd say so. You've no idea who the kidnappers are?'

'None. I don't even know if it's one or many. I get phone calls from mobiles, a scratchy voice making demands. I feel just a little under pressure to get this right and I'm constantly getting it wrong. If you don't mind me asking, who would know that you own copies of the Penny Black?'

He chuckled. 'Many, many people. I was quite an active collector and even people I dealt with in the course of my business had often heard that I collected stamps.'

'What was your business, if you don't mind me asking?'

'Not at all. Bunting.'

'Bunting? Is there money in bunting?'

'Certainly. Decorative bunting, corporate bunting, national bunting, international bunting, point of sale . . . And not just bunting, we did banners and flags and flag-poles. Static flagpoles, portable flagpoles, indoor flagpoles, outdoor flagpoles. But after my wife died I sold the business to a big digital printing firm and retired. I'd only kept the business that long for something to get me out of the house. If you get my meaning.'

I said I probably did. 'It was common knowledge then that you owned a Penny Black.'

'Yes, and you'd be surprised how many people thought it was worth a fortune.'

'So, since I failed to steal yours to deliver to the kid-nappers . . . for a couple of hundred I could just go and buy one somewhere? In a stamp shop?'

'Well, it might not be *that* easy. It might take a while to get hold of a copy, especially a decent one, but then I don't suppose you'd care whether it was a fair one or not.'

'Certainly not. I think the kidnapper has proved that he knows even less than I do about stamps. But I would need it quickly. You did mention earlier that you owned more than one copy?'

'I did. Oh, I see . . .'

'Yes. I'm wondering if you would sell me one of them.'

He looked at me for a moment as though the request I had just made was the most insulting thing he'd ever heard, then he suddenly widened his eyes, shrugged his shoulders. 'I don't see why not. How do you propose to pay for it?'

'Would you accept a cheque?'

For some reason he seemed to find this quite amusing. At last he cracked open the gun. He had only loaded one cartridge, which I decided to interpret as a sign of supreme confidence. He stood it on the blotter and leant the gun carefully against the wall before opening a desk drawer and producing a leather-bound book. From its protective pages he pulled a small clear plastic wallet that contained one of the little unprepossessing stamps. He slid it across. This one didn't look quite rectangular.

'It looks wonky,' I complained.

He snorted contemptuously. 'You're not really in a position to be picky about these things. Yes, it's wonky, as you say. They weren't perforated then, so the postmaster would cut the stamp out of the sheet for you and wouldn't always be very accurate about it. It affects the value now, of course, but then nobody much cared, I should think. A carelessly cut Penny Black is the cheapest, and that's what you're getting.'

I dug out my crumpled cheque book from where it had disappeared into the lining of my jacket, straightened it out and asked to borrow a pen. He shook his head, sighed, opened the drawer again and selected a gold ballpoint pen for me. It looked expensive and felt satisfyingly heavy in my hand. It was about to feel even heavier.

I made the cheque out to Rufus Connabear. 'How much do I owe you?' I asked far too lightly.

'Now, let's see. The stamp's not worth all that much, let's say six hundred? No, make it seven hundred.'

'But I thought you said an indifferent copy might be had for a couple of hundred?' I protested.

'That depends where you buy it,' he said pointedly. 'And not if you're in a hurry. And you're in a hurry, Mr Honeysett, wouldn't you agree?'

I admitted it. He slowly and deliberately rubbed his stubbly chin. 'Okay, then there's the break-in. How did you get in here?'

'Through the kitchen. I broke a couple of little panes in the half-glazed door,' I admitted.

'Well, they'll have to be replaced, I'll have to call someone out and you know what they're like when they have to come all the way out to the sticks. Another hundred at least. And then there's the question of disturbing my sleep. Have you *any* idea how difficult sleep is to come by when you get to my age? A good night's sleep ought to be worth at least a couple of hundred. I tell you what, let's make it a nice round figure, a thousand pounds. Yes, I think I could live with that.'

I took a deep breath, opened my mouth, then thought better of it and made out the cheque. When I handed it over he first read it attentively, then dropped it carelessly into the drawer as though it was just any old bit of paper. 'If it bounces, you'll get another chance to admire the James Purdy. Now ...' He checked the paper-thin gold watch on his wrist. 'You've got what you came for, I've got what you owe me and it's now half past four in the morning. I wish you and the poor boy all the luck in the world but I also wish you'd go home now, Mr Honeysett.'

Which I did. With the Penny Black hidden deep in the lining of my jacket I trudged through the night back to the Norton. The rain had lessened but it was still so black out there that having nothing but a tiny LED light to fight off the darkness seemed a little foolhardy. The cloud might not have been but my mood was definitely lifting. I had achieved what I set out to do, even if the manner in which I'd done it was quite unexpected. Connabear was a very cool customer. As he let me out of the house – through the front like a normal person – he'd asked me to let him know about the outcome and I'd promised to do so, even though I had the irksome feeling that, whatever the outcome, he'd probably see it on the front page of his daily paper first.

180

The Norton was not a happy bike when I got to it. I really should have found better cover for it. I had to pump the kick-starter at least twenty times before the engine decided to catch and it backfired every couple of minutes all the way home.

There really was no point in going to bed at this hour. Annis grumbled from deep inside the bed somewhere when I came out of the shower and woke up just long enough to ask 'Did you get it, hon?' and promptly fall asleep again.

With sunrise still an hour away I assembled a celebratory breakfast – French croissant, Irish butter, Scottish smoked salmon and Ethiopian coffee – that appeared to have more air miles than your average prime minister. We ought to do something about this, go completely local, I thought with a guilty sigh, though finding someone who grew coffee in Somerset might present a bit of a problem. But then later that day I would be presented with a challenge that would make growing your own coffee look like child's play.

Chapter Fifteen

Waiting.

Waiting, smoking, making tea and waiting. The four of us around the kitchen table, the Penny Black, Louis's passport to freedom, lying in the centre. Smoking, waiting, coughing, clock-watching.

Waiting, they say, is the worst part of it, but I wasn't so sure. Could no news really be good news? Would there ever again be good news for Jill?

Tim, who had simply out-raced his shadowers in the TT to get here, dabbing a moistened finger at tiny breadcrumbs on the table and absentmindedly transferring them to his lips; Annis turning the empty coffee mug in front of her between thumb and middle finger, round and round; the nameless cat digging his claws into my sweater every time I moved slightly to make myself comfortable on the hard wooden chair; me, tapping a cheap biro against a notepad where I would write down the next set of instructions. Waiting.

The phone trilled. Tim's finger arrested halfway to his mouth, Annis gripped the mug. I reached for the phone and the cat held on tight.

'Honeysett.'

'Did you get it?'

'I did, but it wasn't easy.' I was thinking of the cheque in Connabear's desk.

'Stop whingeing. Okay, sit on it, and make sure it doesn't get nicked. I've got another little task for you.'

'What do you mean, another task? The deal was that I steal the Penny Black and you let Louis go. Stick to our bargain, I fulfilled my side of it, now y—'

'Shut *up*, Honeysett! I told you before, I make the rules and you do as you're told. Now listen carefully. Your next job. Your last job. I really don't think you'll need to write this down, I'm sure you'll remember this. You will nick the little Rodin sculpture from the Victoria Gallery.'

I stood up and my chair skittered noisily across the tiles. The cat jumped off my lap and galloped away. 'Is this a bloody wind-up? You can't be serious.' Worried faces looked up at me. I bit my lip.

'Oh really.' The voice softened dangerously. 'I somehow thought you might say that. So maybe you would like to write this down so you can remind yourself any time you need to: so far the boy's in one piece. If you don't want me to send you bits of the annoying brat in the post to stiffen your resolve, Honeysett, then you'll do as you're told. You got that?' The faint voice had become poisonous with anger. However much I tried I found it impossible to place it. It could be anyone, anywhere. I had always presumed the owner of the voice to be male, but the more I thought about it the less sure I could be even of that.

'Got it,' I confirmed.

'You're the one who fucked up the Telfer thing, so you've got no one to blame but yourself. So here it is: the exhibition is on for another week. That's how long you've got to get the Rodin out and I'll swap you the kid for it.'

'That's what you said when you told me to get the goddamn stamp.'

'I'm not bloody ready for you. You keep that stamp safe, get the Rodin out and by then I'll be ready to do the swap and I'll be out of your hair. I'll be out of everyone's hair and gone for ever.'

'I can't see how it can be done. It's a museum, not some two-bit private gallery. They've got excellent security, I presume.'

'Nothing out of the ordinary. And you have a reputation to live up to, Honeysett. You got into the Telfer place all right. Just a bit careless on the way home, I'd say. You got the Penny Black out of Connabear's place. You'll manage this one too. And if not then you haven't lost a thing, all you have to do is explain to mummy dearest that you fucked up and her boy is toast.'

'Let me talk to the boy. I must have confirmation that he's alive before –'

'You don't need a fucking thing, all you need to do is shut up and deliver. You do as you're told and that'll keep your letter box free of nasty surprises.'

'I won't need any reminders, thanks,' I assured him.

'Good boy. Now get cracking, you got work to do. I'll be watching.' The connection was cut.

'Well? What did he say?' Annis asked impatiently. 'What does he want now?'

I sat down heavily. 'They want me to steal a sculpture in exchange for Louis.'

'What?' Tim and Annis said almost together.

'There's a temporary exhibition at the Victoria Art Gallery. It's got a bronze of a dancer by Rodin in it and they want me to nick it.'

Tim groaned with heavy premonition. 'What next, the crown bleeding jewels?'

'Our last task, apparently. We'll exchange the stamp and sculpture for the boy.'

Annis looked straight into my eyes and gave a minute shake of the head. 'Victoria Art Gallery, that's . . . big.'

'Big mistake, if you ask me,' Tim insisted.

'I told Jill to expect complications and last-minute glitches, but I'm not sure how she'll take a setback like this.'

'I'll tell her, if you like,' offered Annis. 'I'm better with the tears and tissues.'

'Thanks, I appreciate it. Tim?'

Tim had been staring out of the window. 'Hn? What?'

'The Victoria Art Gallery?'

'Oh yes. Utter madness.'

'This isn't Norway, you know, where you can just waltz into a museum and help yourself to the Munch painting of your choice,' Tim complained. 'How often has it been nicked now? Three times? You get the feeling they don't like *The Scream* much. Perhaps we should see if the exhibition goes to Oslo.'

We were leaning on the balustrade that runs along the Grand Parade, occasionally glancing up at the tall façade of the Victoria Gallery, trying to look casual in the annoying drizzle that had returned after a short interlude of broken cloud. Tim thought the guys who had dogged his steps for the past few days had for some reason given up following him. Who they were remained a mystery to him. I had a different theory, but kept it to myself. I thought it much more likely that after having lost Tim twice the incompetent pair had been replaced with a couple of specimens that knew what they were doing. I didn't hold out much hope that we weren't being watched right now.

Below us the river Avon fell noisily over the weir, swollen with days and days of near continuous rain.

'We've got a few days,' I reminded him urgently.

'So you keep saying.' Tim's dense curly hair had plastered itself around his face in the wet, giving him an even hairier appearance. He didn't look happy. 'It's sheer madness. I mean, look at it. The ground floor of the exhibition space is completely shuttered, the only way in is through the front door. So climbing in at street level is hardly going to work, is it?' He poured scorn over my earlier suggestion that we might just smash a window and be in and out before anyone could shout 'Thief!' 'If it was some piddly item in a glass vitrine then you could try a daylight smash and grab with a stolen motorbike waiting outside and take

185

your chances. Drive the bike into the back of a waiting van outside the CCTV area and Robert's your mum's brother. But a statue like that must weigh three stone if you include the plinth. You can carry it but you won't do much running with it. The first civic-minded art lover's going to chuck her brolly between your legs and send you sprawling. Nah, not a chance. Well, let's have a look-see then. But whatever you do don't take your hat off. They're bound to have CCTV in there. Once the Rodin's gone walkies they're going to have a close look at their videos – they probably keep about three weeks' worth before they reuse them – and ours are going to be the two mugs CID will recognize.' He forced a baseball cap on his own woolly curls. 'Right, put on your reading glasses as well.'

I hesitated. 'How d'you know I have reading glasses?' I'd only got my first pair recently and was still a bit shy about it.

'Annis told me. Let's see 'em.'

'The traitor.' I took the glasses from their case and stuck them on my nose. I'd gone for the old-fashioned horn-rimmed specs. Well, it had worked for Cary Grant.

'Annis was right, they do make you look intelligent. Okay, let's go in.'

We crossed the road, dodging traffic, and entered through the heavy double doors. As soon as I stood in the foyer I felt like a schoolboy planning a prank. Tim pushed through the next set of double doors and into the downstairs exhibition space. I sauntered in after him, trying to look as though I wasn't part of a double act. Immediately to the left was a counter where catalogues, slides and postcards could be bought. Thankfully the blue-suited, tightly permed woman behind the counter didn't give us a second look. Along with half the planet she was too busy staring at a computer screen. There were a fair number of people walking about, silently or talking in low voices. I tried to appear casual and bored but failed miserably. The Rodin bronze in the centre of the room was all I saw. I couldn't take my eyes off it. It seemed to get bigger the longer I looked at it. We were going to steal that? A limb at a time perhaps . . .

It was a male dancer, nude, yet curiously sexless. He stood on tiptoe on his right leg, with his other leg improbably high in the air, the right hand holding the foot; the left arm was flung into the air and his gaze appeared to be following that movement. I tried to imagine making that move and the thought alone made my tendons ache. The dancer's face was deeply serious, which was hardly surprising; the model must have been trussed up like an oven-ready broiler to be able to hold that pose and it must have hurt like hell. It was simply called *The Dancer* and on loan from the foolhardy Rodin Museum in Paris. The bronze was very dark, nearly black in places, and looked extremely heavy. The foot of the figure that was in touch with the ground grew out of a highly polished mahogany base and the whole thing stood on a standard painted museum plinth in the centre of the long room. Several spotlights were trained on it from the gantry above but no particular security features were visible anywhere. It was a tantalizing twelve yards from the door which led to the foyer and the street. Maybe on a couple of skateboards . . . a distraction burglary . . . I fished out my mobile and took pictures from all angles. Photography was not allowed inside the museum, it said so everywhere, but there were enough people making enough noise to mask the annoying little 'ketchee' sound the camera made.

I tore myself away and looked around. The windows in this gallery were blocked off with advertising for this and forthcoming exhibitions. I took pictures of the windows and the position of the cameras. Not that I really thought we could smash our way in and out of the windows. As Tim said, this wasn't Norway and the people living on the other side of Bridge Street might show some curiosity if we tried it. I took a turn round the entire exhibition again and when I'd completed it there was no sign of Tim. It was hard not to look straight into the CCTV cameras once I had spotted them. I walked out into the foyer with its chequerboard marble floor and busts of local worthies and climbed the stairs, past some well-painted trifles. On the first floor another chequerboard foyer gave room to two tables, six black armchairs, a pour-it-yourself coffee bar and three white marble sculptures of women in robes holding aloft meaningful stuff. I turned my back on the marble horrors and walked into the permanent exhibition. Another information desk with another blue-suited attendant, a middle-aged man this time. He looked up but his gaze didn't linger. Tim was there, slumped on the green upholstery of a bench, looking half asleep. I ignored him and wandered about. There was only one other person in the upstairs gallery, a bloke in a Barbour and wide-brimmed hat who was studying a large Gainsborough. I took out my mobile. It was deadly quiet in here. I'd have to mask the sound of the camera. I sneezed unconvincingly while surreptitiously snapping the layout of the gallery. I sneezed up at the enormous skylights. I sneezed at the overhead gantry. I sneezed at the security cameras. The attendant looked up briefly, then returned to whatever he was reading with just the tiniest twitch of the eyebrows. As I walked out Tim came alive and followed me down the echoing stairs and out into the rain.

'Couldn't you have tried coughing? That was the most unconvincing sneezing fit I ever heard.' He stuffed his baseball cap in his pocket and led me to the right, past a takeaway pizza joint and into the shelter of the covered market that adjoined the museum. 'This whole thing is a nightmare and I need a mug of tea. It's your round,' he added as he dropped on to a free chair in the little market café. I queued up and eventually got us two mugs of beige liquid from a tiny serving hatch. I'd forgotten all about this place. Time had forgotten all about this place. Since about 1959. We sat opposite each other at a narrow table and blew on our steaming mugs.

'Told you taking pictures was a bad idea,' I moaned.

'Taking pic . . .?' He waved his hands helplessly in the airspace between us. 'The whole *thing* is a bad idea, Chris. A stupendously bad idea. A fantastically idiotic plan. A desperate, hare-brained venture. And can I just remind you here . . .' He looked around at the shoppers eating and drinking at other tables and lowered his voice to a conspiratorial hiss which I was sure carried further than his normal volume. 'May I remind you that I've been going straight for several years now, except for the stuff I do for you, of course. And I've never been charged, never even been nicked, I have no criminal record whatsoever. But there just happens to be a string of unsolved safe breakings out there and if I get caught in this madness and they fingerprint me . . .'

'You left fingerprints?' I asked indignantly.

He squirmed in his seat and shrugged. 'Might have done . . . And anyway they've got DNA sampling and all sorts of new technologies. You so much as *sneeze* at a crime scene and they can identify you,' he said meaningfully. 'I had a good look at the place just now and I tell you, robbing the museum is complete lunacy, nobody in their right mind would do it.' He took a gulp of tea. 'I suppose that's why their security is twenty years out of date.'

I returned from the lands of doom and gloom. 'You mean . . .'

'I mean nothing, you can stow that silly grin. Yes, we might be able to get in and, yes, we might even get our hands on *The Dancer*. But even twenty years ago alarms meant big and nasty noises and look at where we are: six hundred yards from the police station, smack in the centre of town . . . I bet you my collapsible crowbar they've got silent alarms in there but the moment you trigger it uniforms will gleefully pile into cars in Manvers Street and hare across here to relieve us of the Rodin and our liberty.'

'So don't trigger it. You're the expert.'

'I am. And I say it again: I don't like it. Is there no other way? I mean, are you absolutely sure we can't go to the police behind Jill's back?' He kept his eyes on his mug of tea while he waited for my answer. It was my decision, he had nothing to do with it. You're the boss. And he was right.

'Pretty sure. I think they're local, that's why they picked on us and the police always leak like a sieve, someone'll get a whiff of something. For instance, if suddenly all leave is cancelled, which is what would probably happen, that affects a lot of people *and* their friends *and* relatives and even if they didn't know what it was all about, anyone with their ear to the ground will know something's afoot. And I think the guy has demonstrated that he knows what we're up to. Not to mention you being followed.' Something I didn't tell Tim was the spooky feeling I had that we were being watched even now. *I'll be watching.* I looked around. Sometimes the safest place was in a crowd. Nothing but shoppers everywhere, and no one I'd seen more than once today. I shrugged deeper into my jacket.

'Okay,' agreed Tim. 'You might be right but that doesn't mean I have to like it. Even in my maddest days I wouldn't have considered a scheme like this. Clearing out someone's safe at a private house or an office is one thing. But *robbing a museum* makes front page headlines. Do you realize that it'll get flashed round the world? That the French are going to send Froggy Fuzz across the Channel to catch the guys who stole their beloved Rodin dancer? And you definitely do not want to fall into *their* hands, they have nasty habits by all accounts. Unlike us Brits the French take their art seriously. We could all end up in a chain gang breaking rocks in the Auvergne for thirty years. And I still need a reality check: am I really discussing this with Chris Honeysett, the painter, who hates art theft more than anything?'

'Yeah, well,' I said lightly, 'sculpture is just what you

190

bump into when you step back to admire a painting. And it was a French geezer who said that.'

'That's all right then,' Tim said and rolled his eyes heavenward. 'And here's another thing: what's it for? You can't sell these kind of things, can you? I mean everyone will know it's nicked. So what's the point?'

'No, you can't sell it on the open market because it's too high profile and you'll never be able to stick it in your front room. Unless it's already paid for, of course,' I mused.

'Stolen to order, you mean.'

'Stolen to order and destined for some mafioso dacha in Russia or Turkey. To go with the 7-series Beemer in the garage that was probably nicked from a supermarket car park in Hull and driven on to the ferry to Holland before the owner even got his shopping through the check-out. And how damn clever to get idiots like us to do the dirty work. I bet you my spectacles they got the idea from the Japanese. Last year someone wanted to extract a ransom from a Japanese businessman but they didn't abduct one of his family, they took the son of his *chauffeur*. Now there's obligation for you.'

'Did he pay up?'

'No, he got a new chauffeur. What do you think? How could he not pay up? Who would have done business with him if he hadn't? How could he have lived with himself, for that matter?'

And 'living with it' would come into it for us too. My Accumulated Guilt Quotient was already going through the roof. Louis had been snatched to get to me, to buy the services of Aqua Investigations. Whoever he was, he knew me, at least by reputation. I myself knew plenty of unsavoury individuals and had paraded their mental mug shots through my private gallery but no one stood out as an obvious choice for the face behind the voice. His voice reminded me of nobody and of nothing, it was too distorted over the phone, and if I really had met the bastard before, then that was deliberate.

191

The elderly couple at the table next to ours left and their place was taken by a man wearing a waxed jacket and a matching wide-brimmed hat. I looked across at his face. Around fifty and quite a bit paler than a man ought to be. I'd never seen him before, yet I began to feel uneasy and I motioned Tim with my head: let's get out of here. As we rounded the corner towards the exit I looked back. The man was staring straight at me and from a distance of twenty-five feet our eyes met briefly, then his gaze slid over and off me, not interested, turning instead to the young boy carrying two steaming mugs towards his table.

'What's the matter?' Tim wanted to know.

'Nothing, paranoia's setting in, that's all.'

We had deliberately exited at the back of the market into the courtyard. The old Empire Hotel and the old police station – now thankfully Browns restaurant – the Guildhall and the covered market all backed on to what was now used as a private car park for council workers, restaurateurs and market traders. A man in dirty chef's whites puffed at a small cigar by a door at the back of the Empire, a seagull flew over and scored a direct hit on a shiny blue Jaguar.

Tim sniffed the air and pulled a face. 'This really stinks. There might be a way into the museum from back here but it would mean one hell of a climb.' He turned his back on me and began walking away through the narrow passage between the hotel and the market building.

I went after him and tried to find something optimistic to say. 'If a couple of guys with a ladder can nick a Munch from a museum in Norway then surely we must be able to pinch an itsy-bitsy Rodin in Bath.'

He wasn't having any of it. 'They do things differently in Norway. Must be the long winters. Or perhaps it's the terrible folk music, but this is different. We can't even reconnoitre the place properly. We won't know if there's a way in until we get there and getting there is probably just as risky as breaking in is going to be. I really don't like this,

Chris. I think it's one break-in too far. The chances of getting away with it are minimal – and I just mean away from the *museum*, there's no way we won't get nicked for it later. And don't look at me like that.' Apparently I was looking at him like that. 'It's a lot to ask for a kid you never even met.'

I had never seen Tim less enthusiastic about any scheme I had proposed but I knew that without him my chances were nil. 'If I didn't know you any better I'd say you didn't want to do it.'

'Ha-bloody-ha. I'll have a think but that doesn't mean I'll do it. Now I'm going to work.'

'To work on what?' I asked, too wrapped up in my own problems to function entirely in the real world.

'Work. To *work*, Chris. I do have a job at the uni, you know, the kind that pays my bills. But I might be able to get away early today. I'll come round and we'll have another talk then.'

I opened my mouth for an answer but he was already dashing across the street through the traffic, waving without looking back.

Chapter Sixteen

October rain, what can you do with it? Shopping. I'd picked up a couple of ambitiously priced bottles of French red with deliberate absentmindedness then found myself contemplating the pretend summer of the supermarket. Time-warped summer vegetables from Spanish poly-tunnels and optimistic little salmon kebabs that really belonged on a sizzling barbecue couldn't disguise the fact that people were leaving puddles of cold rainwater on the floor. I heroically turned my back on such anodyne fare, though happily bought the wine, left the supermarket and crossed to Green Street where I picked up a dozen venison sausages at the butcher's. Having strapped my purchases to the back of the bike I puttered through the drizzle to Larkhall where at Tony's greengrocer's things were more in sync with the season. I stocked up with a string of shiny red onions, plenty of dirty carrots, knobbly potatoes, knobblier horseradish and an armful of ruby chard. By the time I pootled out of Larkhall the Norton had taken on the air of a French bicycle wobbling home from the market, with half a kitchen garden tied to the tank. I parked the bike in the muddy yard close to the house, untied my pur-chases and splashed dirt all the way from the front door through to the kitchen, plonking my purchases on the table where they joyfully tumbled from their bags. Yet the unhappy atmosphere seemed evident in the very pine-fragranced and lemon-freshened air. Deep in my irrational self I resented Jill and her son and their predicament, I resented all of it as an imposition and intrusion into my happy-go-lucky lifestyle. Never mind Tim's reluctance, I couldn't *wait* to break into the museum and swipe the silly little Rodin and give it to the bastard who'd snatched Louis.

Out of nowhere the nameless cat jumped on to the table and meowed in a low, self-possessed fashion at my purchases. Zabaglione, I thought, then dismissed it instantly. They'd end up calling him Zab.

I even resented Louis for getting himself kidnapped, the silly brat, although I'd never met the poor kid. I wanted my life back. I wanted to be back at the moment before Annis had handed me the phone, I wanted to be back before the storm when I was happily painting in a studio with a roof on it. The cat pawed at the bags. A horseradish root rolled off the table. I kicked it hard across the kitchen floor like a moody teenager who had been grounded: it's not *fair*. The cat jumped off the table and galloped out of the kitchen. Yeah, that's right, make me feel guilty. Very unlike a moody teenager I crawled around on all fours until I'd found where the damn root had ricocheted and washed it carefully. Then I went and dropped my filthy boots on to a newspaper in the hall where I should have left them in the first place and decided to shower my irritations away. When I got to my bedroom I could hear someone else had got to the en suite before me and my mood lifted instantly. I pulled off my clothes where I stood and dropped them on to the floor, then walked into the steamed-up bathroom. Annis's silhouette moved sinuously behind the glass of the shower cubicle. This was one bathroom scene I was determined would have a good ending. I rapped against the glass with my rings. She slid open the door and pointed her breasts at me, in happy salutation, I hoped.

'Room for a small one?' I asked. The old ones are still the best, apparently.

'Not all that small either.' She grabbed me and gently pulled me into the cubicle. 'I was just going to come out,' she said.

'I was just going to come in,' I pointed out.

'Oh all right then.'

I slid the door shut. The cubicle was ridiculously small and steamy. Annis started soaping me all over but dropped the bar just as she got to the interesting bits, which was a right shame. It slithered into the drain hole and half blocked it. There was simply not enough room to bend down and retrieve it. While the water slowly rose we arranged ourselves first this way, then that. There were bits I was desperate to kiss but couldn't hope to reach without dislocating a limb. I accidentally nudged the mixer with my elbow and the water turned to skin-blistering hot. Annis screamed and I fiddled it back to normal. A few minutes later her knee nudged it into the arctic zone. This time we both screamed.

Eventually we tumbled out of the cubicle with the firm intention of getting into bed but didn't quite make it and somehow ended up on the carpet. Annis managed to scrabble the duvet down on us from the bed while I was otherwise engaged.

'I do love you, Annis,' I panted. And meant it.

'Doesn't count.'

'Eh?'

'Things men say when they're shagging. Blokes say all sorts of stuff. Means nothing.'

'Doesn't, huh?' I didn't really have the breath to argue with the woman. The house phone rang for a while, the old 1940s dialler by the bed making a right racket. We ignored it.

'I love you too, Honeypot. Turn sideways, hon, something's digging into my back.'

'Meaningless drivel. You were lying on my mobile.' I picked it up and threw it on to the bed. It started to ring. Tough.

I pulled the duvet off us again and imagined I could see steam rising from her shimmering, shuddering flanks. Annis's eyes flickered and tilted, always a happy sign, then she buried her face in my shoulder and held tight.

The phone stopped chiming at last. The cat came padding up the duvet and sniffed, then put a possessive paw on Annis's trembling thigh.

'I'm hungry. We could call him Bhaji,' she said, propping herself on one elbow and scratching him under his chin.

'Absolutely not,' I said and slipped away.

When I emerged from my third shower of the day Annis had moved to the bed. So had the cat. Both of them were asleep. I turfed out the cat. 'Don't even think about it,' I informed him. He gave a complaining meow, padded to a pile of Annis's discarded clothes and started nesting procedures there. I turned off my mobile, pulled the plug on the dialler phone and slid under the cover.

When I woke again to the distant ringing of the house phone downstairs I noticed the light had changed. I turned on my mobile and checked the time. Ten to six. Annis turned out to be awake too. 'I'm not moving until I can smell supper, I am famished. Go cook,' she said and pushed me out of bed. I reconnected the dialler phone but the caller had hung up. Tough.

In the kitchen I started with the horseradish. I peeled and grated the knobbly root until I went blind with tears. The entire kitchen had filled with the sharp, energizing smell. Even mixed with thick cream and seasoned it was still strong enough to make your scalp tingle.

To make the red onion gravy I sliced them finely and then chucked them in a pan with oil and butter and sautéed them on the lowest possible heat for what seemed like forever. Long enough, anyway, to stir them absent-mindedly, stare through the window into the rain and wonder how we might get into the museum, how we might get away with the Rodin and how I could make sure that I got Louis in exchange for it. So far I had only vague

197

notions of 'breaking in', 'getting away' and then 'not giv-ing it to them until I had the boy'. It hardly amounted to anything resembling a plan.

I added a spoonful of redcurrant jelly to the pan and once it had dissolved deglazed with a generous slug of port and kept stirring.

Having recently lost my only shotgun to a gangster and having had my handgun confiscated by the fuzz I also felt quite under-equipped in the violence department. Shotguns and kidnapped boys didn't really mix, I quickly told myself, since they were hardly precision weapons, and the Webley .38, while satisfyingly noisy, was about as reliable as everything else made in the 1930s.

My mobile gurgled: text message. *U there? Open door.* From Tim. What was wrong with the bell pull? Nothing, as far as I could see when I got to the hall. I yanked open the door. More rain.

Tim's TT was parked next to the Landy. The Norton was lying in the mud, on its side. Tim was lying in a puddle next to it, also on his side, clutching his mobile. I squelched over to help him up.

'What are you doing down there? Want a hand up?'

'I can't get up, my back's gone,' he said in a pathetic voice I'd never heard him use before.

I knelt down next to him. 'What happened, Bigfoot?'

'Your bloody bike must have slipped off its stand in the mud. I tried to bloody lift it and halfway up my bloody back went bang. And I mean: bang, I think I heard it go. Don't touch me, I think I'd scream. How often have I told you the bloody yard needs recobbling or tarmack-ing or something. It would never have happened if you hadn't neglected this damn place for God knows how many years.'

'You're so right, Tim. And it was very kind of you to try and pick up the Norton but also very stupid, it weighs an absolute ton.' It was raining hard now and even I was getting soaked. 'Can you move at all?'

'It hurts so much when I do, I think I'd rather not, thanks.'

'Okay. In that case, can I bring you out a cup of coffee or something?'

'Ha-bloody-ha. Got any better ideas?'

'No, but Annis might. I'll go and fetch her. We'll find a solution somehow. Back in a tick. Honest.' I ran inside, shouted Annis awake, grabbed my raincoat and an umbrella and ran back out. I laid the coat over him and arranged the brolly so it covered his head.

'This is your solution? Cosy. Please don't bring me a bowl of chicken broth, Chris.'

'The thought never crossed my mind,' I lied. Ungrateful sod.

He groaned, shivering. Half of his face was caked with mud and he was as wet as though he had come down the mill race. At last Annis splashed over. I left Tim to explain while I followed a sudden inspiration and rummaged in a shed until I found a strong plank of wood, about five foot long and twelve inches wide. Together and on the count of three we managed to pull him on to it. It looked precarious but with much groaning, grumbling and several very bad words we managed to carry him inside and deposit him on the carpet between the sofas and the fireplace.

I lit the fire while Annis carefully stripped the wet clothes off him despite his howls of pain. We got him on to some folded blankets and under a duvet at last. Then I called Dr Marland, one of the few practitioners I knew who still did house calls, though she travelled with a minder after dark and charged accordingly.

'Where's the pain?' she wanted to know.

'Where exactly does it hurt?' I asked Tim.

'Lower back. And my left leg, behind the knee. I think I must have torn something there.' I relayed all that.

'Sounds very much like a prolapsed disc. Keep him where he is, in a position most comfortable to him, try it on the side with a cushion between his knees. Give him some painkillers and put a hot water bottle against his lumbar region.'

'Okay. How long will you be?'

'How long will I be? I'm not coming out for something like that and anyway, he's not one of my patients! Get him to his own doctor when he gets some movement back. But he'll need a physio more than a doctor.'

'Why does his leg hurt though?'

'That happens when the prolapse is to the back and the side, it presses on a nerve root. Okay? Bye.'

'Wait! Just one more question: how long before he's okay again?'

'Hard to say. Couple of weeks' rest, then a programme of exercises to strengthen the lower back. His back will be vulnerable for a few months. But the physio will explain all that. Goodbye, Mr Honeysett.'

And that, as they say, was that. I might not have had much of a plan for getting at the Rodin but the little I did have was lying groaning on my sitting-room floor with a slipped disc and would probably remain there for quite a while. I must have looked at Tim with a less than charitable expression because he started to protest.

'I know what you're thinking, Honeypot, but I didn't exactly do it on purpose. And it happened while I was trying to rescue the Norton from the mud, so you can stop scowling at me. I think those guys have stopped following me, I didn't notice anything suspicious today. But better hide the TT somewhere in your outbuildings just in case. Don't want it scratched though. What's that weird smell all of a sudden?'

I sniffed. 'Charred onions. Special recipe.'

An additional layer of gloom settled on my mind as I scraped the onions into the bin and started over again, wielding the knife perhaps just a fraction more ferociously than before. I started off the sausages at the same time and put the water on for the spuds.

Annis came in from ministering to the safe breaker on the floor. 'What now?'

'You can wash the chard and peel the potatoes.'

'That's not what I meant.'

'I know it wasn't but do it anyway. According to Dr Marland he won't be breaking into museums for a while.'

'She said that?'

'Her very words.' It also struck me that he might be unable to perform other acrobatics for quite a while but the unexpected pleasure I derived from the thought instantly made me feel guilty again.

'It's you and me then,' she said, taking the peeler to the first pink-eyed tuber.

'Yes,' I said, looking across at her. 'Just you and me. You and me making love in the shower, you and me cooking a meal together, you and me stealing sculpture from the gallery. The simple, everyday stuff of mature relationships. Got any ideas?'

'One or two.' Annis grinned idiotically as she whittled the potato in her hand.

'Okay, I'll leave it all with you then, shall I?'

I pretty much did exactly that for the rest of the day. Annis looked after Jill and she looked after Tim. She got some painkillers into him and tucked him up with piles of cushions. She even ladled the mash, laced with fresh horse-radish, the venison sausages drowned in onion gravy and the steamed chard into him because sitting up to use knife and fork was still out of the question. This humiliating complication alone convinced me that the man was in serious pain. Later she went up to the studio and worked by the cool light of a couple of daylight bulbs until the wind picked up again and the noisy snapping of the tarpaulin drove her back to the house. I couldn't even think of lifting a paint brush. Annis found me in bed, trying to control my anxieties with a hefty nightcap of Laphroaig. I watched her pull her clothes off and throw them into a pile under the window while she complained away about the draught

201

and noise in the studio. I listened to her hum some atonal nonsense under the shower and admired her taut body as she towelled her strawberry hair by the bed. I simply couldn't *believe* I had never told her that I loved her.

She bounced into bed, took the Laphroaig from me and emptied the glass down her throat. 'Eeeeyuch! Do you know,' she asked as she made her head comfortable on my chest, 'what I like so much about making love in the afternoon?'

'Do tell me.'

'If you play your cards right you get to do it again in the evening.'

The sky was a little brighter when I brought Tim a cup of coffee in the morning.

He declared that his back had improved a bit overnight but soon disillusioned me again by explaining that 'improvement' meant he no longer had shooting pains in the back of the knee, not that he was about to clamber up the façade of the Victoria Art Gallery. Which made me realize once and for all that it would be me climbing into the museum, and since we had already ruled out getting in on the ground floor that meant I would have to acquire some cat-burglary skills pronto. And did I mention I'm not very good with heights?

I discussed it with Tim while we ate one of our favourite breakfasts of scrambled eggs with coriander leaf and huge dollops of brinjal pickle. 'What about Annis?' he asked.

'She's worse than me. She's fearless on the flat but standing on a thick carpet gives her vertigo.'

'You really are a pair of sissies. You'll just have to find a way then. The back of the building is the obvious way in. There's no security guard at night, which should tell you something.'

'Like what?'

'That they think nobody would be crazy enough to try it

right under the noses of all the cops in Bath. Getting out and away will definitely be the challenge. You'd better come up with something soon, you've only got a few days until the exhibition ends. And you'll have to find a get-away car in good time and stash it somewhere safe, not around here where Needham's boys are likely to turn up for a bit of harassment. If you buy the car, or bike if you prefer, and they clock you on CCTV then they'll trace it back to you, so you'll have to steal it. And then you'll need false plates. Not so easy any more but you can still get them off the internet. Make sure they'll exactly match the year of the car or you'll not get very far, the cops are fiendishly clued up on anything to do with plates.'

This was something else I hadn't quite thought through. It would hardly do to turn up in one of our own cars and drive through the thickly surveillanced centre, if we ever got to drive away at all. 'We could of course hold up the place and try and get it that way . . .' I suggested half-heartedly.

'Now you're really talking out of your arse. You'd be a little old man before they let you out of jail again. Even if you used a toy gun. I can recommend it only as the best way of getting yourself shot full of holes you don't require. Think of something else,' he said vehemently.

'I didn't really mean it,' I assured him.

'Glad to hear it, Honeypot. I certainly wouldn't let you involve Annis in a hare-brained scheme like that.'

'Let me?' Something about the way he implied that he had any say in what Annis did or did not suddenly got my goat. 'I doubt you'd have much say in the matter. If she decided to do it then I'd like to see you try and stop her,' my goat said sharply.

'You're probably right,' he admitted. 'She's got too much sense to get involved in anything too crazy anyway. Mind you,' he added after a moment's thought, 'she hangs out with us two idiots and how sensible is that?'

* * *

Later that same morning I was back on Grand Parade across from the entrance to Victoria Gallery in search of a way inside that wouldn't end in one of the many disasters Tim had lugubriously predicted. Mindful of the CCTV cameras at every street corner I had left the Norton out of sight in Caxton Court under the bridge and had picked up a different hat in a charity shop on Argyll Street. Looking up at the façade should have been enough to convince me to just keep on walking until I found a friendly policeman to unburden myself to. Yet there was something else apart from my feelings of obligation and guilt that made me amble along in the weak October sunshine and squint up at the rooflines of the adjoining buildings. If I was honest the answer probably lay in a surfeit of Cary Grant movies in my youth. Somewhere the task of getting in and out of a museum at night – and it would have to be night – struck a hopelessly romantic chord inside me. Thoughtfully puffing on a cigarette I ambled along and mingled with the few tourists who had braved this year's wash-out autumn to admire Pulteney Bridge, Grand Parade with its colonnaded walkway underneath and the river Avon roaring over the horseshoe weir below. For the first time in years the river was in such spate that all boat tours had to be cancelled as simply too dangerous.

I took the cameras more seriously now and tried to behave like everyone around me. On a security tape I would look just like any other visitor, taking only a passing interest in the architecture of the museum and walking in that curiously uncoordinated, aimless way we all acquire as soon as we turn tourist. After ten minutes of hanging around the balustrade on the parade I was none the wiser. I crossed to the other side and walked past the pizza joint, the ladies' fashion shop, the entrance to the market and the Turkish restaurant. At the corner of Boat Stall Lane was a pub called the Rummer. I was going to stroll past slowly and take only a casual interest in the lane which leads to the car park at the back, but the view that presented itself was so arresting that I stood stock still and stared, possibly with my mouth open. There were no cars in the car park. Instead, a sweating and shouting tribe of workmen were erecting an enormous scaffold covering the entire width of the Guildhall building. Another set of men were just manoeuvring a couple of blue and white portable toilets against the back of the covered market. Three huge lorries seemed to fill the entire place.

I forced myself to walk on, past the Empire Hotel. My first feeling had been one of panic but gradually I realized that scaffolding on the building next door might turn out to be nearly as good as a ladder on the museum wall itself. I walked around the hotel until I came to the porte cochère between Browns and the Empire Hotel. And strolled in. For a while nobody took much notice, they were simply too busy to care. There was a definite hierarchy and pecking order among them. Being actually on the scaffold, even ten feet off the ground, which was how high it reached at the moment, obviously allowed you to shout instruction and insult at the mortals on the ground, whose names appeared to be either Moron or Fuckwit. I circled round between lorries to the right, trying to look like I had some business there. I read the writing on the side of the nearest cab with joy. These were proper roofers, not just a scaffolding firm. The scaffolding would go all the way to the top to allow access to the roof and cupola, where the storm probably did some damage. Another hour or so, I noted with satisfaction, and the only two security cameras would disappear behind the scaffold. It was practically a foregone conclusion that the people responsible for security here would be too lethargic to do anything about it ('Hey, it's only for a few days').

I stood near the back door of Garfunkel's kitchen and let my eyes run along the roofline of the covered market. I imagined myself scaling the scaffold, then following the skyline to the roof of the museum, where sooner or later I'd be confronted with the large skylights of the upstairs

205

gallery ... My stomach contracted at the thought. I grabbed the cast-iron railings harder and looked down into what at first sight seemed to be just the basement courtyard of the hotel. Then my eyes travelled further along and down, past silver beer kegs, empty gas cylinders and stacks of plastic crates towards a small cast-iron gate. All I could see beyond it was the swollen turmoil of the river Avon. As I walked back a few paces towards the porte cochère it became clear that this courtyard was in fact an ancient slipway leading in a steady slope from the yard towards the water. At this end it was barred by a larger gate. I tested it casually. It was locked and looked ancient but was obviously in use, so how difficult could it be?

One of the scaffolders shouted and pointed. 'S'cuse me, mate, but you can't hang round here, this lorry's about to move back, all right?' I just nodded and walked off as the lorry started bleeping his reverse warning, not wanting to give anyone cause to remember me. I left through Boat Stall Lane and without a look back crossed the river via Pulteney Bridge, then clattered down the steps which led to the walkway and the imaginatively named Riverside Café overlooking the weir. I stuck my head through the door and ordered Earl Grey from an aproned waitress, then sat outside in the thin sunlight and peered across at the colonnaded walkway underneath Grand Parade. Even from here I could clearly see the wrought-iron door of the slipway leading on to it. There wasn't a camera in sight. Access to this colonnaded walkway used to be from Parade Gardens, the little park bordered by the river. Now the walkway was closed to the public, probably to stop kids jumping into the river there or because of ageing masonry. Between the columns ran wrought-iron railings, easily surmounted, and below them an overgrown drop of twelve or fifteen feet down to the water, which would seem like nothing to a man who had just come down from the roof of the museum carrying a Rodin bronze on his back.

It was obvious. I didn't need a getaway car at all. What I needed was a boat.

The Earl Grey arrived. I slipped a slice of lemon into my tea and raised my cup in salute to the river. There was only a small problem: the Avon was in such spate that all river traffic had been banned until further notice, so it would be complete madness trying to get the sculpture out that way.

Perfect.

Chapter Seventeen

Jake's place had to be one of the few locations where the exhaust note of the Norton remained unremarked upon. At the moment it even remained unnoticed. Somewhere deep inside the workshop an engine was revving freely, unencumbered by any kind of exhaust system at all, judging by the deep shockwaves of sound, and somewhere else the high-pitched scream of an angle-grinder getting purchase on something big and hollow added the top notes to this rhapsody of toil. I left the bike at the entrance and picked my way through the broken landscape of automotive history in the yard.

Originally Jake had bought the farm to breed ponies, but the venture had failed. After that he had changed direction and turned his first love, classic cars, into a thriving business. Restoring and maintaining vintage machinery – as long as it was British and had an internal combustion engine – had made him a modest fortune. You wouldn't know it though, because the place looked like a scrapyard, with bits of pre-1970s cars and vans lying everywhere, some under tarpaulins, some protected by makeshift roofs, some taking a well-earned rest in the weeds. Despite his financial success Jake was still doing most of the work himself, with only one or two assistants, because that was what he enjoyed. At this very moment he was listening with rapt attention, oily bald head cocked to one side, to the unimaginable racket coming from a huge lump of an engine sitting on a workbench in the main workshop, worrying the accelerator with his thumb. He nodded at me and continued his revving, so I sat on an oil drum outside until he had heard enough of the testosterone symphony and joined me, carrying two tin mugs of tea made with a blow torch.

'Still on two wheels, then?' he asked.

'Yes, I'm beginning to get a taste for it. But it's not always practical.' I blew on my superheated tea. 'But then neither is any of this stuff.'

'No, but it nourishes the soul.'

I had to agree. Something went wrong with car design after the 1960s. Too many buttons, for a start. I looked about me. 'Talking of poor souls, is my DS still around?'

'Most of it went for scrap, along with other useless crap I had hanging around.'

'Do I owe you?'

'I made a few pennies on engine bits, so no, we're quits.'

'That's good, because I've a favour to ask.'

'You surprise me.'

'Do you remember, a few years ago, you went on this trip down some wild Welsh river in a snazzy motorized dinghy with your then girlfriend?'

'I haven't got Alzheimer's yet,' he bristled.

'And she fell out the boat and it took you half an hour to notice and when you finally went back to pull her out she dumped you?'

'Your point being?'

'Still got the boat?'

He scratched his scarred scalp with oil-blackened nails. 'Now there's a good question. I know where I've got the engine – never mislaid an engine yet – but the inflatable ... It'll be somewhere, sure, but it might have,' he made a sweeping gesture at the farmhouse and the endless outbuildings, 'some stuff on top of it, if you know what I mean.'

I knew exactly what he meant, since I used the same filing system at Mill House.

'What you want it for, messing about on the river? Just remember what happened with Sally, is all I say.'

'She did marry you in the end.'

He sniffed. 'Yeah, but she still mentions it.'

'I need it for a job. A tricky one.'

'I won't ask then. When d'you want it for?'

'Yesterday.'

'There's a surprise. I'm busy now, but I'll see what I can do later,' he promised.

Leaving the matter in Jake's oil-stained hands I rode back towards Bath. The rain had returned in the shape of a depressing drizzle that rendered me half blind trying to peer through the goggles and slowly soaking me, making me seriously consider such stylistic horrors as rainproof trousers. Before I could skid too far down that dangerous road to sartorial oblivion a sudden impulse made me go past my turn-off for home and rumble on through the misty afternoon to the Lam Valley.

Needham hadn't bothered pulling me in again because, as he had hinted when he came to inspect my pantry, the latest thinking was that just possibly I might have nothing to do with the killing and it had all been some weird coincidence that Albert Barrington had exhaled his soul in the back of my car. But even at my age I still had some problems believing in a random universe where all was coincidence and meaning a matter of personal choice. I sensed method behind all this. Unfortunately it wasn't my own. At the moment my own style of detection resembled blind man's buff more than any methodical investigation, but then I was just a little distracted by other events. I didn't believe in the joyrider theory of how the DS had landed in Lam Valley. Whoever had nicked my car that night hadn't gone very far in it. It was perhaps less than ten minutes' careful drive from Larkhall to Blackfield's meadow, or a five-minute drive at the kind of speed that makes you crash through a five-bar gate and carry on another forty yards up the hill. Not much joy, anyway.

Someone had found my keys where I had dropped them that night in my inebriated state or, much more likely, had swiped them off the table at the Rosie while I was away from it, checking out Mr Lane's reading material.

There was now no evidence left that my DS and the late Mr Barrington had ever met in the dank little meadow. Even the smashed five-bar gate had been completely cleared away and replaced with a lot of nothingness. As I came up to it I slowed and stopped. The sudden fall in exhaust noise allowed me to catch a similar noise behind me, like an unwholesome echo. I looked swiftly around and just saw the top of a motorcycle helmet disappear over the rise as someone frantically turned their bike around and hared back in the direction from which I'd come. I heard the bike's engine accelerate away fast. If I didn't catch him last time then I wouldn't catch him this time. The memory of missing Jack Fryer's enormous tractor by a couple of inches as I screamed round the bend was still fresh enough in my mind not to need refreshing.

The Norton's noise made a handful of sheep bolt from where they'd been grazing near the lane as I grabbed a handful of throttle and accelerated away. I crossed by the little bridge and turned towards Spring Farm. This time I found the gates closed but I could see light behind the kitchen window. I leaned the bike against the fence and opened the gate. Unfortunately, between me and the front door of the farmhouse stood a large, dark, wet dog who seemed to be as mesmerized by my every move as I was by his. Where had he suddenly come from? He was huge and he sniffed in my direction. Why did people always let monsters like this run around, free to eat harmless visitors? And why had I yet to see a farm with a doorbell? And why was I so scared of dogs? I made a tentative step forward. The dog barked and ran straight at me. His rank smell travelled before him. I stopped and stood, petrified, while the huge wet thing sniffed my boots, my legs, then stuck his snout firmly into my crutch. What was all that doggy

211

sniffing supposed to be for anyway? What if he decided he didn't like the smell of me? What if he decided he liked it lots and lots?

A face appeared briefly at the window. A few moments later the door opened and Brian, the farm worker, filled the frame. 'What are you doing standing in the middle of the yard?' There was genuine puzzlement in his voice.

I didn't take my eyes off the dog. 'I've come to have a word with the farmer. Mr Fryer.'

'Yeah, I know that's his name, no need to remind me. You'd better come in then.' He stepped aside to let Fryer squeeze out of the low door.

'What is it, Brian?'

'It's that *private* in*vesti*gator again.' I had never noticed my job had that many syllables before.

'So it is,' he confirmed. 'What are you doing here again?'

'I'd . . . just like a quick word, that's all.'

'Well, I don't really mind the rain but wouldn't you feel more comfortable inside?' he asked. By now he must have had little doubt as to what had rooted me to the spot but he made me spell it out for him.

'You couldn't call off your dog first, could you?'

'Call him off? Just push him away, the soft bastard's not going to bite you, he's the most useless guard dog on the planet. I'd be better off with one of my chickens patrolling the place.'

'What's his name?' Being on sniffing terms I thought we ought to be introduced.

'Grot. Though I'm not sure he knows it.' He disappeared inside, followed by the farmhand. I walked forward, closely shadowed by the dog who did in fact wag his tail now and tried to jump up at me. 'Make sure the dog stays outside!' Fryer called.

'Sorry, Grot,' I apologized as I squeezed the door shut behind me.

The kitchen, which I'd last seen in the grip of form-filling depression, had normalized to the point where the floor

212

was no longer covered in dirty pots and pans and the big table in the centre was merely cluttered with mugs, newspapers and a crate of gnarled quinces exuding the most delectable perfume. Fryer himself looked less dishevelled and had shaved sometime during the last twenty-four hours. Brian stood by the sink and Fryer on the other side of the table. Both held chipped mugs and began sipping what looked and smelled suspiciously like instant soup. No wholesome stews bubbling on the Aga in this household. No one offered me a mug, so I couldn't tell them just how revolting I found the stuff. And how much I'd appreciate some.

'Still sniffing around? What's it this time?' Fryer asked, sipping from his mug and pulling a face at the hot soup.

'Oh, same thing really. I just wondered . . .' I gave him a description of Cairn and Heather, told him their names. 'Ring any bells?'

'Not in my church. You think they have anything to do with the murder?'

'They might well have. I wonder, have you come across anything strange in the valley lately?'

'What, apart from yourself, you mean?' Fryer said drily. Barry guffawed at this as though it was the funniest joke he'd heard for years. Perhaps it was.

'Apart from me, yes.'

'No, not really. What do you mean? People?'

'Someone killed Gemma Stone's dog up in the wood by Blackfield's place. Bashed his head in.'

'Did they?' He pursed his lips and nodded. 'That's not nice. I wonder why.'

I had the suspicion he wouldn't spend too much time wondering. 'I think someone's trying to get to Gem Stone.'

'Why would they try a thing like that?' He shrugged. 'Stone can look after herself. When she first turned up I thought she wouldn't last three months, down there by herself, no phone, no nothing laid on. But she's made a go of it, give her that.'

'Yes, you have to be pretty tough to live down there, I imagine, in a caravan, all through the winter. Lonely at Christmas, too, I should think.'

Fryer shot me a look at that but I returned it levelly, as though I had never heard of his Christmas lunge. 'Farming's a lonely business these days,' he agreed. 'Not so long ago farms needed lots of labour, there'd be twenty-odd people in a field doing a job one man does by himself with a tractor now.'

I wondered how lonely Fryer himself felt. No woman would have tolerated the state of this kitchen for long, so I assumed he was living alone or with Barry here, who struck me as rather a dour companion. 'You seen her lately?'

'Who?' This seemed rather disingenuous, since we had only just mentioned Gem Stone, so I didn't elaborate. 'You mean the Stone woman? Not for ages. Have you, Barry?'

Barry sniffed, shook his head. 'Nah.' He turned to rinse out his mug with elaborate care.

I changed tack. 'I went up to Blackfield's place the other day.'

'Oh yeah? Meet him?'

'Met his son.'

'That's who I mean. Dad's not all there by all accounts since his wife died. Did you ask him what the fuck he's turning his bit of land into?'

'Yup, secure storage.'

Both Barry and Fryer guffawed at that. 'That's it,' Fryer said. 'Secure fucking storage, that's what he told us at the public meeting, I just wanted to hear it again. Ha. And he got planning permission, can you credit it? Have you seen the mess he made out there, even a bit of road, massive fucking crane and all to shift his tin boxes around. I'd gladly store something securely up his . . .'

I felt we had probably explored that theme as far as it would go and made to leave when I remembered why I had come here in the first place. 'Oh yeah,' I asked by the

214

door, 'do you know of anyone riding around on a trailie in the valley?'

'Lots of people use trail bikes around here, it's a good way of getting around. Trailies and quad bikes. We've got both. Why the interest?'

'Do you remember the other day? One must have nearly collided with you in the lane, couple of seconds later I nearly ran into you.'

'Didn't see any trailie, all I saw was you carrying an idiotic amount of speed round the corner. You were very lucky not to become a smudge on the side of my tractor.'

I had to agree with him, though just how he could have missed seeing the bike I was pursuing was a little mysterious.

The door slammed unceremoniously behind me as I stepped into the worsening rain. Grot was lying amongst sacks of something or other under a shelter of wood and corrugated asbestos and sensibly lifted no more than his head as I left. As I rode away from the place the gloriously useful heating arrangements at the Rose and Crown insinuated themselves into my mind, irresistible like the mirage of a lake to a man dying of thirst in the desert. Well, something like that, anyway.

Only a few early regulars were perusing newspapers or studying the empty space on the other side of their pints. The landlady wasn't about. The barmaid, a brawny young woman with blonde hair permed to within an inch of its life, furnished me with a mug of black coffee. I described the Cairn and Heather duo to her. Had she seen them lately?

'Yeah, they were in last night,' she confirmed. She yanked open the dishwasher and thick steam rose briefly between us.

'They come in here a lot then?'

'Not really, no. What you want with them, anyway?' She began stacking the glasses on their shelves below the bar top.

'They ... kind of hired me to look into something for them and I'd like to give them a progress report.'

'Mm, kind of hired? I thought you'd have enough employment explaining away the dead body in the back of your car.'

'Does everybody know about that?' I wondered.

'Yup.'

A couple of the regulars nodded sagely without bothering to look up.

'Did you know the man? Albert Barrington?'

'Never heard of him. Not known in these parts until after his demise.'

The regulars shook their heads. I realized what it was. It was altogether too quiet in this place, there was no music playing yet and not enough customers. Cosy, but perhaps a bit too cosy right now. 'Do you know where the kids might live?'

She shook her head and continued stacking. 'Somewhere in the valley perhaps. Not in Larkhall, never seen them around except in here sometimes. Definitely not regulars.' The regulars shook their heads like a bunch of radio-controlled toys.

'You wouldn't know their surname, then?'

She didn't. I pushed my card across the bar. 'Could you give me a ring next time they're in? I'd appreciate it.'

'As if we didn't have enough to do in here without ... yeah, all right, if it isn't too busy and if I remember and if they happen to be in when I'm in, I only work three shifts now.' She swiped the card off the bar and stuck it into a pile of papers wedged next to the till. Not much point in me waiting by the phone then.

I finished my coffee and left. I had stuff to do. I dialled Jill's number, wanting to reassure her that I thought I could pull the museum job off, but there was no answer. Then I armed myself with some cash, rode to the catalogue showroom place on the Upper Bristol Road and bought a large black rucksack, a pencil torch, a bolt cutter, two

216

combination bicycle locks, a padlock and a couple of aluminium fire escape ladders since I had no illusions that I could learn the rope work of abseiling in just a couple of days. In fact the less I thought about climbing the better I was able to suppress the panic trying to bubble up from behind my navel. These long ladders made from light-weight chains and treads, designed to get you out of a burning building, appealed to my low-tech mind.

Back at Mill House Tim was still presiding over the sitting room from his nest on the floor in front of the fire. The paraphernalia of convalescence spilled out around him like flotsam from a shipwreck: painkillers, box of tissues, his phone, his laptop, his iPod and headphones, bottles of Pilsner Urquell ('I got bored!'), a bag of doughnuts and a stack of Annis's M.C. Beaton novels.

Since Tim couldn't join us anywhere else it only seemed natural that headquarters moved into the sitting room. Soon Annis and I added to the chaos by spreading maps and pictures I'd taken of the museum on the floor and dumping other paraphernalia of the forthcoming heist everywhere. Annis and I pored over the large-scale map of Bath. While I had been at Jake's to scrounge the dinghy Annis had scouted out a place to launch and recover it from. The closest place where we could get access to the Avon upriver from Pulteney Weir was a long way out, opposite Kensington Meadows and the playing fields. Here Annis had found a farmer's access road to the meadow we could use. It still meant carrying the inflated dinghy and its engine a hundred and fifty yards through the meadow to the water, but we might manage to do it unobserved. That side of the river appeared completely dark at night, especially when viewed from the well-lit Kensington side.

None of this seemed quite real, it felt much more like planning a movie sequence than something we were going to attempt in the real world of police, courts and crowded prisons. Tim's lugubrious comments didn't help.

'Well, it's been nice knowing you two . . .'

'Rubbish, we'll pull it off, no sweat. The more unlikely, the more James Bondian, the better. No one will expect it and we'll be out of there before they know what's hit them.' I didn't feel any of this excessive optimism. I felt absolutely certain that one day I would write about it from a prison cell, or even a hospital bed en route to a prison cell. Still, all in a good cause . . .

'They'll scoop you up and bag you before you'll manage to lay a finger on *The Dancer*. The whole thing stinks. Somebody, and it stands to reason it was the fuzz, followed me for days. They know something. They know Aqua Investigations is up to something.'

'I didn't notice any surveillance while I was out.' Annis munched thoughtfully on one of the dozens of mini doughnuts she had brought back for Tim. 'And I really looked, tried to catch them out.'

'Neither have I.' I didn't say that even now I had the distinct feeling an invisible net had already been thrown over us, that whatever I did, wherever I went, someone was watching. The darkening windows suddenly made me feel exposed. I got up and closed the curtains on all of them. I tried to be casual about it, but looked hard into the gathering darkness, looking for any sign of movement beyond the rain. A hopeless thing to do. A whole battalion could hide out there and as long as they weren't wearing Day-Glo uniforms I wouldn't see them.

'The river is so swollen you won't be able to navigate your little cockleshell. You'll drown like rats and I'll lie here unable to get up, and I'll starve to death. Right, you can't have any more of these.' He swiped the family-size bag of doughnuts and stuffed it under his blanket. 'It's all that stands between me and death by starvation. They'll find my emaciated body when eventually they open up the house after your bloated remains have washed up in Avonmouth . . .'

I let Tim witter on because in some weird way it was

beginning to cheer me up. 'You're just jealous because you can't come along, dear.'

'I told you when you first suggested it that it was an idiotic scheme.'

'You're just scared that I might find out I can do without your criminal expertise and hand you a redundancy notice.'

'Ha! Redundancy implies employment. You haven't paid me for ages. Anyway, you're scared of heights, remember? Halfway up there you'll crap yourself with fear and the fire brigade will have to come and fetch you down like a kitten from an apple tree.'

This was so close to the centre of my own fears that I nearly told him to shut up, only I knew that the resulting silence would scare me more. 'I'll cope.'

'You'll never even get there. You'll get swept away or your dinghy will turn turtle and you'll drown.' Tim was getting into his stride now and obviously enjoying his role as gloom-dispensing oracle. He had even acquired a familiar; ever since he'd settled down in front of the fire the cat hadn't left his side.

I coughed as I lit yet another cigarette and wondered how long I could stay afloat for. 'We can both swim.' Annis nodded her agreement.

'Not in the weir you can't. It's become eroded and the changed shape creates a fierce suction pulling you down to the bottom and preventing you from coming up again. Might be all sorts of bodies already down there. And with the river in spate like this your chances will be zero anyway. You'll both be dead a couple of minutes after hitting the water. What's for supper, by the way?'

It was Annis's turn to cook. While I watched her boil fettucine and drown a few handfuls of prawns in arrabiata sauce straight from the supermarket ('You didn't think I was going to knit you a *cassoulet*, did you?') I called Jill. A lot could go wrong but if it didn't then it looked as though within a couple of days we might at last be able to exchange Louis for the Penny Black and *The Dancer*. There was no answer.

'I tried before and didn't get any answer then either.'

Annis elaborately licked a large wooden spoon, then waggled it at me. 'Mm, yeah, meant to tell you: I swung round her place earlier after I picked up some of Tim's stuff and she didn't answer. I don't think she was in, I leant on the bell for a while, it would have woken the dead.'

'I'll try her again later.' I slipped the phone back into my pocket and decided to do rather more than that later.

We had just sat down to keep Tim company in front of the fire and begun to slurp fettucine and chase prawns round our bowls when I sensed more than heard a vehicle approach. I wandered off with my bowl of pasta into the dark hall and opened the door a crack, from where I could watch the entrance to the yard without showing a backlit silhouette of myself. Now I could clearly hear the slow, distinctive rattle of a large diesel approaching down the track. A few moments later headlights appeared and soon I recognized Jake's vintage Land Rover. He was pulling a Rigid Inflatable Boat on a trailer, complete with outboard engine tilted up, into the yard. I turned on the outside light, which at the moment consisted of one feeble light bulb. There was more light coming from Jake's Land Rover. He climbed from the cab, still in his overalls.

'Hold this.' I handed him the bowl of pasta and went to admire the boat. I walked around it, patting its sleek black flanks. It was far bigger than I had expected, a lot more substantial. Surely this would stand up to any amount of current, any kind of weather. 'Can it be carried? With two people?'

'Just. Without the engine. It's a good little boat, that. I'll leave you the trailer of course. Got anything to pull it with?'

'Annis's Landy.'

'You're sorted then. Cheers, Chris.' He handed me back the bowl. Empty.

I stared at it in consternation. This had to be some sort of conspiracy.

Annis had appeared in the doorway but preferred to stay dry in its shelter while Jake unhitched the trailer.

'It's got a twelve horsepower engine, I know that doesn't sound much, but it's perfectly adequate. I filled her up, you can return her dry though, it'll only go back into storage anyway. Give us a hand.'

We unhitched the trailer and pulled the boat as far as it went into the incomplete shelter of one of the crumbling outbuildings. The one adjacent to it, with most of its sagging roof still complete, hid Tim's black Audi, under bits of tarp, carpet and cardboard. Jake spotted it instantly with the trained eye of the obsessive. 'I won't ask.'

'It's just Tim's Audi. He's come to stay for a few days.'

'Blimey, does he always park like that? Right, gotta go, car to finish.' He climbed into his cab, waved a goodbye and cranked the Land Rover out of the yard.

In the kitchen I made myself a tuna sandwich, closely watched by the cat who had suddenly appeared out of the ground beside me. How do they know? He was there before I got the tin-opener in. After explaining to him the merits of opposable thumbs when it came to the acquisition of tinned tuna I relented and dropped some in his cat bowl – and where had that come from? – just so I got some peace in which to munch my sandwich.

And think. And the more I thought, the more uneasy I felt. The feeling that my life was controlled by outside forces, that events and people might pop in and out of the ground like a nameless cat, was beginning to get to me. The museum robbery was of course an utterly ridiculous and doomed undertaking, even if the couple attempting it had not been a pair of painters with a fear of heights. Now that I was by myself and I didn't have Tim's ridicule to cheer me up the depressing realities of our situation crowded in on me.

Reluctantly I put on my still-damp leather jacket and boots, got on the bike and rumbled through the drizzle into town. The Norton never liked being parked on steep hills so I left it in Portland Place and walked the few yards down to Jill's little house in Harley Street. No lights were showing. The blinds at the upstairs windows were drawn but I seemed to remember they'd been like that when we first arrived at the house. I checked my watch. It was only half past eight. The doorbell was shrill and remained unanswered, even after the fifth time of ringing. I called her mobile again without success. Bending down I pushed back the tin flap of the letter box. Only the dim glow of the street lights that fell through the doors leading off it illuminated the narrow hall. I hunted round my jacket pockets for my Maglite without success. What I wanted to see was in complete darkness. I turned on my mobile and, using the bright display as a torch, stuck it through the letter box. I had to hold it at an awkward angle and it slid from my rain-slickened fingers and dropped down the other side of the door, emitting a bleep of protest as it hit the large pile of uncollected post on the other side.

That decided it. It was only a Yale lock but my lock-picking expertise, despite Tim's efforts to train me, was pitiful. The houses next door showed light behind their front room curtains. From the one on the left I could hear snatches of TV sound. I hoped the people on the other side were equally busy and didn't suddenly decide to leave by the front door. I worked for a nerve-tingling minute, during which several people walked past on the pavement behind me. I forced myself not to look over my shoulder but to concentrate on the inner workings of the lock. At last it clicked open and I pushed through into the hall. The pile of post made it difficult, as some of it slid under the door. I picked up my mobile, closed the door and turned on the light. At my feet lay mainly junk mail, leaflets and take-away menus and stuff addressed to The Householder, but there were other letters as well, most bearing the name

222

A. P. Downs. Presumably the previous tenant. There was no post for Jill, since she had only lived there for one or two days before tragedy struck. I simply couldn't see how Jill could have entered her house without sweeping most of the mail to the side as I had done when I opened the door. Unless she had used a rear entrance. I dropped the letters back on the floor and looked into the sitting room on the right. In the orange glow from the street lights I could see that nothing had changed in here, the ashtray overflowing, the half-emptied boxes, the china pigs on the telly. I was still feeling for the light switch when a police car pulled up outside, without siren but blue lights flashing. Two officers jumped out. Now was a good time to find out if there was another way out. One of the officers made straight for the front door, already flashing his torch at the window, the other went to the next door neighbour's, presumably to cut off any escape from the back.

I turned off the hall light and ran to the small kitchen at the rear. A narrow, half-glazed back door led to a tiny garden. It was locked. There wasn't the time to try and unpick the lock. I lifted one of the wooden kitchen chairs, hoped it was solid enough to break through the glass, took a good swing back and spotted a key hanging on a hook in the door frame. I put the chair down and tried the keys. Behind me the front door was being rattled, then a powerful torch beam, aimed through the letter box, jumped about on the kitchen furniture. The lock disengaged, I pulled. Bolted. I released the top bolt and pulled. I swore and released the bottom bolt, which was stiff because the wood had warped. At last I managed to get the door open, only to see a police constable's head bob over the fence to the right. The fence was overgrown with brambles and the copper was looking for a way across without getting shredded. I ran straight down the middle of the strip of garden, cracked my ankle against something in the dark but kept running.

'Halt! Police! Stop right there!' The authority of his voice was subtly undermined by the quieter addition of 'Shit.' I took a run at the fence at the back, ignoring the padlocked door, and scrambled over it. It landed me in the narrowest of alleyways full of crud. To my right a puffing police officer rattled at the high back gate of the neighbour's fence. It was topped with rusted barbed wire. I jumped over what looked like a collection of empty paint cans and sacks of rubbish and ran past him uphill. It was a dead end. The back-to-back gardens of Harley Street and the much posher Northampton Street converged and soon I found myself at the bottom of an eight-foot sandstone wall. Fortunately someone had neatly piled large sections of a dead fruit tree under it for me to climb up. Behind me the constable crashed through the pile of paint cans, getting awfully close. I clambered up the pile of logs, which began to move precariously. It seemed to take me forever. When I got one leg on the top of the wall I gave the wood pile a good kick with the other one. I didn't wait to check the results. I dropped down between a brick barbecue and a glass greenhouse into the sudden glare of a security light high above on the back wall of the house. This was a much larger garden, belonging to the last house on Northampton Street. The light was helpful, though. I spotted the door to the car port on the other side and when I got there found it open and squeezed through the two cars to freedom. No time to hang about. The Norton was parked twenty yards up the road. When I reached it I was so out of breath I wanted nothing more than to bend double and throw up. I worked the kick-starter instead. One of the constables was back in the street in front of Jill's house and, seeing me frantically trying to start the bike, began running uphill towards me.

The Norton never did like the damp. Only on the fourth attempt did the engine come to life. Realizing that he wouldn't reach me in time the officer changed his mind and ran back to his car. With the thunderous noise the fifty-year-old bike emitted I had no chance of giving him the slip quietly and I certainly couldn't outrun him. I pointed the bike left and roared along Portland Street straight at a large complex of council flats. I squeezed the bike past the beam that barred the car park and rode the few yards to the pedestrian underpass. Blue flashes of the police car's beacon pulsed on the wall above me as I negotiated the metal barriers designed to stop people from driving through it. It was an agonizingly slow squeeze through it but once on the other side I was home free. For a couple of seconds the Norton's exhaust noise was ear-splittingly amplified in the short tunnel, then I hustled the bike up the curved tarmac path to the top where it spat me out on to Lansdown Road. I turned left uphill and opened the throttle all the way. There was no sign of pursuit, even when I reached the long straight on top of Lansdown.

Taking the long way home along dark and deserted country roads allowed my adrenalin levels to readjust themselves and gave me time to subdue my paranoia. The arrival of the police at Jill's house had nothing to do with the kidnapping or our planned robbery; someone had watched me spend ages breaking the lock and sensibly called the fuzz. If they'd been after me personally, they'd have been CID.

The much more important question was now: what had happened to Jill? I hadn't had the chance to search the house but it seemed obvious that no one had been there for a while. Quite apart from the evidence of the junk mail pile what had convinced me that Jill hadn't been back for a couple of days was the smell. The place smelled uninhabited. Nobody had smoked there for a while and Jill was a heavy smoker.

Had she decided she needed company after all? Had she gone to her sister's? She said she didn't know anyone in Bath; had she gone to Bristol, perhaps even back to her ex-boyfriend?

In the valley I approached the turn-off to my house from the east instead of the usual west. I hid the Norton as best I could by the side of the road and walked the last quarter of a mile, this being the approximate distance the bike's engine sound travelled at night. I was thoroughly wet and tired but kept on my toes by a brain feverishly trying to compute all the possibilities, all the alternatives, any exit strategies or plan Bs. If I found the yard full of police the answers would become painfully obvious. If not, then our plans had to be put into action as soon as possible. I cautiously crept along the last bit of track, darting from tree shadow to tree shadow. The outside light was on, there were no police cars in the yard.

If it was still empty by tomorrow night, I would go and steal a Rodin.

Chapter Eighteen

'Pack everything in the right order, so what you'll need first is at the top.'

'Yes, Grandma Bigwood.' Now that we were definitely going Tim had decided to stop dispensing gloom and be helpful instead. I wasn't sure what I found more irritating, but I realized how helpless he felt and I also knew that despite his myriad objections to the scheme he would eventually have done it, and done it well.

'Cereal bars? What, are you going to hold a picnic in there first? What other nonsense are you taking?'

Annis sighed. 'Ham sandwiches with the crusts cut off, camping stove for making hot soup and a gramophone, if I'd have let him.' Annis was long ready and only waiting for me to see that really, so was I. It was three o'clock in the morning, the city centre would be as quiet as it would ever get, and there was no moon. We were dressed in black, with black trainers, and I'd be carrying a black waterproof rucksack I deemed large enough to carry the little Rodin in. Outside, the dinghy on its trailer, disguised with cardboard boxes and tarpaulin to give it a different shape, was hooked up to the Landy.

I thought I had everything. I thought I was ready. 'Let's do it.'

Annis knelt down to kiss Tim goodbye. A bit longer than was strictly necessary, I thought. Then we were off. We hardly spoke on the way. We'd gone over it countless times and in my experience it never paid to labour your plans.

Nothing ever worked out quite the way you'd imagined it anyway. We met few cars on the London Road and soon turned off, crossed the river and disappeared into the quiet suburbs. Here for a while we were at the mercy of insomniac neighbourhood watch schemers but it wasn't long before we left the houses behind and Annis manoeuvred the Landy down a narrow lane that ended at a gate set into the low stone wall bordering the riverside meadows. It was only held shut with a loop of nylon rope. I opened it and stepped back to let Annis drive in. She killed the lights and bounced past me towards the river, far into the boggy meadow. I wasn't convinced of the merits of this; the last thing we could afford was to get stuck in the mud here. I ran after her in the thin rain and was relieved when her brake lights came on at last.

'I checked it out, it only gets really soft closer in,' she said when I protested. 'We don't want to have to lug the boat any further than absolutely necessary. We'll be all right from here.'

'You're the expert.' Which she was. Annis could manoeuvre a Land Rover with dreamlike ease. Learnt it on a driving course somewhere.

Untying the tarpaulin in the rain was harder than tying it on, especially since my rope craft was nil. Those beautiful secure knots that untangle themselves when you pull on them were quite beyond me. My knots were the muttered-curses-and-broken-fingernail type. Everything took longer than expected, was more difficult, wetter, windier, colder. When eventually we managed to get the thing off the trailer the RIB proved spectacularly heavy. Fortunately dismounting the engine was easy. We first carried, then dragged the inflatable to the water's edge, aiming for a dead-looking tree in the gloom. The river was in noisy spate; I had to use my torch to make sure we didn't slither down the steep bank and pitch straight into its swirling waters. Launching the boat didn't look to be at all easy. We were in the middle of a shouted discussion about it when the thing displayed a watery will of its own and launched itself, aided by the wind and me slipping in the mud. We both dived for the long trailing rope and managed to stop the boat from disappearing into the darkness. After we managed to tie it to a fallen branch of the dead tree we trudged back and got the engine. By the time we had carried it to the boat and mounted it again I was too wet, scratched, bruised and narked off to even complain about it and Annis was grimly quiet. She got the engine started easily and ran against the current while I untied the rope from the log and climbed back in.

As we turned away from the shore the current swiftly pushed us along into the wet darkness. The engine puttered bravely but at this stage was mainly used to provide steering. Any legitimate night traffic on this stretch of the Avon would run navigation lights of course, unlike us, but there was nobody out on the water. Not running navigation lights was the flotsam: the fallen branches, the wooden crates, the plastic dustbins blown into the river, some of which we bumped into on the dark water. It doesn't take much to pierce the skin even of a RIB – what can inflate can deflate – but so far we were lucky. The current brought us downriver much faster than I had anticipated. The centre of town with its lights, police patrols and security cameras suddenly reared up out of the dark. If anything, the current speeded up. Now it was possible to see just how much debris the river was carrying downstream with us. The three arches of Pulteney Bridge loomed dark and low above us as we inexorably drifted towards it on the swollen river. The roar of the weir beyond echoed through them. The black water swirled and eddied, producing a wave against the mossy stone of the bridge. Not until it was nearly too late did I see that the right-hand arch for which we were aiming was blocked with a plug of massive branches and an assortment of flotsam.

'Steer left, quickly, left!' I shouted to Annis.

'It's called *port!*' she shouted back irritably as we just missed colliding with the cutwater. We were speeding up alarmingly as the middle arch swallowed us. 'Grab the chain or we'll go over the weir, the current's too strong.'

Leaning as far as I dared over the edge I managed to get my right hand on to one of the chains hanging from the masonry. I gripped one of the handholds on the rib hard as the drift tried to pull me out of the boat. I felt my joints pop but managed to stop us racing ahead.

'I can't hold this long,' I shouted over the roar of the weir. Its thundering mouth seemed to be inches away. A plastic beer crate shot past us and seconds later disappeared into the swirling, sucking waters.

'Well, you'll just have to!' Annis wiped strands of wet hair from her face with a gloved hand. 'We're pointing the wrong way, I need to run full throttle against the current to get us across to the other side. I'm not sure we can do it!'

'I'll let the boat turn round on the current, get ready for when I let go!'

First slowly, then rapidly as the current caught the starboard side, the boat swung round as I pushed. Annis opened the throttle further and further. 'Let go!'

We slipped backwards, away from the bridge. As soon as we cleared the cutwater on the downstream side she opened the throttle all the way. The little engine strained and screamed. We were suspended in mid-stream, unmoving despite our bow wave. I refused to turn around and stare into the roaring waters behind us. Then, hardly perceptibly at first, with agonizing slowness, we began to make headway. But after only a few seconds of progress the boat slipped sideways, caught by a different current, and got pushed back several yards before Annis managed to bring it under control. Our engine was battling away, just ten yards or so from our objective, a rusty old landing stage and a set of iron steps that led up to the colonnaded walkway. Normally well above the waterline, it was in danger of becoming swamped.

'Just aim for the wall, we can pull ourselves along!' I had spotted a garland of cables running along the base of the walkway, just above the waterline.

Annis did as I asked and the slimy walls seemed to advance on us rapidly. We rammed inelegantly against the side and the manoeuvre had pushed us another few yards back, but with the engine going at full throttle and me pulling hand over fist we reached the landing stage after only a couple of minutes. I hastily tied the painter to the ironwork.

The plan had been for Annis to set me down, retreat and then return at my signal but it was obvious that it took both of us to land the boat. 'I'll be here!' she assured me. 'Just don't be bloody ages. It only takes one copper with good eyesight to come along and look over the parapet and we've had it.'

She stopped me as I made to climb out, grabbed my face in both hands and kissed me goodbye. I ran up the steps, climbed over the little padlocked gate and moved along swiftly in the deep shadows of the walkway. I reached the slipway's wrought-iron door and half unslung the ruck-sack. Subtlety costs time. I'd bought the biggest bolt cutter in the shop and made short work of the padlock. I flung it into the river, stowed the bolt cutter and moved into the slipway. It was dark down here in the narrow canyon into which the jetsam of Garfunkel's cellars had spilled. Once I had negotiated the gas bottles, kegs and crates I arrived at the elevated end in front of another locked door. This one had its original lock, though well maintained and used, as I discovered when it surrendered to my picklocks after less than a minute.

The car park was cluttered with building materials, mobile toilets, a corrugated metal lockup, a portable shelter for the work gang and heaps of stuff under tarpaulins, all of it only dimly lit by the distant street lamps. I hugged the left side and peered through the porte cochère into Orange Grove. Not a soul to be seen. I hurried across the exposed expanse and gratefully slipped into the shadows at the foot of the scaffold. From the bottom to the top it was covered with pale blue tarpaulin, bleached of colour by the orange glow from the little street lighting that reached into this sea of grey. The scaffolding had swallowed both security cameras that used to cover the car park. Nobody had thought it worthwhile to have them repositioned while work was being carried out. Heads would roll . . .

Some effort had been made to secure access to the bottom of the scaffold by building a twelve foot cage around it, but since it was only as secure as the padlock on the wire door it could only keep out the opportunist climber. I kicked the cut padlock out of sight. From the inside I replaced it with a similar one I had brought by sticking my hands through the wire mesh, just in case someone decided to check while I was up there. I stashed the heavy bolt cutter out of sight. Then it was time.

I took a deep breath and gripped the bottom of the first ladder. My strategy for coping with my fear of heights was to take everything in stages. This was just one ladder. Nothing to it. Nothing. I took it steady and stepped out sideways on to the first of the four levels. It was dark in here but relatively dry under the tarpaulin, which creaked and snapped and dripped with the wind and rain. As my eyes adjusted to the darkness I could see that the next ladder was at the opposite end. I traversed the level on the narrow boards, which moved ominously under my weight as I walked on them, by pulling myself from handhold to handhold until I made it to the other side. At the bottom of the next ladder I stopped to collect myself. If I started each climb in a calm frame of mind I would be fine.

Level two. Perhaps I could treat it like a computer game. It occurred to me just how cosy the world of virtual adventure was. It also occurred to me that scaffolders the world over would laugh at my palpitations as I climbed further into the darkness.

Level three. The wind was stronger up here and made me grip my handholds harder each time the tarpaulin filled with air like a giant sail threatening to pull me from the wall. I was sweating with the exertion of the climb and my breathing never seemed to slow down even when I paused. There was definite movement in the structure when the wind freshened and I wished there was someone to ask whether this was normal or not.

Last ladder. There was no longer any point in trying to calm myself, I was panicked and listening to my heart pounding as I stood there didn't help at all. My legs, unused to climbing, had acquired a slight tremor. I might stand here all night, it wouldn't get any better. I simply couldn't turn back. I had to go forward. Last ladder, last ladder. Surely this one was longer than the others. There was more construction above me, looking complicated in the dark as it stretched away towards the cupola of the Guildhall, where the storm damage had occurred, but I knew I was now level with the roof of the covered market to the right of the scaffold. With my pocket knife I simply slashed through the tarp from head height to the bottom and carefully stuck my head through the gash. I was staring into a yawning chasm. I had climbed too high and was an entire level above the market roof. I withdrew my head sharpish and worked my way hand over hand along the side of the building to the ladder and climbed down. I was happy about no longer being so high up – though falling from the third floor wouldn't be much more fun than from the fourth – but it was merely a cerebral happiness I didn't feel in my diaphragm, and was very short-lived. I cut a hole into the tarpaulin on level three. I stuck my head through. There was the market roof. And there was the *gap*. There shouldn't have been a gap, a four-foot gap between the scaffold and the neighbouring roof, a black gap into which rain and people and darkness fell and disappeared from view for ever. The roof was glistening with wet and might as well have been twenty feet away. I withdrew my head into what suddenly felt like a cosy protective shell, before the view could scare me witless. Calm down, it's not a big gap. Four feet. Four feet was nothing. It was just . . . the width of a man with a full rucksack.

I fumbled for a cigarette, lit it, sucked on it hard. Sod forensics. There was no chance we'd pull this off and get away with it anyway. Even if I'd ever manage to leave this scaffold. My legs screamed for me to sit down, just for a little while, just for a minute, but I knew it would make it worse. It seemed ages since I'd last eaten and the cigarette made me a little dizzy. In a side pocket of my rucksack were a couple of cereal bars but perhaps Tim was right, this was not the time or place to be picnicking. I teased the glowing tip off my cigarette and stepped on it as it fell and pocketed the fag-end. Time to have another look. Just a look, no obligation. I pulled the flapping tarp aside. I looked at the roof opposite. I looked down. I suddenly slipped, grappled hopelessly for a handhold, fell into the darkness, my head smashing against the boards as I passed on my way into the chasm. I could taste blood in my mouth, my flailing legs grazed the side of the building, the air rushed past and didn't leave me enough breath to scream before I dashed myself to pieces and crumpled on the tarmac below and died.

Chapter Nineteen

I stepped back and stood, panting, gripping the struts to either side of the loose tarpaulin. Four feet. Four feet was nothing, a long stride, a hop and a skip, a skip and a jump, a jump and a fall. Unenthusiastically I slashed more of the tarpaulin away until I had a clear opening. There were no snags, nothing my rucksack could catch on. A simple jump. Less, a hop. On the count of three. One, two, three, four, five. Pathetic. Four feet. Nobody needs a running jump for four feet.

I jumped, with three times the necessary force, and hit the roof running. I was free of the scaffold. Crouching down I worked my way forward over the gently curved roof towards the octagonal central structure of the market. I forced myself to admire the cast-iron construction of the lights. Lovely intricate ironwork, needed painting here and there but otherwise, oh, who was I kidding. I felt naked up here, opposite the old Empire Hotel. Row after row of darkened windows faced my way, watching me scuttle like a big black beetle into the darker shadows at the back. A minute to get my breath back. Another minute to get my breath back. A cigarette, I needed another cigarette. They said an enemy bomber could see the glow of your cigarette from fifteen thousand feet. What about enemy insomniacs in the Empire Hotel? No cigarette, then. Go forward. Stage by stage, up a slate incline, down into a leaded trough. I followed its curve, counted off the three sets of skylights above, reached the end. Nearly the end. Climb up before the end. I had memorized every detail from the aerial photographs I'd found in my guide books. The details were all there, yet the scale was so immensely different it was hard to believe the landmarks when I came to them. Up, passing the last skylight on the left, and down again on the other side, sliding on my bum, feet first, until I reached a parapet, a level piece of masonry, a reprieve. I took my time but tried not to check my watch. Every minute I delayed increased the danger of Annis being discovered clinging to the landing stage. Below. Far below.

A dark chasm opened on my left as I followed the curve of the roof space towards a three-storey addition to the back of the museum, lower than the original and stuck on at a curious angle. Deep below, it created the strangest-shaped, darkest canyon into which Private Investigators traditionally threw themselves head first during sudden attacks of vertigo . . .

Despite the tremor in my legs I managed to walk, as far from the edge as possible, never taking my eyes from the wall ahead. When I got there I leant against it. Wet, but solid. Now I had to get up it. It was only two feet or so higher than me and a round metal vent gave me a good foothold. I pulled myself up on to the next flat bit and lay there for a moment. Two tall chimneys reared to my right. The next bit was easy. Here the roof was constructed in giant steps; I climbed up easily. I had reached the corner where the southern cupola of the museum joined the roof over the upper exhibition space, with its pitched, old-fashioned skylights, beloved of burglars. To reach them, I would have to heave myself up to the flat, outer rim of the roof, twelve feet above me, which would have presented me with considerable difficulties had it not been for the tangle of downpipes, aerials and lightning conductors in the corner. I tackled this climbing frame quickly and methodically, spurred on to greater heights by the closeness of the goal, and heaved myself gratefully on to the roof of the gallery, panting and sweating despite the wet and the wind and the cold fear of being blown off it if I moved even one muscle up here. From this vantage point one could see the river Avon wind its way west through the town, or look south and see the entire length of Great Pulteney Street as far as the Holburne Museum and Sydney Gardens, and the dark mass of Bathwick Wood and Bathampton Down beyond; if one dared look, which I didn't. When I recovered the will to move it was on all fours and as far as the edge of the skylight. This was where all my theories about the quaint old museum and its robbability hinged on the yet unanswered question: were these skylights alarmed or not? I fully expected to set off the alarms as soon as I opened any doors inside – the first on the upper floor, the second on the ground floor – but calculated I'd have just enough time to make my escape before it occurred to the police to surround the place. These were not the kind of calculations made with military precision, they were done on my fingers and quite probably contained a large measure of unfounded optimism. They had also been done before I realized how long it would take me to traverse all that roof space just to get here.

There was no point in delaying. There was nothing to be seen through the streaming wet glass as I peered down, but I knew what was there. Three large iron beams braced the roof structure below the skylights. I counted off the right number of panes and knew I was above the first, nearest the door. Then I attached a professional climber's suction pad left of centre by pulling the little lever in the device, which created a strong vacuum. These panes were large, heavy duty items, and they were ready to tumble into the void as soon as I completed the cut. I had to cut in two stages to be sure I could hold them. After having scored the glass all around I held tight to the suction pad and tapped the glass. Nothing. I tapped harder. Still nothing. I repeated the cut all around, though it was difficult to see where the diamond had scored the surface before, then thumped the glass hard. No alarms, no whistles or bells. It snapped off and hung heavily but the suction cup held. I levered the glass out and released it on to the roof. I stuck my head into the opening. Warm air rose towards me.

The next part of the pane came away more easily and cleanly. I pocketed the suction cup and glass cutter and, thrusting my arm deep into the opening I had created, chanced a flash of my pencil torch. There was the beam, just below me. I killed the light and swung my legs over the edge, braced myself on the frame either side and lowered myself down until my feet made firm contact with the beam. This felt easier. Even though there was a twelve-foot drop below the beam this was *in*side and inside wasn't half as scary as *out*side, don't ask me why. The beam was broad and felt solid under my feet. I managed to persuade my hands to let go of the skylight and straddled the beam. With the pencil light in my mouth I removed the first fire escape ladder from my rucksack, hooked it on to the beam and let it go. It rolled out with a high metallic tinkling sound and hit the hardwood floor below with a startling bang.

My legs took some persuading but I managed to get first one foot on to a thin aluminium tread, then the next. The ladder swung inwards, being designed to work against the walls of a house, but it got me down, next to a glass vitrine full of . . . stuff; china and glass and antique knick-knacks. I had no time to browse. If I had set off an alarm already then I had probably three minutes until the first police car came to a screeching halt in front of the main door. I didn't bother to take the torch from my mouth and crossed to the double doors. The lock was an old-fashioned one. It engaged bolts top, bottom and sides, effectively defending the door against being rammed open, but it wasn't sophist-icated enough to defeat a man with lock-picking skills. Even my laughable skills. Tim would, no doubt, have been on the other side of the door by now, whereas I had three picklocks inserted and tried and jiggled while first long seconds, then an entire minute ticked away. At last the lock

238

snapped open with an echoing din and I pushed through. I had trouble keeping myself from screaming all the way down the stairs to the next door. I'd gone through the first door and the clock was ticking. No alarm bells. That meant a silent alarm had been triggered at Manvers Street station and police were at this very moment pouring out of the doors towards their cars.

I skidded to a halt in the small lobby in front of the next set of doors. The glass panels tempted me with their apparent fragility, yet smashing all the heavy panes and removing enough of the framework to squeeze myself through would take longer than defeating the lock. Quite apart from being a lot noisier. It was a race against time, a contest, police driver against lock breaker. This was an identical lock to the one upstairs. I already had the right picks out and knew in which order to insert them, only my hands were shakier and my nerves thinner. Sweat was running into my eyes as I stood in the little lobby, my back to the entrance door. One moment all I could hear was the metallic clicking of my picks, then suddenly behind me the sound of an engine and the crunch of brakes being applied hard, car doors opening, muted voices. Ignore it.

The lock snapped open under my efforts, the door yielded to the pressure of my shoulder. I stowed the picks, taking the few steps up into the exhibition space at a run. The piercing beam of my torch picked out the exhibits, scowling shapes with jumping shadows. The little Rodin was there, standing in the centre, in pride of place, waiting for me. I grabbed the dancer by the cold scruff of his neck, pulled him off the plinth and lowered him into my rucksack, secured the top with the speed cords and heaved it on to my back. And I nearly staggered backwards. It was surprisingly heavy for its size and one of its sharp angles poked painfully into my back. I wouldn't get much running done while carrying this load of junk. Crossing the lobby I could hear voices and the nasal whine of a police radio on the other side of the main entrance door. Ignore it. I climbed the stairs steadily, using the handrail, pacing myself. I had a long way to go carrying this thing and it was no use running out of puff halfway to the boat with the police already here.

Back on the upper floor I pulled the double door shut behind me. I fished my cheap combination bicycle lock from my jacket pocket, slipped it through the brass loops of the door handles, wound it round tight and clicked it shut. That would keep them out until they decided to break the door down or send some poor bastard on to the roof.

This was it. I tugged the escape ladder tight, took a deep breath and started climbing. The heavy rucksack made me swing nearly horizontal as soon as I had both feet on it. It was an awkward operation. Halfway up, my left foot got tangled in the links and treads of the ladder. I couldn't look down to see, it was too dark and the angle was wrong. My arms started to ache while I thrashed about until at last I was free and could start moving again. Still no noise of pursuit, which was puzzling me but I wasn't about to complain. I heaved myself up on to the beam, breathing hard, unhooked the ladder and let it clatter to the floor. As I stood on the beam and slipped the rucksack off my shoulders so I could push it out of the skylight I could hear noises below me. Ignore. Once rid of the weight I felt featherlight and pulled myself up easily. The sound of hammering came from somewhere, probably the cops trying to get through the upstairs door, as I let the second ladder roll down the side of the building towards the next level down. I shouldered my burden once more and swiftly climbed down. A vigorous shake dislodged the hooks by which the ladder had held on to the masonry with worrying ease. Leaving it lying where it was, I retraced my steps, down another level, then across the semicircular parapet. The extra weight made the mossy surfaces difficult to negotiate and I slipped back twice before I gratefully slithered down into the leaded trough around the cast-iron lights surrounding the central roof structure of the market.

Here I paused and tried to subdue my breathing so I could listen for any sound below. It remained quiet. Reluctance to move on to the edge of the roof rained down on me like treacle. The longer I cowered in the dubious shelter of the roof's damp valley the harder it would get. I wanted this done, I wanted to be away. Above all, I wanted to be *down*. I pushed along to the furthest corner. In front and above me the grey giant of the scaffold stood ready to swallow me. I could not afford to stand on the edge of the market roof, in full view of anyone on the ground in the car park, and dither. I'd simply have to do it instantly: line up opposite the hole in the tarpaulin and jump across. Jump. Jump across. Jump across the gap. I stood and stared down into the canyon into which the weight of the sculpture on my back would pull me if I stumbled. The level of the scaffolding was higher than the roof on which I stood, not much but it was enough to make the jump look impossibly hard. Hard. So hard. Too hard. I'd need *wings* to get up and across with this sodding lump of metal on my back. Unslinging the rucksack I briefly wondered how resilient bronze was – didn't they once make swords from the stuff? – got a good swing on it and flung it across the gap on to the scaffold. It disappeared into the dark beyond the tarp with a reverberating bang.

'What? No, I heard something . . .' Voices below and to the left, coming nearer.

'Check the back entrance to the market.'

'I already did.'

'Well, check it again.'

'Yes, sarge.'

At this distance the combined noise of the wind, rain and river might mask my jump, if I let them come any closer it might no longer. It wouldn't be long before they got men and lights on to the roof. I could hear a surge of engine noise from the direction of Grand Parade.

'Super's just arrived,' said the first voice.

I jumped. Before I knew it I'd landed awkwardly on top of the unyielding rucksack. During the jump I had the briefest impression of torches being waved about to the left.

'Did you just hear something?'

I lay very still. My jump had been in the darkest corner of the yard, where the two buildings met. I had been heard but not seen. Now I had to move on before they got bodies down here. The Super? What on earth was Needham doing down here in the middle of the night? They couldn't have got him out of bed and down here from his house in Oldfield Park this fast unless these days he travelled with a rocket pack. Perhaps he'd been at Manvers Street anyway working on something else. Perhaps he was one of the Friends of Victoria Art Gallery, if there were any. Or perhaps he'd been expecting me.

It is hard to shrug off your paranoia standing three floors up on a narrow scaffold in the dark with a stolen Rodin on your back and police running around below. I moved slowly, setting my feet carefully each time, until I reached the ladder. I was safe from view and the snapping tarp and drumming rain helped mask my descent. No more voices, no sounds at all while I worked my way steadily down the levels.

The sudden shout close by nearly made me fall off the last ladder. 'It's secure, sarge, padlocked! They didn't come through here.' A constable rattled the cage.

Bending down, hanging on the ladder, I watched his legs move away. I stood and panted in the dark at the foot of the ladder, getting my breath back and my nerve up for the next lap. Keeping my body as far back in the shadows as was possible I pushed my hands through the grid of the cage, got the key into the padlock, let it snap open and unhooked it from the latch. The constable had moved off to the left. My route of escape lay more or less straight ahead: through the wrought-iron gate on the opposite side and down the slipway. There was no point in delaying. I had no idea where the constable had gone nor if there were any other bodies in the car park, but every second would make the situation more dangerous. I expected at any moment to hear the cry go up as someone discovered Annis clinging to the landing stage.

I opened the wire door wide, took a deep breath and loped across the car park like a demented Quasimodo. My legs ached and the lump of bronze on my back seemed to try and push me into the ground. Just as I reached the slope of the slipway that would take me out of view of anyone searching the car park the beam of a torch swept across the back of the Empire Hotel's walls and passed over me.

'Hey, stop! Police!' The shout I had feared went up as I dived into the darker slipway and shouldered open the door. I fumbled for the next bicycle lock to close the gate against my pursuers but when I heard the pounding of police boots echoing towards me I panicked and ran on, down the narrow canyon of the alley, dodging the stacks of crates and rows of empty beer kegs. I could hear the clang of the gate opening behind me as I strained to reach the little door at the other end.

Unencumbered by any Rodins the constable gained on me quickly, no longer shouting but saving his breath for the sprint and leap. I skidded against the little gate and had to step back to give it room to open and squeezed through. The dark shape of the officer filled my vision as I put the gate between us and fiddled the bicycle lock through the iron staple. He threw himself against it, breathing hard, just as I managed to shut the lock and twist the combination lock. He reached through the bars of the gate and made a grab for my jacket but I yanked myself free and staggered on along the colonnade, with the shouts of police and the roar of the weir in my ears.

Annis was waiting for me at the end of the walkway. 'You got the damn thing then. You've been ages,' she hissed and vaulted lightly back over the balustrade. I didn't dignify her comment with an answer since, as usual, I didn't have the breath to argue. I clambered over and gripped the handrail hard to steady myself. Everything seemed to be moving in the wind, the dinghy bucked, the river swirled. I practically fell into the boat and simply wanted to lie where I was but had to shrug out of the rucksack to untie the painter. Annis pulled the starter on the engine. There was no time to fiddle with the knot so I cut the rope. Annis pulled the cord again. Nothing. I lunged at the landing stage but it was too late, we were slipping away, accelerating fast in the current. Annis ripped the starter cord ever more frantically, again and again. Against the backdrop of the thunderous foaming of the weir it looked a soundless, futile exercise. The boat started its unstoppable race. It slewed sideways towards the drop of the weir. There were two paddles at the bottom of the boat. We both grabbed for them simultaneously while exchanging monosyllabic comments on the situation and started shovelling at the black water.

'Not upstream, that's hopeless!' Annis called. 'We can't get away, the current's too strong. We'll have to go over the weir, but bow first or we'll capsize!'

She was right. Without engine power we had no hope of fighting the greedy suction pulling the boat into the dark. We had to ride the chaotic white water that boiled and thundered and waited to engulf us.

It happened in a matter of seconds. Both of us paddled on the same side now, trying to point the boat bow-first at the weir, but we were carried across the side of the horseshoe before we had managed to change direction even a fraction. It felt like being swallowed by a screaming monster with an excess of saliva. For a moment I was deaf and blind and the boat appeared to be completely submerged. I gasped for air, swallowed water instead and reappeared coughing and spluttering, with a coughing and spluttering Annis next to me. By some miracle we were both still in the boat. Then we seemed to skate across the surface, the swirling waters twirling the dinghy round and round until we hit a calmer stretch alongside the bank of Parade Gardens. The boat was brimful of water but still floated on.

I quickly summed up the situation. 'Blimey!' I looked back. I couldn't make out much detail in the rain but imagined I could see two figures peering down over the balustrade of Grand Parade into the spume and foam of the weir. We had come a long way very quickly and the current was still pushing us along. We added paddle power to that and soon disappeared from sight under North Parade Bridge, the curve of the river taking us all the while further from the museum.

'Now what?' I complained. 'If we keep going this way we'll end up in Bristol. Home's the other way.'

'Typical. A minute ago we nearly drowned but already you're quibbling about my driving. We've got to get off this river pronto or they'll scoop us up like a rubber duck.'

'There's bound to be a landing place coming up soon.' At the moment the sheer sides of the river banks didn't offer the faintest hope of getting out. The old railway bridge hove into view but when we passed under it there wasn't even a handhold. Annis was right, we had to get off the river quickly and disappear into the night. As the Avon gently curved right I spotted an irregularity in the uniform dark of the left bank. 'On the left, let's make for that darker splodge.'

'Dark splodge coming up.'

I recognized the place. 'I know where this is, an arm of the Kennet and Avon joins here, there's a lock on the other side of that opening.'

'You want to go in there?'

'No, a bit further, is that steps? Up ahead.'

I was right. Only a few yards beyond the gloomy arch of the lock a series of concrete steps led up to the towpath. Kneeling in the bows I managed to grab the handrail and steady the boat while Annis heaved the rucksack on to the steps and climbed out after it.

'What about the boat? We can't leave them the boat. They find that, they find us.'

'I know. Shame though,' I answered and started stabbing the dinghy with my pocket knife. It deflated quickly and crumpled under me. I made it on to the safety of the steps just before the weight of the outboard pulled the entire thing bubbling and hissing into the murky depth of the Avon. The two paddles took off downriver into the darkness.

'Jake will be pleased.'

'Perhaps not. His wife might be though.' Yet I couldn't help feeling that Jake would be unsurprised at the outcome. He tended not to expect things he lent me to come back in any usable format.

'Now what?' Annis asked as we gained the towpath.

'Now? Now we'll take the long way home.'

She shouldered the rucksack and expressed her disapproval of Monsieur Rodin in words of extreme yet eloquent economy.

Chapter Twenty

'Dysentery, cholera and dengue fever is what you'll get,' presaged the oracle by the fire. 'How much river water did you swallow?'

'Enough to last me a lifetime, thanks.' Annis shivered theatrically and followed it up with a very real sneeze and a trumpeting blow into a wad of tissues.

It had taken us hours of staggering about in the rain through dark side streets, hiding from every car engine we heard, before we eventually made it back to the Landy and finally home. What we had feared most during our wanderings, the sound of a helicopter overhead, never materialized. Perhaps the weather was too bad to fly, perhaps they'd been attending elsewhere. By the time we got to the Land Rover we were both frozen and shivering.

'I'd happily kill you for a mug of hot soup,' Annis admitted. I gave her a muesli bar and told her to drive us home before we perished from hypothermia.

After a shower, some hot coffee and an awful lot of toast I was beginning to revive but Annis seemed to have come off worse. As she pointedly pointed out she'd waited around in the cold and rain for me *for ages* while I clambered all over roofs and scaffolds, *keeping warm*.

'Is it too early to try Jill again?' she asked. 'I worry about her. If she hasn't been home as you say then what can have happened to her?'

I dialled her mobile again. This time I got her voicemail service and left a message. 'Hi Jill, just letting you know that everything went fine. We got the . . . item and hopefully we'll swap it soon for . . . something more interesting. But we're a bit worried, not having heard from you at all. Give us a call when you get this message.' I put my phone away and shrugged, but secretly I'd been worrying about Jill's nerves.

'She might have gone to stay with her sister,' Tim suggested. 'It must be lonely for her in Harley Street, with her son's stuff all over the place and no one to talk to.'

Annis nodded. 'True. Her sister's in Trowbridge, that's not so far. Or she could have gone to stay with friends in Bristol. She might even have decided that Craig, her ex-boyfriend, had his uses after all. Have we got an address for him? We haven't, have we?'

'She never mentioned it. Somewhere in Bristol.'

Annis looked thoughtful. 'Unless . . .'

'Unless what?' Tim propped himself up on one elbow and pulled a pained face as his back reacted.

Annis took her time answering. 'I don't know. Unless she no longer believed that her son was alive. Perhaps she gave up.'

'Give up, how?' I asked.

'How would I know? As she said, none of us have children of our own, so perhaps she did feel that something had happened, something changed.'

'And chucked herself in the river.'

'It's possible,' she admitted.

There was another possibility that began nagging at the back of my mind but seemed too remote to give it much house room. All three of us looked thoughtfully at the little Rodin. At the museum it could inspire hushed voices and admiration on its spotlit plinth, here it looked prosaic standing next to a potted yucca on my floor. Context was everything and as ornaments went I preferred the yucca.

The morning drifted on and slipped into afternoon while I ghosted about the house and studio, carrying both cordless phone and mobile, waiting for the call, listening out for the crunch of police cars braking hard in the yard. I was getting increasingly worried about Jill not being in touch.

Tim had been right about the newsworthiness of the stolen Rodin: it got top billing on the lunchtime news. Hearing my rooftop antics being described as a 'daring raid' and Annis and myself as a 'well-organized gang' would have been almost funny if the bulletin hadn't started with the words 'A nationwide police hunt is today under way'.

I tried to distract myself by clearing up in the studio. The painting on my easel had been only half finished when the storm and Haarbottle's call had interrupted. Looking at it now I could barely make out my own intentions, even less feel the emotions that had driven the image across the canvas. It would never be finished now. Too much had happened since then.

The Stanley knife is the painter's best editing tool; four slashes quickly empty a stretcher of canvas and make sure of rigorous quality control in his oeuvre. But I was under no illusion that I could start a new canvas before this mess was resolved. The pointed blade slid seductively from the grip of the knife. The phone rang and effected a stay of execution. I slid the blade back in, dropped the knife into the tool box and pressed the talk button on the phone with a heavy heart.

'Well, congrats, shithead, told you you could do it.' The grating voice held a sour edge of feigned amusement. 'And now listen very carefully to what I have to say. The hand-over will happen tonight. You will be by yourself. There will be nobody with you, there will be no police and none of your mates. And you know why you'll do exactly as I tell you? Because now I've got the brat's mother. That's right, shithead, mother and son reunited, only not the way you expected. And you don't want anything to happen to *her*, because how could you live with yourself? You still listening, shithead, or did you faint?'

249

I sat down heavily on my painting stool. This was exactly what I had feared but hadn't allowed myself to say out loud. But the question that weighed heavier on me was this: why would the kidnapper go to the trouble of snatching Jill if he already had the boy? Why would he need another victim, unless . . . 'I'm listening.'

'You'd better. Because now I'm ready for you. Here's what you do, very simple. One: you'll secure the Penny Black inside a padded envelope, reinforced with cardboard. Then you'll tape it safely to the statue. Two: you'll wrap the lot in several bin bags and secure them with tape so they don't flap about. Three: you load it on the back of your Land Rover and drive out of your yard at eight o'clock *precisely*, with your mobile phone charged up and switched on, ready to receive instructions. Four: you talk to no one. You'll be by yourself and you'll bring no weapons and no wires. Oh yes, and just so I'll know you'll have no weapons or microphones, you'll be wearing nothing but a pair of boxer shorts. Just to make sure there are no hidden surprises. Do anything differently and the woman dies.'

I drew breath to answer but he had already hung up.

Jill. We should never have left her alone all these days. What happened to the sister . . .? This might still come out right of course but there remained one question that seemed to make this unlikely: why would the kidnapper bother to take Jill, when he already had the boy? Unless the boy was dead.

Chapter Twenty-One

Five minutes to eight.

I felt chilly even though I was still only standing in the hall of my own house. Annis pulled me hard against her. 'You make sure you come back to me, okay, Honeypot? No heroics, just do as you're told for once and bring them back. Promise?'

'I love you, Annis.'

'I know, Chris.'

This time, apparently, it counted. It also saved me from having to make promises I might not be able to keep.

In the yard, parked as close as possible to the front door, the Landy had been 'warming up'. I got in and mentally went over everything again. There wasn't much to check. The stamp in its envelope and the Rodin were on the back, wrapped in black plastic and covered with a bit of old carpet. I myself was wrapped in a scratchy grey blanket, the only one I could find, making me already feel like the survivor of some kind of disaster. Despite the kidnapper's warning I was wearing basketball shoes. If he objected he could always make me take them off. I had my mobile, as instructed. I had also purloined Tim's far flashier mobile, and his Bluetooth headset, without bothering to tell him, because I had made no decisions yet about what to do when I got there and was literally going to play this by ear. I put my mobile on the dash, stuck the Bluetooth set on my right ear and let my hair fall over it. I set Tim's mobile next to me on the seat.

Eight o'clock.

I waved to Annis in the doorway, silhouetted against the warm light of the house, put the engine in gear and rumbled out of the yard.

The heater in a 1960s Land Rover was a well-known joke and Annis's decrepit example was no exception. Only most people who complained about how bad their Landy's heater was didn't usually drive it half-naked through a late-October night.

My mobile chimed its hateful little tune. I answered it. 'I'm on the move, so where am I going?'

'Patience. You're on your lonesome, like I told you?'

'I am.'

'And you are unarmed and in your shorts?'

'Unarmed, freezing cold and half-naked, apart from a pair of basketball shoes.'

'Who said you could wear those?'

'You want me to slip on the brake and drive your Rodin into a ditch?'

He grunted reluctant agreement. 'Where are you?'

'Top of my drive.'

'Turn left and keep going until you get to the London Road. Keep the line open. If you disconnect your mobile even for one second then the deal is off and the woman will feel the consequences.'

I turned and drove slowly along the unlit, narrow road through the valley. The worn blades of the windscreen wipers squeaked as they ineffectually scraped at the renewed offering of rain falling out of the blackness. I was once more on the move, on my own, with the spoils from a robbery. My memories of the hold-up on Charlcombe Lane were still vivid in my mind. What was to stop the kidnapper from taking the plunder off me by force when I got to my dark destination, and go on indefinitely with his demands? Now that he had abducted a second victim he could afford to kill one of them simply to demonstrate the seriousness of his threat, if he hadn't already done so.

252

As I reached the sodium-lit London Road at Batheaston I put the phone to my ear. 'I'm there.'

'Turn right. Drive carefully and at legal speeds. Don't attract attention. When you reach Bailbrook Lane, turn into it.'

There was not a lot of traffic on the road, it was dark and the rain was hammering down; chances were that no one would remember a dirty old Landy. The goose bumps on my arms were an indication not just of how cold I felt but also of the hideousness of the realization that this time I really was in deep shit, just as Needham had predicted. I had let myself be drawn into the deepest mess of my dubious career and my only backup was Tim's dinky little Bluetooth mobile. The turn-off into narrow Bailbrook Lane came up quickly. Bumping the car into it I asked for instructions.

'You know this lane? You must do. Just keep going until you get to the highest point from where you can have a good look over Larkhall and the rest. Then stop.'

He was right, I knew the lane well. It skirted the bottom of Solsbury Hill, made famous beyond its stature by some dippy song. Dark, evergreen hedgerows whizzed past on either side as I hustled the Landy along. A particularly nasty pothole made my load jump on the back and I slowed down a bit. Soon after I'd passed the rusty corrugated iron mission church the view opened out. The lights of Larkhall and Lower Swainswick twinkled below. I stopped. 'I can see Larkhall below. Now what?'

'Turn off your lights.'

I did as I was told. At least it might save them having to bash them in with baseball bats. It was baseball, last time, I remembered it clearly. Unlike poor old Albert who'd apparently been hit with a cricket bat. Same result I should think.

'Now turn them on again and flash your lights. Very good. Just wanted to be sure you were where you said you were. I can see you. Which means I'll also be able to see any monkey business. Well, what are you waiting for? Come on down.'

It was quieter in the cab because the engine was still in neutral and I thought I heard an engine start up at the speaker's end. I put the phone on the dash and kept on driving downhill, over the bypass and plunged further down until I reached the bottom.

'Where exactly are you now?' he asked after I'd announced my arrival.

'St Saviour's to the left. Dead Mill Lane to the right.'

'You've gone too far. Take Dead Mill Lane. Then turn left and take the second turn on the left again. And keep going.'

I had suspected it since he made me leave the London Road and this confirmed it: I was heading into the Lam Valley. Soon the now familiar tracks swallowed me up. I recognized this one in particular. Very soon it would bring me to Jack Fryer's farm. I slowed down, fingering Tim's mobile beside me on the bench. The farm buildings hove into view on my left.

Dimly illuminated by a single watery bulb fixed to a telegraph pole in the yard the main structures of Spring Farm squatted in the wet darkness like black cattle depressed by the rain. I speed dialled the number for Mill House on Tim's mobile while driving slowly up to the gate, peering into the gloom beyond. The dial tone snarled in my ear via the headset. I stopped. This didn't feel right at all.

'Hello?' Annis's voice in my ear.

A door opened in a concrete shed on the other side of the yard. Fryer's farmhand shielded his eyes against the glare of the Landy's light, looking puzzled.

'I'm at Spring Farm,' I said into the mobile.

'Hello? Is that you, Chris?' Annis spoke into my ear.

'Keep going, follow the sign, don't stop until you get there,' came the impatient voice on the other mobile.

This was the wrong place. I hastily reversed back into the lane and drove on.

'Did you say Spring Farm? Hello? All I can hear is noise now,' Annis said in a faint voice, to Tim, presumably. Both mobiles started crackling as I drove deeper into the darkness of the valley, then reception died. How would I get my instructions now?

The answer stood at the turn to the narrow track on the left. A roughly made blank finger post had been rammed into the soft verge. It pointed forlornly down towards the ford of the Lam brook. This slippery track led to only one place: Grumpy Hollow. One way in, one way out.

I cranked the wheel over and plunged the ghostly signpost back into darkness as I followed its direction down towards the Hollow.

When I reached Gemma Stone's herb farm I turned off both mobiles. I no longer needed them.

I had arrived.

Chapter Twenty-Two

I let the Land Rover crawl slowly down the slope to where Gemma's old Volvo was parked. The narrow beam of my headlights picked out her car, with its hatch at the back wide open, the shepherd's hut and the caravan in sharp, rain-glistened detail, while appearing to pour black ink over everything else. When I had brought the two cars nose to nose I killed the engine but left the lights on and cranked down the window. Earthy smells of dank vegetation rushed into the cab, replacing the oily fug thrown up by the engine. All I could hear was the thrumming of rain on the cab's roof and the splashing and trickling all about. I got out into the mud and rain, pulled the blanket closer around me and approached the caravan. The door was wide open, a rectangle of blackness against the dirty white of the exterior.

'That's close enough,' came the commanding voice from inside. 'Stay right there.'

The surge of a powerful engine behind me made me turn around. Headlights on full beam dazzled me as I tried to make out what and who was approaching from behind. What eventually slowed and stopped close to the Land Rover was a black luxury van with wide tyres and permanent four-wheel drive. The engine stopped, the lights remained on, sending their beams deep into the plantation.

'Who said you were allowed to wear a blanket?' the voice from the caravan demanded as quiet returned. 'Drop it!'

256

I let the blanket slide into the mud.

'I see. Give us a twirl then, we all saw *Die Hard*.'

'No, that's all right, love, he hasn't got anything squir-relled away up his backside,' came the much-loathed voice of Detective Inspector Deeks from the side of the van. He coughed. 'I'm glad I don't have to speak in that stupid voice any more.'

Jill stepped out of the caravan, wearing a blue plastic rainproof and jeans with knee-high boots. She was holding a big lump of a revolver with both hands and gestured with it towards the Landy. 'Go on, fetch the Rodin and stick it in the van.'

'Watch where you're pointing that gun, love, keep it on him.' Deeks slid open the side door of the van.

To say that I felt exposed, cold and narked would sum it up neatly. ' Where's Gem Stone, Deeks? What have you done with her?'

'I'm all right, I'm in here.' Gemma's voice came muffled from inside the shepherd's hut. 'Sorry I couldn't warn you, the bitch said she'd shoot you on the spot if I did.'

'That's okay then,' I called back. I turned to the bitch in question. 'Your son, Louis?'

'There's no such person, thank God.'

'Jill's not the least bit mumsy,' Deeks said cheerfully. 'Good at amateur dramatics, though. Go on, you heard what she said. Move the statue into the van.'

Jill gestured with the big revolver which seemed a little heavy for her. I stared at it hard.

Deeks noticed. 'Looks familiar, doesn't it? Stuff goes missing from police stations all the time, you know. Like your confiscated gun.' Jill was pointing my own Webley at me. How annoying were these people?

'You've given up on being a copper then? I'd heard you were bent but this is insane. You'll never get away with it.'

'That's exactly what I'll do, get away. Internal affairs have been sniffing about, I was warned by a loyal soul at Manvers Street. Time to get out, we thought, with a good starting capital. You'd be surprised what sterling still buys in some countries. Just a sec.' Deeks tore a hole into the covering of the Rodin bundle and felt about until he had the envelope containing the Penny Black. 'Carry on.'

I lifted the Rodin off the back and squelched across to the van. 'You might find that the proceeds from this lot won't go very far,' I hinted.

'That won't matter much. I only wanted the stuff in Telfer's safe because after we put his brother away he claimed to have video evidence he would use against me if he was ever arrested. Which was possible since I'd taken a bung from them more than once. I hate that arrogant shit so I came up with the idea of killing two birds with one stone, and you're just as arrogant a shit as Telfer.'

The van was crammed full of boxes and one or two small pieces of antique furniture but there was just space for the Rodin near the door. I dropped it heavily into the van. 'That haul disappeared into the night, presumably back to Telfer's. So where's your starting capital coming from?'

Jill waved the gun towards the shepherd's hut. Deeks pulled an irritated face and took it from her, then pointed it firmly at me. 'Go on, in the hut. Speed is of the essence, as they say. Amphetamines, Honeysett, is what they made at Lane End Farm, supplying Bristol and half the West Country. A nice little laboratory hidden among all those shipping containers. Only they're a load of chemistry nerds, so Blackfield and I managed to rip them off to the tune of half a million each. Then I managed to rip Blackfield off, only he doesn't know it yet, and now it's time to go.'

Shivering and dripping, with Deeks prodding me from behind with my own revolver, I stumbled up the little steps and into the shepherd's hut. Gemma, wearing nothing but black knickers and T-shirt, had been firmly tied with rope to the narrow armchair in the corner. Her black eye had turned a hellish shade of yellow now but I was glad to see there was no fresh evidence of violence on her face.

'Take a seat, Honeysett,' Deeks invited me.

I sat on the chair by the little table full of books. Jill squeezed into the overcrowded hut with a roll of nylon gardening twine and started by tying my hands behind me, then winding the thin but strong twine around me with an irritating grin on her face. 'There you go, you can keep each other company for a while.'

Deeks growled. 'Stop enjoying yourself and get on with it.' There came a dull rumble, like distant thunder. 'There goes the lab. Bit early. Time to go.'

'Okay, I'm done.' Jill ruffled my hair. 'Nice knowing you.'

'Just one thing,' I asked. 'Who killed the old guy, Albert?'

'No time to chat, I'm afraid, that little woomph was the speed factory catching light.' Deeks scooped up an armful of Gemma's books. 'You won't need these any more.'

The moment the door was slammed shut, leaving us in semi-darkness, we both started trying to struggle out of our bindings. Jill really had enjoyed herself too much, the cord cut deeply into my chilled skin.

'It was Blackfield,' said Gemma.

'What was?' I was too busy wriggling to pay attention. I hadn't liked the sound of 'You won't need these any more.'

'Blackfield hit Albert to discourage him from cycling along his fence in search of mushrooms. He came off his electric bike. But he didn't kill him, at least that's what Deeks said.'

I could hear van doors sliding and slamming, then the sound of the big engine starting. Deeks and his girlfriend were leaving.

'I'm a bit ahead of you in the wriggling game,' Gemma said, grunting with effort. 'I had a lot of time to try and get out of these while they were waiting for you and this is rope, there's always some give. I think I'm nearly there.'

The engine of the van surged outside as Deeks turned and churned it up the hill, taking most of the light that fell through the little window with it. I had stopped shivering, not feeling quite so cold now. It took me only a few seconds to realize why when the first wisps of smoke rose from the floorboards.

I stated the obvious. 'Shit, we're on fire. I can smell paraffin, too.'

'I use it for heating the greenhouse. At least it's not petrol.'

The nylon cut my skin as I pulled and pulled. I didn't manage to snap it but the twine stretched a little around my ankles. 'It's still raining, that'll slow it down a bit.'

'It's not raining under the hut, though, is it?' Gemma argued.

'Good point.' The hut began to fill with smoke and both of us started to cough. We'd die of smoke inhalation about five minutes before burning to a cinder. 'Those gas bottles outside, they're empty, right?'

'Yup. All except one.'

'Great. If I know Deeks at all then he'll have stuffed it under the hut. At least it should be quick. '

I rocked the chair back and forth on to the front legs, hind legs, front legs, until on the last swing I ended up on my feet with the chair attached to my behind. I waddled the short distance across and threw myself at the cast-iron stove as hard as I could. I heard an encouraging crack and despite the pain joyfully threw myself at it again. One chair leg came adrift. It was enough to loosen the entire net of twine around me and I managed to kick and pull myself free. I opened the door. Flames were kindling the steps. The inrush of cold air helped me breathe easier, though every lungful made me cough. I grabbed Gemma's armchair and dragged it to the door, yanked it outside with one big heave while the flames licked about us and we both tumbled over.

An eerie light reflected on to the Hollow from the rim behind the polytunnel, far too bright for just one burning laboratory. I ran into the caravan.

'On the draining board!' I heard Gemma call. I grabbed the bread knife and seconds later had cut her free of the tumbled armchair. I was trying to drag her away from the fire while she dragged me the other way. 'No!' she cried. 'The gas bottle's not in the fire, we can save the hut!'

She ran off towards the nearest water trough while I cut off the rest of the twine from my limbs, then I followed her.

'What are those lights?' she asked, throwing an empty watering can at me.

I could now see two blinding light sources shining down into the valley further on where Blackfield's stalag amphetamine lab was. Had been. I wondered if the chemists had been inside when that went up. 'No idea what they are.' We ran back and started throwing water on to the fire, Gemma from a bucket, me with the plastic watering can. The floor of the hut was completely on fire now.

'What's that sound?' she asked.

'Helicopter.' Even as I spoke the word a helicopter swooped across the Hollow, turning night into day with its powerful night-sun focused on us. I presumed it was friend, not foe, so I gave it a quick wave, then went on firefighting. A combination of rain, mud and Gemma's determination to save her hut eventually defeated the fire. The helicopter remained hovering above the rim of the Hollow, shedding light on our labours. At last we realized we had done it and stopped. We were both still coughing, we were wet, covered in mud, and steam rose from our bodies in the cold light of the night-sun. We sank against each other, not quite in an embrace, just keeping each other from falling over. I was still too hot from running back and forth to feel the cold, despite being half naked. There were emergency sirens in the air.

A leather-clad Annis arrived on the Norton only half a minute ahead of her pursuers, slithering the Norton to a stop beside the Land Rover. 'Blimey, looks like your usual style, Chris,' she called over the helicopter noise. 'I won't ask why you're both half naked but where's Jill? Where's the *boy*?'

261

My answer was drowned out when the helicopter swept closer and Detective Superintendent Needham and his convoy roared into the little herb farm, doors opening even before the cars had squelched to a halt.

I shivered as the cold began to get to me, but before I could even suggest to Gemma the loan of a towel Needham's irate form hove into view from among the cars. 'Chris Honeysett, you're under arrest. And you, and you,' pointing at Annis and Gemma. 'Sorbie,' he called to his Detective Sergeant who was following in his considerable wake, 'read them their rights and arrest them properly, I just can't be arsed today, I cannot be arsed.'

Epilogue

At least this time we hadn't shot anyone. But that was about the only law we hadn't broken, according to Detective Superintendent ('Two-sugars') Needham. The shock was not of being arrested – I had always expected that – but being arrested for all the right offences: breaking and entering, theft of the Rodin, obviously, the attempted theft of the Penny Black from Rufus Connabear, and the Telfer burglary. My suspicions were aroused even more when DS Sorbie seemed to have more detailed memory of the items we had nicked than I did.

Needham admitted it. 'Deeks was bent. He was under investigation but we didn't want to spook him by suspending him. We wanted to find as much evidence as possible and catch all his contacts, in and outside the force, that's why I gave him DS Sorbie to run with, who did an excellent job of pretending to be his loyal sidekick. Deeks was under constant surveillance, of course. And then suddenly, though not atypically, I might add, *you* turned up in the middle of it all. We had to find out what was going on. So we put you and your lot under surveillance too for a while. I couldn't really see you and Deeks working together. So we took a step back. I wanted whatever you got out of the Telfer place but had to make it look like a mugging. We got some of our esteemed colleagues from Bristol to do the job and I'm afraid they went a bit over the top, sorry about that. But amongst the crud you stole was a secretly filmed video of Deeks accepting money from

Telfer, which will be enough in itself to put Deeks away for a while.'

'Glad to have been of service.'

'His involvement with the amphetamine factory on Blackfield's land and six counts of attempted murder and two counts of arson is going to age the man even more.'

'He tried to fry the drug chemists too?'

'Tied up just like you. They were lucky we'd decided to give them a tug that very night. But it's a huge place to raid. We had brought searchlights and generators on flat-back lorries and sixty officers, but Deeks and his woman had already rigged the place to burn and he was sitting in his van, waiting for you to drive into the Hollow, where Jill was waiting for you. The helicopter crew realized that your lives might be in danger when they detected the fire and stayed overhead to direct us to you. Otherwise Deeks would never have managed to give us the slip.'

'You let him get away?'

'Don't worry, we'll get him. I'd worry about myself and my mates if I were you.'

'Hey, without me you wouldn't have the video. I was helping.'

'As they say: tell it to the judge.' Needham was in suspiciously high mood which led me to conclude that he was once more lacing his cop shop coffee with the sweet white poison.

'Deeks and his woman conned me. I believed I was saving a boy's life. Isn't that moral coercion or something like that?'

'Why don't you ask your solicitor?'

Which I did. Grimshaw gave a withering speech but it was me she was withering. For having failed to inform at least my solicitor before embarking on such imbecilic etcetera etcetera.

Those imbecilic etcetera became less likely to send me to prison when the Rodin was recovered from inside the van as it was pulled from a ditch a mile and a half from the Hollow. There was no sign of Deeks or Jill.

The Rodin Museum got their sculpture back, though were embarrassed when for insurance reasons they had to admit that it had only been a copy they had sent to Britain. I paid for the damage to the museum's skylight and thus found out that they cost an absolute fortune. In the end the only one who had been robbed was myself, since Deeks had made off with the Penny Black for which I had written a cheque, though to this day Rufus Connabear hasn't thought to cash it.

The real loser was Albert Barrington, who had died from being knocked over with my car after an attack by Blackfield, who had bumped into him while inspecting his fence one night. Blackfield had also disappeared.

It was shortly after Annis, Tim and I were acquitted of all charges, like obstruction, perverting the course of justice, resisting arrest and littering (deliberately sinking the dinghy), leaving me owing Grimshaw a wealth of paintings, that another piece of the jigsaw fell into place, and again in the Lam Valley.

It was a bright and deceptively mild November day when a microlight plane ran into engine trouble while circling the area. The plane crashed into a shed on Spring Farm and the injured pilot was rescued from the wreckage by Jack Fryer and farmhand. The pilot turned out to be no other than James Lane, whose balance problems, according to him, didn't affect him in the air. He later admitted to defrauding the insurance company in order to finance a correspondence Open University degree in British and European History. Summing up, the judge suggested he might find it easier to concentrate on his studies in a prison cell. The crash left Lane walking with a real limp.

Late December, and a rare snowfall had dusted the Lam Valley, softening the edges of farmhouse roofs and adding an insulating blanket to the cloches, polytunnel and glasshouse down at Grumpy Hollow. Annis and I had delivered a load of logs, cut from the branches shed by the trees at Mill House during the October storm. We had stacked it under a tarp and now Gemma served scalding coffee in her caravan. The little wood burner, moved into here from the badly damaged shepherd's hut, singed the air around it. I gratefully wrapped my hands around a steaming mug.

'I have a couple of things for you,' Gemma announced.

'Presents?' I mumbled something about how it really wasn't necessary.

'Found objects, really, and a bit of a mixed bag, I'm afraid.' She reached up into the cupboard space over the bed alcove and produced two metal items which she set in front of me, one of which I instantly recognized. It was the big lump of my Webley .38 revolver.

'I found that in the mud when the foliage of my coriander collapsed in the frost. I cleaned it up, it was filthy.'

'Deeks must have thrown it there. Probably wise, Jill might have accidentally blown his head off with it one day.' I cracked it open. It held a full complement of rounds.

'And this?' Annis picked up the little blue tin, hand-painted with stars and moons. 'Tobacco tin.' She shook it. It rattled. She prised the lid open. Inside, among the dregs of hand-rolling tobacco and cigarette papers, nestled the missing keys to the DS.

Gemma nodded her head at it. 'I found that when I was collecting cob nuts in the hedgerows, on the opposite side of the valley from where Albert died. I thought of giving it to the police, but I'll leave it up to you. Your call.'

Annis handed it to me and I slid it into my coat pocket. The teenage girl who had lost it was probably better at riding trail bikes than handling left-hand-drive classic Citroëns. Cairn and Heather, rightly assuming that I had really no intention of looking into their story, had pinched the DS and driven it deep into the Lam Valley to make sure I would eventually go there. Irony pushed into their path

266

the very man whose life they thought they were helping to save, stumbling about after having been hit by Blackfield.

I shut the tin and pocketed it. I would take it out later in a quieter moment and think very hard about whether anyone would benefit from Cairn and Heather being dragged in front of the courts.

Gemma walked us through the crunching snow to the Land Rover. Annis performed her arcane start-up ritual and despite the cold the engine started first time.

'I meant to ask,' Gemma said, sticking her frozen nose in at the driver window. 'What name did you give the cat in the end?'

Both women looked expectantly at me.

'Derringer,' I said with only the faintest hesitation. 'The cat's called Derringer.'

Author's Note

Thanks again to Krystyna and Juliet. I'm especially grateful to Clare and Imogen for making my manuscript readable. Special thanks to Chris for giving me Derringer. No thanks at all to Asbo the cat for sharpening his claws on a pile of signed hardbacks.